PAMELA AARES

Love on the Line

LOVE ON THE LINE
Copyright 2014 Pamela Aares

Ryan and Cara --*The Tavonesi Series*, Book #4

http://www.PamelaAares.com
Sign up for Pamela's newsletter
http://www.pamelaaares.com/newsletter-signup

Cover design by www.jdsmith-design.com
Interior Layout by www.formatting4U.com

Hiding her identity was a small price to pay for freedom...

Heiress Cara Barrington fled the opulent world of her rich and famous family to carve out an idyllic existence on the California Coast. In the sleepy town of Albion Bay, she's embraced the simple way of living she's always craved. No one knows her identity, and she's free from the pressures of wealth... until her sexy new neighbor threatens the unpretentious world she's worked so hard to build.

All-Star athlete Ryan Rea enjoys his high-profile status. He's used to charming his way into the heart and bed of any woman he desires while keeping his own heart secure behind a steel wall. When he meets Cara, she throws him a curveball—she's unlike any woman he's ever met, and he has to have her.

Cara's growing attraction to Ryan endangers her hard-won anonymity, and when she inherits the family business, she must choose between the world she left behind and her new life in the community she's come to cherish. But facing up to her responsibilities could destroy her freedom and cost her the greatest love she's ever known.

Books by Pamela Aares

The Tavonesi Series:

Love Bats Last (Book #1, Alex and Jackie)
Thrown By Love (Book #2, Chloe and Scotty)
Fielder's Choice (Book #3, Alana and Matt)
Love on the Line (Book #4, Cara and Ryan)
Aim For Love (Book #5, Sabrina and Kaz)
also available:
Jane Austen and the Archangel

For a complete list visit www.PamelaAares.com

Dedication

For my mother who taught me to treasure my dreams and for readers everywhere who believe in the power of love.

CHAPTER ONE

A HIGH-PITCHED SCREAM WAS ONCE SOMETHING THAT stopped Cara's heart. But not anymore. After two years of driving the Albion Bay school bus, Cara found it would take blood or the report of an injury to have her take the antics of the children seriously.

A quick glance in the side-angled mirror over her head told her that Sam Rivers was up to his usual tricks. His repertoire included dropping lizards down the backs of girls' hoodies and the other occasional pranks of a typical twelve-year-old.

Sam and his friends liked nothing more than to get a rise out of Cara as well. Though she was twenty-three, the older kids sometimes treated her like a buddy. She walked a careful line with her charges, happy that they liked and accepted her, while taking seriously her responsibility for their safety.

Secretly she was glad they had the spunk and verve that they did. Some days their enthusiasm rubbed off on her, their innocent, youthful energy wrapping a snug web of delight around her heart. But today the curving coastal road to the Albion Bay middle school was littered with rocks that had slid down the cliff side during the night. Dodging obstacles and getting her charges safely to school was foremost in Cara's mind.

1

She glanced back up to make sure the boys hadn't done any harm and was surprised to see Sam race to the driver's side of the bus and throw open a window.

"There! I told you I saw it!" Sam pointed to a red car parked in the driveway of a newly renovated ranch house.

Not just any red car.

Cara knew a Bugatti when she saw one; her brother had two, although he preferred muted colors.

She maneuvered a curve that brought them closer to the ranch house. Whoever had bought the old Smith property had done a speedy job of putting a new face on the dilapidated old ranch.

"It's a Ferrari," Timmy Brown said as he stuck his face out the window.

"It's *not*. It's an Aston Martin," Cara heard Sam say with definite authority.

She smiled to herself. What did the name of a car matter? But hearing the awed voices of the boys did give her pause. Money could buy such a car, but unless the owner was part of a racing circuit, there was usually only one reason someone needed a two-million-dollar sports car in a rural coastal California town.

Ego.

Well, that and the desire for the flash that went along with it. All one and the same, really.

The high-end sports car was a visual reminder of the world she'd spent three years fighting to escape.

And only because she knew that novelty was scarce in Albion Bay did she slow the bus and give the boys a good look at the car.

But as she drove closer, it wasn't the car that caught her eye.

A ridiculously handsome specimen of male was unloading a hay bale from the passenger seat of the Bugatti.

2

He was tall, maybe six-foot-three, and handled the hay bale as if it were a sack of feathers.

Hay?

Now, *that* did make her smile. A sports car wasn't a sensible vehicle for transporting hay bales. The guy was crazy, desperate or just lacked everyday common sense.

Whatever his foibles, his broad-shouldered physique and rugged good looks were likely to cause a town buzz that went well beyond a group of preteen boys. The man looked up and flashed a wave toward the bus. When he followed his gesture with the most beaming smile she'd ever seen, a smile that zinged into her core, she was sure of it.

Cara threw her keys onto the kitchen counter. It'd been a good day. No fights on the bus and a good turnout to help with the harvest in the Albion Bay community garden. Over the next two weeks they'd can the surplus and take it down to the community food bank for distribution. For some residents, the extra food from the canning sessions got them through the winter.

She poured a glass of iced tea and glanced around the small cabin that had become her sanctuary. For all its faults, the simplicity of the cabin suited her. She'd had to put in new pipes in the bathroom so the shower wouldn't leak through the floor, and the kitchen had been a challenge, but two refurbished burners in the stove and an overhaul of the fridge had made it serviceable. A coat of bright paint that she'd applied herself had spiffed up the bedroom upstairs.

The rest of the cabin she'd left mostly untouched, although before the winter rains set in she'd have to hire Adam Mitchell, the local carpenter, to shore up the roof over her bedroom and replace the worst of the sagging boards on the front and back decks.

Her one indulgence had been a set of floor-to-ceiling bookcases that housed her most precious volumes. The books were her best company on rainy winter nights.

There were only two doors in the cabin. The front door was a bit battered, but the two glorious rose bushes that flanked it made up for the sagging beams and peeling paint. The paned windows at the top of the back door that led out from the kitchen provided a view of her vegetable garden and the small deck where she loved to drink her coffee on lazy Saturday mornings.

Cara walked out that back door now and set the glass of tea on the redwood stump that served as her outdoor table.

Turning her head left and right, she pulled the elastic band from her hair and let it swing free around her shoulders. She tried to stretch out the worst of the kinks in her neck and then rubbed at her temples. The din of thirty kids crammed into the bus, bursting with energy after a long day at school, had made her head throb.

The stem of a ragweed poked its head up out of her herb bed. She knelt at the side of the garden box and tugged the weed out, careful not to disturb the roots of the basil plant growing next to it. She'd dry the basil and send it to her family in ribbon-wrapped jars for Christmas. Though they poked fun at her homemade gifts, she liked to imagine they appreciated her efforts.

Working in the garden after her afternoon shift of bus driving usually relaxed her, but all the talk in the community garden that afternoon had been of Albion's newest resident, Ryan Rea.

As she'd suspected, the boys on the bus weren't the only ones who'd noticed the flashy Bugatti of their town's newest resident, and Cara wasn't the sole woman to have noticed his rugged good looks.

Ryan Rea.

His name made him sound like an extra from a Texas Western. And the smile he'd flashed as she'd driven past him had made her pulse leap, surprising her. She didn't need the complication of a flashy man in her life. No indeed.

She put both thumbs to her temples and pressed hard.

An earsplitting ring sounded from the room that doubled as her dining room and living space—she'd forgotten to turn the ringer down. For a moment she considered not answering. No one local would be calling since she'd seen nearly everybody in town during the course of her day. And anyone calling from the world outside Albion Bay just brought trouble to her quiet slice of paradise.

On the tenth ring she remembered she'd also forgotten to turn on the answering machine. Whoever was trying to reach her was damned persistent. She stubbed her toe on a protruding deck board as she ran to answer. She'd better call Adam and see if he could come out to work on her decks this week. They'd had a dry September, but the rains wouldn't hold off forever, and if Adam didn't get started before the rains did, the decks would never get done.

"Cara?"

Alston Patterson might be nearing eighty, yet he had the voice of a much younger man. But her attorney's voice always meant trouble. At least it had lately.

"No, it's Glinda, the Good Witch of the North."

"*Just* the person I was looking for. Facing the news I have might require a bit of magic."

"Alston, I'm bordering on a headache and—"

"The news will be the same whether I tell you today or tomorrow," he said in a gentle voice.

She'd known Alston all her life. He'd been her grandfather's attorney, and when she needed wise counsel a few years back, she'd asked him to be hers.

5

"Might as well tell me now then. After wrangling thirty hyped-up school kids, dodging the latest rock avalanche that the gods of nature have thrown upon us and harvesting the world's most stubborn earth-hugging carrots, nothing could faze me."

"Your grandfather's estate has finally been settled."

There was a long silence. One of those silences that made time feel unreal, one of those silences that Cara imagined was intended to prepare the listener for the news to follow but never did. She missed her grandfather; Alston knew that. That he was calling her rather than just mailing information told her that what was to follow wouldn't be welcome news.

"His will sets you up as president of the Barrington Foundation." He inhaled and exhaled a heavy breath. "Its current assets are just under two billion dollars."

Two *billion* dollars.

Cara groaned and sank into the stuffed chair, one of only two seats in her tiny living room. For three years she'd lived simply, quietly, anonymously in the little town of Albion Bay. The townspeople had accepted her as one of their own. For the first time in her life people looked at her and saw just Cara, the school bus driver and community member, not Russell Barrington's daughter, not a woman born into one of the richest families in America.

She'd driven the bus, quilted beside the women of the town when someone had a baby, farmed the Albion Bay community garden, gotten dirty, and laughed and cheered at the middle school baseball games.

She'd fit in. She'd carved out a life that felt right. Felt right to her. She'd learned to live with her family's protests and lack of understanding. She'd found meaning for her life in Albion Bay, meaning that buoyed her in her darkest moments, meaning that made it possible to face her days without fear.

And she'd managed, with Alston's help, to hang on to her anonymity; he understood that it was crucial to maintaining her carefully structured new life. For the past three years she'd met with him in the city and found clever ways to disburse the two-hundred-thousand-dollars interest from her personal foundation, granting the funds anonymously each year.

And though she was tempted—she liked providing funding to projects that made a difference in people's lives, even had a knack for it—stepping up to head a two-billion-dollar foundation would push the game into a new arena. A very public arena. Being responsible for giving away that much money in any fashion—and especially in a prudent and well-thought-out manner—would be more than complicated. It would push her back into the world she'd fled and would destroy her quiet, happy life.

"He's also bequeathed a matching two billion to you directly. That is, *if* you accept the position as president of the foundation. But you won't be able to touch that money until you're twenty-five."

Four billion dollars.

She could do even more good with four billion dollars.

But the thought had barely materialized when she saw Laci's face—cold, white and surrounded by the silk blankets that Cara had tucked into her coffin. She would never forget the waxy feel of Laci's skin and the bruises that showed through the mask-like makeup the undertaker had slathered on her friend's face. Unlike Cara, Laci hadn't escaped.

"I won't do it, Alston. I can't. *What* was Grandfather thinking? What about Quinn? He can take the helm."

"Your brother has a bequest and a foundation of his own to run, although his is far smaller than this one. And the legal language is very clear. You have two months to decide, or the foundation will remain under the control of the present board and its current president. As will the funds of your private bequest."

"Who *is* the current president?"

"Your father appointed Dray Bender to that position, just after your grandfather died."

Cara knew from Alston's tone and what he didn't say that he didn't like Dray Bender. All she remembered was that the man was one of her father's golf buddies. Her dad probably owed the guy a favor or something. A big one. Her heart fell at the thought. They'd probably fund golf scholarships for Ivy League preppies.

"I see." She suppressed her desire to curse. Alston always clucked in disapproval when she cursed. "Can't we dump him and hire someone else? Someone"—she searched for a positive way to frame her remark—"someone who would honor my grandfather's legacy?"

"Only if you're at the helm."

"This is worse than blackmail."

"Blackmail's a harsh term, my dear. I doubt that's what your grandfather intended." He paused. "Think about it, Cara. There's a lot at stake here—lives, possibilities, values. Your grandfather liked your values—he trusted you. I'm sure he wouldn't have wanted a man like Bender stewarding his legacy."

Her head was splitting. "Look, can I call you in a few weeks? Can you stall? There must be a way to pry Dray Bender out of there and find someone good to head up the foundation."

"We already have someone good for that. You."

"What happened to *no pressure, my dear?*"

"That was before you were willed the control of two billion dollars and a private fortune to match it. Like I said, think about it. And I promise I'll see how deeply we can bury this for the time being so you can maintain your anonymity, at least for a while. But I warn you, it may not be possible."

Alston had never criticized her choices. He'd even helped her get through the fingerprinting and paperwork at the county level so she'd been able to take the school bus driving job under her mother's maiden name. The guy was a wizard with the law and with government forms. She'd known that someday there'd be bumps, tasks she'd have to handle, responsibilities that Alston couldn't hold at bay. But not this soon. And not at this level.

"I can keep it out of the press, if that's what you're worried about," Alston added. "That'll buy us some time."

She had that, at least.

A loud knock at her front door made her jump up.

"There's someone here, I have to go." She started to hang up, but stopped. "Thank you, Alston. I know you understand what I'm doing. That's better than anybody else who knows me."

"You might be more ready for this than you think," Alston said.

"*My* side, Alston, remember?" But his words rang through her as she hung up the phone.

The front door banged open before Cara could reach it. Albion Bay had an open-door policy, one Cara was still getting used to. Molly Rivers, Sam's mom, breezed into the living room carrying a tissue-wrapped bundle.

Molly came up to Cara's chin. She was beautiful in a delicate sort of way, but the years of being a single mom on the edge had taken their toll. Molly's husband had died in an oil-rig accident two years before Cara moved to Albion Bay, leaving Molly and Sam just enough to scrape by every month. She had a part-time job at Grady's feed barn, but even with that income, Molly and Sam relied on the food bank in town.

Molly unwrapped the bundle and held out a beautiful slate-blue sweater, hand knitted.

"I saw that ratty sweater you had on last week, Cara."

Cara fought down the lump rising in her throat as she took the sweater from Molly's outstretched arms. People in town had been so kind to her. They were the sorts of people who chipped in and helped—it didn't matter if they didn't always see eye to eye on the bigger issues of the world or agree about how to run the town.

"I knew you'd never go out and buy yourself something. Belva had some yarn she'd spun, left over from last year's shearing, and we dyed it to go with your eyes."

Cara slipped the sweater over her head.

"It's perfect," Molly crooned. "Even if it's me admiring my own work."

Cara looked at her reflection in the two foot by two foot mirror she'd hung on the wall next to her door. She hoped the emotion she was unsuccessfully swallowing down didn't show in her eyes. But it did. Cara wrapped her hands around her elbows.

"It's lovely, Molly. It's so soft."

"And it fits you *perfectly*. Belva said you were bosomy— that's a funny word, isn't it?—but I told her that you were slim in the waist. I measured you from behind one day when you were working in the garden. If I'd listened to her, I would've had you looking like a sack of rice."

She stared for a moment, and Cara braced under the scrutiny.

"You *really* should let Mary Brown see to that hair," Molly said. "Maybe just trim off a couple inches and get it away from your face. You have such a beautiful face, Cara. You shouldn't be hiding it like you do. How are you ever going to meet a good man if you hide away like that?"

Cara was accustomed to Molly's occasional mother-henning. But she drew the line at matchmaking. Her first year in town, just to fit in, she'd accepted a blind date Molly had set up. The evening with a mechanic from a nearby town was a disaster she wasn't going to repeat. But she had to admit there were times when the hunger for a man crept through her defenses and swept loneliness into her soul.

For the moment she was glad that the focus was on her hair and not on the pulse she'd seen racing in her throat when she'd looked in the mirror. Deceiving the good people of Albion Bay was a burden she bore alone.

She talked Molly into taking two big jars of her homemade strawberry jam with her as she left. Only after Molly turned up the lane did Cara break down and cry.

CHAPTER TWO

THE CROWD IN DETROIT WAS ROWDY. ONE THING about playing in center field, Ryan got a taste of the hard-core fans and their energy. He'd stolen a home run from the Tigers' best hitter in the eighth, so he wasn't on their happy list.

Ryan crouched and focused on Romaro, their closer, and tuned out the catcalls and obscenities. If Romaro did his job and struck out Hobbs, the final Tigers hitter, the game was theirs. But there was nothing comfortable about a one-run lead. Ryan had played against Renaudo in the minors—the guy had power and, more than that, he could put the ball where he wanted it.

Romaro's pitch was too sweet. Hobbs connected and shot it through the gap.

Ryan was too far back to scoop it on a hop. He waved off Paxton in right field and dove, rolling, and then sprang to his feet and fired the ball to Alex Tavonesi, poised and ready at first. Ryan's throw was on the mark, and Alex stayed on the bag, but the umpire called Hobbs safe.

Ryan cursed. Sometimes close calls didn't go your way. But Hobbs should've been called out, ending the game.

When the next Tigers hitter shot a line drive into shortstop Matt Darrington's glove, the crowd booed. Usually Ryan could translate the negative energy of the opposing team's fans into what it was—love of the game. But tonight the echoing boos just dragged him into the gloomy, black feelings he hated to give the upper hand.

They'd won—he should at least feel happy about that. But he didn't.

He was miserable and pissed because he had to jump on a plane, fly to Boston, and sit in a courtroom publicly facing more lies and accusations. Worse, for the first time in his Major League career, he'd miss a game.

He boarded the plane and swore that no matter what happened, he'd never miss another game. There were thousands of guys out there hungry to take his job, a hundred of them lined up, ready and waiting. But more than that, the game was sacred to him. But the law was the law, and this time he hadn't had a choice.

The next morning Ryan grabbed a coffee from the corner kiosk and headed for the courthouse. Usually he took the time to admire the architecture of the city; he loved Boston. Playing there for four years had been a dream. But he loved San Francisco more. Maybe it was the unconventional, pioneering spirit from the Gold Rush that still bubbled there, or maybe it was just the stunning beauty of the hills, the Bay and the way the western light played on the sea. Whatever it was, when the Red Sox traded him to the Giants, he'd celebrated.

And had sex that night with a woman he should have steered clear of. The champagne and the headiness of celebrating had made him tamp down his trusted warning signals.

People hurried along the corridor of the courthouse, their footsteps clacking on the marble floors and echoing through the hall. How many people would have their lives and future decided in this building today? How many would face injustices like the one he faced?

"You look terrible," Tom Stevens, his attorney, said as he caught up with Ryan outside the hearing room.

"Late flight, bad bed and bad dreams," Ryan said. He didn't have to elaborate. Tom knew what they were up against.

"She's upped her request to twenty thousand a month," Tom said.

Ryan took the papers Tom held out. "What could anyone possibly spend that much on?"

"Maybe she's going to have the kid dipped in gold."

Tom wasn't a cynic, but in the past three weeks, the woman's demands had made them both rethink their vision of humanity.

"Did the judge take into account that she had the kid more than nine months from the date I had sex with her?"

"She had a doctor swear that she had a late gestation."

"Six weeks late?"

Tom shook his head. "The judge bought it."

"And overlooked the fact that I used a condom." Ryan clamped his hands into fists and held them still at his sides, resisting the urge to strike out at the wood paneling of the hallway. "Maybe he hates athletes."

"Worse—he hates baseball players. His youngest daughter was jilted by one of the Yankees. I doubt I have to tell you who."

"I still don't get why the judge subpoenaed me, why I had to come in person. I'm missing a game."

"He couldn't care less. Maybe he wanted to torture you."

"He's succeeding."

They took their seats in the courtroom. Ryan breathed

easier at finding that the woman wasn't there. Elaine—he had to look down at the papers in front of him for her last name—Elaine Mooney.

But he'd sighed his relief too soon. Elaine walked in flanked by four men in high-styled business suits. She looked like a pilgrim, wearing no jewelry and her black dress with its white lace collar right up to her neck. But what riveted Ryan's attention was the baby she held in her arms.

Because he hadn't been able to turn away from thoughts about the baby, he'd made decisions that had more than frustrated his attorney. If she'd kept to their original paternity settlement, he'd never have seen the child. But evidently greed had grabbed her. Or maybe his high-paying contract had put more dollar signs in the eyes of her well-dressed attorneys. She'd dressed the tiny boy in some sort of cute outfit and now displayed him in over-the-top motherly ways in front of the judge. She couldn't have known what that did to Ryan; he suspected she wouldn't have cared. Ryan had listened to Tom and resisted the urge to request to see the child after it was born, but now he had a face to fuel his warring thoughts.

She'd already made it clear that it was money she wanted, not Ryan. That she didn't want the kid to have a father bothered him.

As the judge began the proceedings, Elaine Mooney never once glanced at Ryan, though her attorneys kept him in their hawk-like stares. He was pretty sure they thought they had his number. Maybe they did.

Ryan sat in the coffee shop down the street from the courthouse, watching Tom eat a hearty steak and cheese sandwich.

"How can you have an appetite after that?"

"In my business, Ryan, that was a two on a scale of ten. And besides, we succeeded. You have ninety days to show evidence and to appeal the judge's decision. We can do a lot in ninety days."

"I'm not doing it, Tom." Ryan pushed his bowl of chowder away. The sour feeling in his stomach wouldn't take well to food.

"Did you ever wonder how I got in this business?" Tom took another huge bite out of his sandwich.

Ryan shrugged.

"I like justice. Have a passion for it. And while I admire your feeling for that kid, it's not your kid, Ryan. We know that. *She* knows that. I think even the judge knows that." He took a huge slug of his iced tea. "I'm asking you to rethink my request. It'd save all of us a lot of trouble."

"The part you don't get, Tom—the part that I haven't been able to let go of—is that if I have the DNA test and the kid's not mine, then what? Then what happens to that kid living with that kind of woman?"

"That's not your problem." Tom dipped his sandwich into his side of sauce. "And maybe if you step out of this, maybe the real father will step up. He'd have rights to the kid, rights he could prove, rights he could exercise. The kid would have a chance at having a dad."

"I shouldn't have signed off on those original papers saying I'd pay and stay out of her life."

"That was before you had me. Baseball agents should never substitute for attorneys. Yours steered you wrong."

"He was trying to protect my image." And the contract Ryan was hoping to sign with the Giants. A messy, public paternity trial wouldn't have helped his agent's bargaining power.

"Yeah, yeah. Look, it's a quick cheek swab. One swipe, and you'll know for sure. Justice has mysterious paths, but the one you're on isn't right."

Tom pulled a card out of his pocket. "This is Dr. Garrett; he's in San Francisco. He'll take care of the details." He nudged the card across the table. "Think about it, Ryan. Think really, really hard."

"I'm paying you to think."

"That's right. And you're paying me to get you to where you won't go yourself." Tom crossed his arms and leveled his best attorney stare at Ryan. "It's not just this thing with Elaine, is it?"

When Ryan didn't answer, Tom shook his head. "Whoever tangled you up like this—whatever happened— it's time to move on. A guy like you should be enjoying his life, not stewing over the past and creating problems that aren't there."

On the flight back to San Francisco, Ryan wrestled with his conscience. Tom was right about one thing: if the father of the kid stepped up, the kid might have a dad. Every kid deserved a dad, even if the guy wasn't perfect.

Exhaustion tugged at him. He propped his head against the tiny window and gave in to a fitful sleep. The flight attendant woke him to ask that he bring his seat upright for landing. He stared down at the vast expanse of the San Francisco Bay, his eyes tracking the whitecaps whipped up by the afternoon winds.

Tom's words slid across the back of his mind. Maybe he did need to get a grip and focus on what was going right in his life.

But as the plane circled to land, the thready voice that rose from the depths of the dark recesses called to him, taunted him—told him that whatever he did it would never be enough. Nothing seemed to ease the gaping hole that lurked in his heart even on his best days.

He'd distracted himself with the pleasure of spending

some of his multi-million-dollar salary on things he'd always dreamed of having. The Bugatti was off the charts, but he'd paid it off. And still he had enough left over to buy the ranch in Albion Bay outright and renovate it.

But those pleasures hadn't filled the hole.

And the incessant gnawing hadn't made life outside the stadium any easier to wrangle. When he'd first come up to the majors, he'd been like every other rookie from a small town who'd made it to the show. The accolades and the attention had been like a drug. The attention from women, lots of women, had gone to his head. And everywhere else. Like some of his buddies, he'd played fast and loose the first couple of years. And the plentiful sex almost made it possible to forget Terese.

Almost. Until he got burned by Elaine Mooney.

Lies.

He'd never had any tolerance for lies. Lying stole the freedom to make real choices out from under the person being lied to. A gentle white lie? Maybe those were okay— he struggled with those himself. In eighth grade, when his older sister had asked if the jeans she'd worked months to save up for looked good, he'd told her he liked the color. But he hadn't told her they made her look like a linebacker for the Cowboys. He probably should have, but it would've broken her spirit.

A well-intentioned white lie was one thing, but a deliberate, life-changing altering of the truth? He'd never run up against a reason strong enough to support twisting reality like that.

Elaine's lie had cost more than attorney's fees and lost time.

The paternity suit had shut him down again, numbed his heart and eroded the buoyant trust he'd fought so hard to wrap around himself. Elaine's lies pushed him into cynical mode, snapped him back into the head spin that had first gripped him on the hot summer afternoon he'd raced out of a grueling minor league team game and ridden four hours on a crowded bus to meet Terese. She hadn't been happy to see him. With a blank expression she'd told him that she needed some space. That she needed time to think. She hadn't given him any explanation, just handed him the key to his apartment and told him she'd be in touch.

He'd found out the next week that she'd already moved in with a big-shot plastic surgeon from Atlanta. A month later his sister told him she'd married the guy.

Space, my ass.

What bothered him most was that he hadn't seen it coming. Maybe love was blind, but it didn't make him feel any less the fool when she sent a letter six months later telling him that she'd needed a stable life, a life in the city where she could feel part of a bigger world. He could read between the lines; she hadn't believed he'd make it to the majors. To her he was just another ranch foreman's son who'd end up stringing barbed wire and mending fences. She'd wanted a sure ticket out of East Texas, and she'd bagged one.

He'd loved Terese from as far back as he could remember; they'd grown up together. She'd been his first kiss, his first love. His first everything. He'd given her his heart. Evidently it wasn't worth much.

The irony was, he still yearned for the power of the love he'd felt for her, but the voice that drove his yearning wasn't one he trusted anymore. Maybe he never would again.

CHAPTER THREE

RYAN DROVE LIKE A MADMAN FROM THE BALLPARK. His Bugatti took the curves of the country roads heading to Albion Bay like the finely engineered machine she was. She might not have been the wisest expenditure, but she was a darn sweet pleasure on the country roads. He needed a name for her—something so special needed a really hot name.

He pulled the car into his barn and closed the door. Though he loved driving the Bugatti, he didn't want the people of Albion Bay getting the wrong impression. He jumped into his Jeep and headed over the ridge that separated his ranch from the town of Albion Bay.

He pulled into the dusty parking lot next to the Albion Bay middle school. A freshly painted sign sported an image of a peregrine falcon, the team mascot. He'd seen parents and kids painting the sign the previous week. He'd watched their progress from the window of Nick's Place, the local diner where he ate hurried breakfasts before charging off to the stadium. One thing he'd noticed about the town—if something needed to be done, everybody rose to the occasion.

He felt the wave of energy flow out from the kids and parents as he headed toward the rough-hewn bench that served as the home-team dugout. He'd gotten used to the stir his presence caused; most times he did his best to ignore it. He'd learned the hard way to put public admiration in perspective. Players who didn't went down hard.

It was one thing to respect fans—their energy was part of the game, certainly part of his, and they loved baseball as much as he did. But twisting the love of baseball into something else, into something personal, into something you craved, that road was paved with misery.

Outside the stadium, turned heads and comments in public didn't bother him, not usually—it was part of the price he paid to play for a championship team.

But out here in Albion Bay he wanted to be just a citizen of the town, accepted for what he could contribute and not for the fantasies or projections he inspired.

A week after buying the ranch, he'd volunteered to help with the middle school baseball team. He'd warned the coach, Dave Jenkins, that until the Giants' season was over he'd have little time, but promised that in November he'd be able to do more. Right now they had to settle for him showing up when the team had a day off or for him arriving late after a day game.

"Hey, Ryan," Perry Norman hollered out to him. Albion's mayor was called *Perk* by his constituents. "Nice shot in the third."

His triple had been a thrill. The runs he'd batted in had given the Giants a lead they'd held to win the game. Ryan was still buzzing from the rush. The team had lost the day before, while he'd sat in that damned courtroom. And his performance today hadn't dissolved the inquiring stares in the clubhouse. Usually somebody had to die or be the equivalent of mortally wounded before a guy missed a game. When he'd suited up for the game that day, Ryan had felt that he'd experienced the sting of both.

He nodded toward the visitors' bench. "Let's see if we

can duplicate that play against the Hawks tonight."

"The Hawks have a good lefty," Perk said. "Our boys don't hit him well."

The boys on the Albion team were a rather scrawny crew of twelve- and thirteen-year-olds playing with outdated equipment. Ryan knew too well the feeling of being a scrawny kid on a team with subpar equipment. During his own early middle school years, he'd been the scrawniest kid on his team—until he'd had his growth spurt. He'd shot up and filled out, but the shame and frustration of those early years still clung to him like a cloying octopus.

But he'd been a twelve-year-old with a mission. He'd been determined to make it to the big leagues. And he had made it. He was living his dream. And it was a good life.

He'd made up his mind to show the local boys a few tricks that might whet their interest and entice them into practicing the basics. The thought put a smile on his face. These off-season intramural games didn't count against the Falcons' team record, but they built up a player's skills and experience. He'd set up a batting cage in his second barn and put in a practice diamond behind the ranch house. By the time the spring season started, he was pretty sure he could help Dave get the boys into shape. *If* they practiced. And maybe grew a few inches and put on some muscle over the winter.

Ryan's stomach grumbled.

He'd skipped out on the spread in the clubhouse after the game and driven faster than he should have to get to the middle school game before it started. And he was starving.

"The taco stand open for business?" Ryan nodded toward the tables set up near the parking lot.

"*Five* bucks a shot." Perk shrugged. "We need new bats. If they sell out tonight, that should do it."

Ryan had been tempted to plunk down the money for the bats, but he'd learned early on that the citizens of Albion

Bay had very definite ideas of self-sufficiency. Maybe it was pride. He understood the power of pride, wrestled with it himself. He'd have to settle for buying a few fish tacos and find a diplomatic way to help out with equipment expenses.

But he wasn't giving up on talking Dave into letting him pay to have the field rolled and seeded. Convincing the stubborn coach might require a few nights over beers at Nick's, but he'd manage it. If he didn't, the field would be a muddy mess after the winter rains had their way.

Ryan slipped past a group of moms and over to the taco stand fashioned out of folding tables and camp stoves. Cain Bryant, the best fisherman in Albion Bay, was filleting a salmon on a worn cutting board. The prospect of a fresh salmon taco made Ryan's stomach growl louder.

"Had to go out ten miles for this big guy," Cain said as Ryan approached. "Want the usual?"

Cain and he had gotten to know each other over stacks of pancakes at the diner; one meal Ryan had never learned to do well was breakfast. At least not the kind of breakfast he wanted to eat. He and Cain had developed an unspoken respect for each other. Ryan played the game Cain loved and played it well. And Cain fought off elements out in the open ocean that Ryan could only imagine facing. In the winter, waves could top fifteen feet and fog and storms made for treacherous fishing. To do what they loved, they both pitted their bodies against the elements of speed and force.

"Yup," Ryan said, leaning in to savor the aroma of the sizzling salmon. "Make it three."

"We don't need bats *that* bad," Cain said with a grin. He poked Ryan's rock-hard abs. "Tubby center fielders don't win pennants."

"In that case, make it four. I'll save two for breakfast."

"Fish shouldn't be left out without refrigeration," a woman said as she walked up to Cain. Though her voice was like velvet, her tone smacked of authority.

Ryan had seen the woman around town and driving a school bus. She was tall, almost model-like, but she wore simple clothes that hid her body, and her unruly hair made her face hard to see.

"It's fifty degrees out, Cara," Cain said with a laugh. "But if it makes you feel better, I'll put Mr. Rea's breakfast on ice until the end of the game."

Cara brushed her hair away from her face and smiled at Cain. She didn't look at Ryan; instead she studiously started chopping onions. But Ryan had glimpsed her haunting beauty, and felt the ping of attraction he hadn't felt for a long time.

Cara showed none of the usual posturing to capture his attention. He was grateful to the good people of Albion for giving him a chance to be considered for his qualities as a person, as a member of the community rather than for his stature as a sports star. Though he knew it wasn't real, the *feeling* of anonymity was refreshing.

And Cara's lack of regard intrigued him. He saw through the transparent gloves she wore that she didn't sport a wedding ring.

She plated his tacos and handed them to him with barely a glance. But enough of a glance to tell him that she was a puzzle he'd like to explore.

As Perk had predicted, the Falcons fared poorly against the Hawks. In the bottom of the ninth, Sam Rivers attempted to steal second but collapsed, gasping, halfway there. The Hawks second baseman ran over and tagged him out, ending the inning and shutting down the Falcons' chance to even the score.

Sam's mother, Molly, ran onto the field brandishing an

inhaler. Sam waved her off, clearly embarrassed.

"There's no telling that boy anything," Dave said over his shoulder as he jogged out to where a crowd of players and moms had gathered around Sam.

"Kid's got one of those asthma conditions," Perk said as he helped Ryan stash the bats and balls in a burlap bag. "But Molly's right to let him play. A boy's gotta have a life."

Sam got up, still struggling for breath. He shooed his mom away and trudged over to collect his gear bag.

"Hey, nice dash," Ryan said, going for a casual, offhand tone.

"Hardly," Sam said. His shoulders had the defeated hunch Ryan hated to see on anyone.

"Hey—I've been thrown out lots of times trying to steal second," Ryan said, conveniently leaving out the fact that he'd succeeded more than a hundred times. Though he was tempted to pat Sam on the shoulder, he didn't. "You never get anywhere if you don't give it a go."

Sam didn't say anything, but Ryan saw the boy's shoulders relax. He remembered being Sam's age. Every mistake loomed like the end of the world.

After the Hawks loaded onto their team bus, the parents and the Falcons' players began to disperse. Ryan headed over to collect his breakfast tacos. Cain wasn't there, but Cara was. She didn't see him approach, and he had a moment to study her. Her dress was worn and faded, but the light evening breeze made the sweater she wore over it hug her very fit body. Her movements were efficient but graceful, like a dancer's or an athlete's. She smiled as she worked, and Ryan was pretty sure it was the sweetest, freshest smile he'd seen in years. When she looked up and caught him staring, her smile faded fast.

"I came to collect my iced-down breakfast," he said, suddenly feeling awkward. There was something about her that made his body stand at attention and his brain go into alert mode.

She turned to the cooler and pulled out a plastic bag. She started to hand the bag to him, but then pulled it back.

"You'll need an outer bag with some ice to keep these cold until you get home."

"It's a short trip," he said. And then his next idea had him changing his mind. "On second thought, more ice would be great. Especially since I'm hoping you'll join me at the diner for a beer before I head home."

She stiffened.

Okay, maybe his approach was too forward. He was still adjusting to the ways of the people in the town.

"No, thanks. I have to clean up here."

"Then let me help." Ryan stepped around the table and picked up a cleaning rag. The scent of fish rose up from it, but standing next to Cara he also detected the scent of honeysuckle. He knew that scent. Bowers of it grew on the ranch he'd been raised on.

"I can handle this," she said. "I'm sure you have more important things to do."

"Can't think of a thing." Ryan swapped out the fish towel for what appeared to be a clean one and began wiping down the table.

"I'm still not going to have a beer with you," she said.

She said it softly, but he heard the restraint and confidence in her tone. It told him she was a woman who had very clear ideas of what she did and didn't want in her life. That she wasn't jumping on a chance to go out with him was as refreshing as her gentle but firmly straightforward manner.

"Then how about a cup of tea?" He knew women liked tea; his sister and mother did. He'd snagged a couple of unlikely dates by suggesting an outing for a cup of tea. There was something about the drink that must signal safety to women. Nothing racy like, *Hey, join me for a magnum of Dom Pérignon at my place*, even if that might be what he wanted.

She looked up from the ice chest. "It's been a long day," she said, melting him with a sigh that told him it was true.

He busied himself with scraping down the grilling skillet with a wire brush and considered his next-best approach. He was aware of her studying him, and tamped down the zing of arousal that had him imagining scenarios well beyond a cup of tea.

"But maybe tomorrow," she said, surprising him. "Just tea."

He had a ten-day road trip. Ten days without seeing her was a painful penalty for failing to woo her into joining him tonight. But he could see the fatigue in her eyes, so he didn't push.

"I'll be away for a couple weeks," he said. "How about the tenth? That's my next free day."

"There's an all-day canning session for the food bank that day," she said as she packed up a box with utensils and condiments. "Then a party at Grady's feed barn after, to celebrate."

"I know a bit about canning. My grandmother used to lasso me to help out with the heavy lifting."

"You're a man of many talents, Mr. Rea."

Her smooth response didn't fit his image of a small-town woman. And he wasn't sure if she was poking fun at his blatant attempt to ask her out. Right then it didn't matter. All he knew was that he craved to know more about her.

Molly Rivers walked up and stacked napkins and paper plates inside the box Cara had packed. "I'll take this, Cara. I'm on taco duty next week."

"How's your boy doing?" Ryan hid his concern with a level tone.

"Recovering. No boy wants to cart an inhaler around the infield. But he pays the consequence when he doesn't." She looked over to where Sam stood talking with Dave Jenkins. "If I could get him to spend one-tenth the energy he puts into baseball on his homework, I'd feel I was doing my job."

Her words rang in him, echoing memories of his dad saying the very same thing. But he wasn't his dad, and he had an opportunity to support the kid's dream.

"He's got a solid swing," Ryan said.

It was true, the kid had talent. So Molly had her work cut out for her. Ryan knew too well the allure of the diamond. Reading books and scratching out numbers on homework pages might get Sam ahead in school, but study couldn't compare to the buzz of smacking a game-winning hit or stealing a base. He grimaced as he remembered the fights with his father on nights when he'd sneaked out of the house to hit balls into the piece of chain link he'd set up as a practice fence behind their house.

"Maybe you could tell him that his studies are just as important as practicing his swing," Molly said in a quiet voice.

"I'm afraid I won't be much help in that department," Ryan said with a shrug. "I'm not much for bending the truth."

Molly shook her head and hefted the box.

"Let me help you," Ryan said, taking the box from her.

"My truck's the green one." She grabbed a stack of paper cups and dropped them on top of the overflowing box. "Last chance to tell Sam the importance of doing his math homework."

Ryan laughed. "I'll put in a word about the geometry of the baseball field. Worked for me."

"Mr. Rea here might be joining us for our canning session," Cara said.

Ryan heard the unspoken question in her tone.

Molly looked from Cara to Ryan. "We could use some brawn," she said with a grin. "But did Cara warn you about Belva? She's mighty picky about outsiders in her kitchen."

"He *lives* here," Cara said quickly.

"Yeah? So does Martha Stewart. And you're not going to see Belva inviting her to anything, at least not yet." She studied Ryan. "But since you're helping with the ball team, Belva might make an exception."

That he was concerned about being approved to help a bunch of ladies can their vegetables struck Ryan as ridiculous. But as he looked at Cara and saw the smile curve into her face, he hoped he'd make the cut.

CHAPTER FOUR

ACEDOWN ON THE TRAINER'S TABLE WAS NOT THE place Ryan preferred to be. But the pain in his right shoulder had cost him at the plate that afternoon.

He'd smacked a double in the first inning, but the hitch in his swing had him late on the pitches in later innings. What should've been a home run in the eighth turned into an off-the-pole foul.

But worse than that, his subpar throw to home in the ninth had cost the Giants the game. At least that's how he saw it. Sure, he could run a mental replay of all the at-bats and fielding moves, point to any number of split-second plays and come up with a dozen variables that added up to a loss. But *he* hadn't played well. Not like he could.

"I can shoot that shoulder up with some cortisone," Mark said after another unsuccessful kneading of Ryan's muscles.

Some days the pain just went away—it didn't matter whether he played or had a day off. On days when it hurt so much he thought he'd have to pull himself from the lineup, the trainers tried everything. Ryan's pain stumped them. Right now, he was the team's hottest bat and their arm in center field—they'd try anything to keep him in the game. But he drew the line at injections; shots and painkillers would be a last resort. He'd seen what cortisone had done to a buddy on the Red Sox. For now he was going with ice, massage and disciplined physical therapy.

And sucking up the pain.

At twenty-four, he was the youngest center fielder to be in the running for a Gold Glove. An honor like that would put him in a category with Jones and Kemp and would be a dream come true. That it might help settle a score with his father wasn't an outcome he could count on.

With a month left to go in the season, he already had three hundred and sixty-seven put-outs and eighteen assists, and he'd climbed his fielding percentage to .988. Only two players were close to his stats, and both were veterans with more than a decade in the game.

But the season wasn't over.

He'd have to work out the kink in his shoulder if he was going to stay on top, if he was going to be a solid asset for the team.

And he'd have to get more sleep.

He woke too many nights in a tangle of covers and sweat, nagged by nightmares. Some nights he felt like a ghost had decided to settle in his muscles and haunt him.

When the Giants bought out his contract with Boston, he'd been sure that that'd be the end of sleepless nights. He'd arrived, hadn't he? He was playing for the team he'd always dreamed of playing for in a city that loved the game. His agent was negotiating a sweet deal that could bring him a six-year, fifty-million-dollar contract. The early rumors about the contract were probably what had ramped up Elaine's lawyers' greed.

Ryan sat up on the trainer's table. "No injections. I'll work it out."

"Walsh would like me to convince you," Mark said. "The playoffs are ahead."

Playoffs were ahead only if the Giants kept their lead in

the division. Of course Hal Walsh wanted him to try anything that might work; it was a manager's job to keep his team playing at their best. And Ryan had an obligation to the team to do what it took to play strong. But he knew his body. Cortisone injections weren't the answer.

"If it's not better when we get back from the road trip, I'll think about your needles," Ryan said, hoping it wouldn't come to that. Right then he'd say anything to get the trainers off his back. They were trying to do their jobs, but they couldn't know the nature of his problem. Hell, he wasn't sure himself.

Ryan grabbed a towel and headed for the showers. He inhaled the steamy warmth and let the hot water beat down on his neck and back.

"Table time help any?" Scotty Donovan, Ryan's buddy and the Giants' star pitcher, asked from the shower next to him.

"I'm not a friend of the table."

"I get that," Scotty said. "My grandmother gave me some arnica. I have some if you want to try it. It works for me. Sometimes."

Ryan nodded. He'd try almost anything, as long as it didn't involve scalpels, needles or drugs.

Ryan turned the handle on the shower and ramped up the heat, giving the shoulder even more attention. When he got to his locker, Scotty handed him a blue and white tube.

"Arnica. Salve of champions."

Ryan squeezed some of the ointment onto his palm and spread it across his shoulder. "Did you ever hear about that pitcher—the starter for the Reds—that guy that said he had a phantom pain in his shoulder?"

"Henderly? I call him the Love Boat," Scotty said with a grin. "Any guy who can solve his problems with a beautiful woman is pretty intelligent in my book."

Henderly had been hot; he'd won the Cy Young the year the pain had tormented him. Ryan had heard that nothing had showed up on MRIs or X-rays. Henderly married the next summer and announced that the pain had gone away. Tales flew around the clubhouse that he'd said he'd been battling with a force in his soul and falling in love had changed everything for him. He'd taken a lot of razzing in the press, but his twenty-one and three record said it all. Ryan shrugged. He didn't want to believe that pain in his body had anything to do with forces he couldn't control.

Scotty tilted his head and surveyed Ryan. "If you think it's a phantom pain, maybe you should see a psychic."

Ryan was pretty sure he was kidding. As a pitcher, Scotty knew about shoulder pain. But Ryan wasn't so sure his teammate knew much about psychics.

Ryan shook his head. "Not in the market."

"Or try Love Boat's solution. Find a wife."

"Definitely not in the market." At least he didn't think he was. He wanted to get married, of course. But there was no rush.

Pain zinged along the back of Ryan's shoulder as he turned out of the players' parking lot at the stadium. He adjusted the seat in his Bugatti and tilted the steering wheel down. The pain eased.

He'd beat it—he had to. He didn't believe in phantom pains, not unless there was an amputation involved. He already wished he hadn't mentioned the whole phantom idea to Scotty.

He drove along the Embarcadero and glanced across at Alcatraz. It appeared to float in the tossing waves of the Bay, a reminder of how bad decisions could derail good ones. Had some of the inmates who'd done time there made split-second decisions that landed them in the infamous prison, or had their sentences been the result of repeated poor judgments over a long period of time? Sitting in the courtroom in Boston had made him think hard about the repercussions of bad decisions. And about people and their motivations.

There was a time that he'd thought the best of everyone, had learned from his mother to give others the benefit of the doubt. But the naive man who'd held those values in the past wasn't driving a Bugatti and thinking about prison inmates. Or paternity suits. Or being dumped by the first and only woman he'd loved. He'd left that gullible man behind. But the wall he'd constructed to keep foolish decisions at bay sometimes closed in on him, closed in too tight.

Jeez.

And there he was, thinking about the downside again.

He had to stop.

He knew how to recognize a pattern and change it. He did it in baseball all the time. Just last year he'd adjusted his batting stance and adjusted his grip. The careful tweaks had changed everything—his approach and follow-through and his stats. And he'd trained himself to sink into a meditative state when he stood in the batter's box, had learned to let everything but his body, his concentration and his awareness of the movements of the pitcher drop away.

Flow.

That was what the scientists called the zone he could drop into. With practice he'd found he could shut his eyes and focus, call up the flow and stay with it. Let his striving and worries drop away so he could sink in.

But since the night he'd met Cara, when he shut his eyes and went for ramping up his flow, her face would float in front of him. It spooked him because he didn't even know her. And it didn't help that the images of her quickly morphed into hot fantasies that had him wanting to do more than buy tacos.

Perhaps Scotty was right. Not that he should find a wife, but it couldn't hurt to have a woman in his life. The right kind of woman. He didn't need the surging images of Cara to remind him that it had been way too long since he'd held a woman in his arms.

Like oxygen blowing onto embers long covered by layers of cold, dark ash, meeting Cara had sparked life into a place inside him that he'd thought his caution and wariness might have snuffed.

Maybe he could date her, keep it light, keep it simple. Maybe they could enjoy each other and do things around town.

But as he merged onto the Golden Gate Bridge, his cynicism tightened its grip, locking him into a war that his brain fought against the urgings of his body and heart.

He'd have to be careful not to lead Cara into thinking he was her road out of Albion Bay.

A rescuing Prince Charming he wasn't.

And he likely never would be. The experiences with Terese and Elaine had left long, dark skid marks. Nope, he wouldn't be anyone's road out.

CHAPTER FIVE

RYAN LOOKED THROUGH THE SCREEN DOOR AND into Belva's cavernous kitchen. Steam hung in the room, hovering among the women stirring pots on a commercial-style stove at the center island. Tables lined a far wall and held camp stoves, and those too sported massive, steaming pots. Four women tended those while others chopped vegetables on a wooden counter that reached across the back wall.

He didn't bother knocking. No one would hear over the clattering utensils, the laughter and the sound of knives chopping against wood. He stepped through the door. It was twenty degrees hotter in the kitchen than the warm autumn day outside.

His eyes sought Cara. She was studiously stirring a pot that came nearly to her shoulders. Her hair was pulled back into a ponytail and for the first time he saw the beautiful, heart-shaped frame of her face. She swiped the back of her hand at the beads of perspiration on her brow and held her lips in a half-smile, half-frown.

She had beautiful lips. They were full, but not too full. And the rosy red color was like something out of the fairy tales his sister used to love. But fairy tales weren't what he had in mind as he watched her purse her lips to sip from a spoon she'd dipped into the pot. She closed her eyes and savored whatever she was tasting. Then she cut her gaze to where he stood in the doorway, and her hand froze, midmotion. Molly Rivers stood beside her. She saw Cara freeze and turned toward the door. Like a herd of startled antelope, the rest of the women stopped what they were doing as a silence fell over the room. The only sounds were the boiling pots and the hiss of gas burners.

Flee.

Ryan swallowed down the impulse and shrugged.

"For God's sake," a heavyset woman called from the end of the kitchen island. "Get that boy an apron, Cara," she ordered as she walked over to Ryan. "You're just in time. My husband, Roy"—she crossed herself—"God rest his soul, always helped with the heavy lifting." A smile crinkled in the lines around her eyes as she wiped her hands on her apron. "You'll have to do. I'm Belva Rosario."

She shook his hand with a firm grip. From the look of her and the grip of her handshake, he wasn't sure she really needed him to lift anything. She had biceps nearly as big as his.

"Ryan Rea."

"I know who you are," she said. "I don't let strangers wander into my kitchen." She tilted her head toward Cara and Molly. "The girls here say you'll be handy."

He wouldn't want to face the price she'd exact if he wasn't.

Cara handed him a yellow apron.

"The only other one left is pink," she said with a laughing light in her eyes. "Not your color, I imagine."

He ignored the ruffle at the bottom and strapped it on.

"Looks like he has a strong hand," Belva said.

Being sized up by an Italian grandmother was worse than facing the scouts in college. That she referred to him in the third person brought all those edgy days swooping back.

But when she took him by the elbow and led him over to stand beside Cara, he forgave her for stirring anxious memories.

"Back to work, ladies," Belva said with a loud clap of her hands. "Perk's picking the canned food up at three."

Belva handed him an eleven-inch cleaver.

"Our squash has tough skin this year. Usually we'd bake them in the oven, but we don't have the time. See if you can carve through these babies, and we'll have squash soup for canning."

Without a backward glance she marched to the other end of the kitchen and began giving orders to two women peeling pears.

This was not his grandmother's canning scene. Not even close.

The days when he'd helped put up watermelon-rind pickles and stolen cherries before they went into jam pots seemed very distant. These women were serious. Cain had told him at breakfast that morning that they put up nearly six thousand dollars' worth of food for the food bank every year.

As he surveyed the crates of vegetables and fruits stacked around the kitchen, Ryan didn't doubt Cain's estimate. When he'd asked Cain why he didn't pitch in and help, the other man looked at Ryan like he was nuts. He'd rather face a tsunami in the open ocean than make a wrong move around Belva, he'd said. Ryan was beginning to see why.

He squared off with the first of the two dozen or so squashes spread before him on the table. He tried using force to press the cleaver into the tough skin, but it glanced off. He tried turning the squash on its end and pushing the blade down with both hands. No go.

He heard a light giggle.

The last time he'd heard a giggle was from his sister Eve when her boyfriend had asked her out in tenth grade. He looked up from the cleaver. Cara smiled. He hadn't imagined her giggling. Laughing, sighing, moaning when he... He stopped himself. Recalling some of the fantasies she'd starred in while he'd let hot water drill into his shoulder in the clubhouse wasn't going to help in this situation. Nor likely in any other.

"Try this." She put her hand over where his rested on the handle of the cleaver. "See the seam, the gap between the ridges? Just edge the blade in there. Give it a little wiggle."

His pulse picked up at her touch. Giggles and wiggles were not what his body had in mind. He tried to squelch the new fantasies racing through his mind. Sometimes a good imagination was not a guy's best asset.

She leaned closer to guide his hand, and he felt the curve of her breast barely touch his forearm. As if reading his mind, she backed away.

He put the cleaver exactly where she pointed and pressed. Again it glanced off.

"A pickaxe would be my tool of choice here," Ryan said through clenched teeth. Though there was humor in his voice, he couldn't believe he'd been bested by a squash.

"I heard that," Belva said as she strode over to him. "Those are my prize Burgess Buttercups."

She took the cleaver and lined up a squash in front of her on the cutting board and muscled the cleaver in between the ridges. To his delight, she had no more success opening the squash than he had.

"Okay, so maybe not a pickaxe," Ryan said, keeping any gloating out of his voice. "But maybe you have an ax nearby? Or a different species of squash?"

Belva puffed up like a cornered adder. "These make the best soup."

He trusted her on that. He'd had a bowl of her soup at the diner.

"I'll set you up outside," she said. "Cara, let Molly take over there. Help Mr. Rea with these darn squash."

"Please, call me Ryan."

Belva gave him an assessing look that could've halted a Cape buffalo stampede. He was used to being called Rea—some guys on the team did it and he'd asked the kids to call him Coach Rea—but *Mr.* Rea? It bugged him coming from an adult.

"Follow me," Belva said.

As he watched the swing of Cara's hips as he followed her and Belva out into the back garden, Ryan squelched a smile and thanked the heavens for his brusque, Italian, cleaver-wielding angel of mercy.

Belva set them up with some squares of cardboard and handed Ryan a battered but serviceable ax.

"I don't suppose I have to show you how to use this," she said, squinting into the sunlight. She reminded him of his grandmother. Only his grandmother didn't put the fear of God into him like Belva did.

"No, ma'am, you don't."

"I'm too old to be running around doing away with volunteers, so don't go letting any of those seeds scatter in my garden."

He wasn't sure if she meant doing away with him or the squash seeds that might escape and sprout unplanned. Whichever was true, he'd be careful not to rile Belva.

But as he knelt beside Cara and saw how the dampness from the steam had made her blouse cling to the curve of her breasts and felt the heat from her body, he didn't much care what Belva or anybody else thought. For the next few hours, he'd be in heaven. As the breeze stirred and wafted the scent of honeysuckle and woman to him, he was sure of it.

Cara scooped seeds from the fifth squash Ryan had opened. The man wielded an ax as if he'd done it all his life. Maybe he had. She knew little about him. Sure, everybody in town talked about his All-Star status as the Giants' hot, young center fielder, but that was about it. Except she'd seen the Bugatti. But the flashy car didn't fit with the down-to-earth guy who helped out with the local team and came to lend a hand with community canning.

Maybe she should've warned him that the sessions were hard work. She still felt a little guilty about taking him up on his offer. But this was Belva's first year without Roy around. Having Ryan there not only helped, it filled the gap Roy left. Sort of. That she'd converted Ryan's obvious interest in her to lure him to participate wasn't *such* an underhanded ploy. After all, helping out the ladies of Albion Bay wasn't Gulag duty.

But she hadn't counted on the visceral, physical presence of the man. Or on her reaction to him. She'd always thought ads and commercials with manly men doing manly activities were aimed at women other than herself.

She'd been wrong.

When he took off the apron and then removed his T-shirt, folded it and laid it on the ground, she felt her heart stutter. Never had she imagined that real men had six-pack abs. And the fine line of golden hair that dipped into the top of his jeans hadn't been airbrushed on.

The man was lip-smacking hot.

And focusing on him took her mind off the looming deadline that rattled through her thoughts even when she was trying to forget about it.

Blushing, she turned back to scooping seeds from the squashes he'd expertly split open and tried to turn her mind to the task at hand. Ryan worked fast. Or maybe time had sped up. Within what seemed mere minutes he'd surrounded her with perfectly halved squashes. Cara's arms were tiring as she scooped out the seeds and tried to keep up with him.

"Break time," Belva said as she arranged a tray of lemonade on a table near the door. She surveyed the pile of cleaved, seeded and hollowed-out squashes. "Not bad for beginners."

Ryan laughed.

Cara had seen him smile but hadn't heard him laugh. Part of her wished she still hadn't. Ryan Rea had one of those laughs that went beyond words to wrap into a woman's heart and leave her wanting more. He could prove to be real trouble if she let him.

He rested the ax against an oak tree at the garden entrance and walked over to pour out two glasses of lemonade.

"You don't say much," Ryan said as he handed her a glass.

His fingertips brushed hers, and her pulse leaped. Maybe she'd gone too long without a man, but she couldn't just import one into Albion Bay, even if she wanted to—it'd be the talk of the town. And since she'd left her life back East behind, there weren't any prospects there. There were a couple of interesting men in the city, but getting close to any of them would just pose problems she wasn't ready to face.

She sipped her lemonade and told herself it was just good manners to engage Ryan in conversation. She swallowed the tart, cold liquid and dug around in her mind for a safe question.

He squatted down on his haunches near where she sat cross-legged surrounded by the scooped-out squashes. "Where're you from?" he asked before she came up with a question of her own.

The advantage to being the one doing the asking was that she could move the flow of words toward or away from difficult subjects. But some topics were just so basic, they came up no matter how carefully she orchestrated the conversation.

"I grew up in a small town back East," she said.

That much was true. That fact that her family basically owned the entire town of Hudson Manor and that most of the townspeople worked for her family's estate was a detail no one needed to know. Nor was the fact that when she hadn't been in Hudson Manor, she'd lived in her family's sprawling three-floor apartment that soared high above Fifth Avenue in New York.

"My mom's from Boston," Ryan said, gulping down the last of his lemonade and wiping the sweat that had beaded on his face onto his forearm. "Is it always this warm out here in September?"

"It's the most beautiful time of year." She tried not to stare at the planed muscles of his chest. "I've tried to explain how lovely it is at this time of year to... to my friends. I've never succeeded."

Thank God for conversations about the weather. Always a safe topic.

"It'd be hard to describe the light out here," he said with a dreamy stare out across the hills behind Belva's place. "Sometimes when I walk the beach and see the light dancing on the water, and the colors it fires on the hills, it takes my breath away. I've never seen anything like it."

Between the effort she was making not to stare at his body and the disarming way he had of describing exactly what she hadn't been able to put to words, she was feeling more than a little unsettled. Maybe the weather wasn't such a safe topic after all.

He unfolded from his crouch with astonishing ease and

walked toward the table that held the lemonade. Cara tried even more unsuccessfully not to focus on the sweat glistening down his back and highlighting the stretch of muscles that rippled as he moved.

His powerful yet graceful movement brought to mind the panther she'd seen in Guatemala. The panther had surprised her and her guide that morning. If they hadn't been upwind, one of them might've been breakfast. Maybe it was the thrill of being in a presence that had no regard for her as anything other than intruder or prey, or maybe it was the sheer beauty of the panther's primal movements, but the memory had seared deep. Her chest tightened as she remembered the rush of awe and fear as she'd crouched, unmoving, and watched the panther circle, sniff the air and then prowl off into the jungle.

That Ryan called up the same energy she'd felt staring into the eyes of that big cat made her haul in a deep breath and try to gain perspective. She was seeding squash in a small town on the California coast, for goodness' sake. No danger or panthers here.

But as Ryan turned and walked toward her, her breath caught and her pulse pounded. His jeans had that worn-in, perfect fit that hugged his thighs, and they sat perfectly poised on his hips, resting just below the vee of muscles that disappeared below the line of his belt. And just below the buckle of that belt, his jeans pouched out, holding what she could only imagine lay beneath. He was easily an advertiser's dream. No amount of professional fussing could've created the casual, devastating effect of a real man—vital, toned, misted with the sweat of work and obviously very comfortable in that devastating body.

She shifted her eyes to the ring of squash that circled her and shivered with the want coursing in her veins.

"You want more?"

His question startled her out of her fantasy. It took her a moment to register that he was nodding toward her near-empty glass.

Another display of him walking to the table just might do her in. Though she was thirsty, she shook her head.

"No, thanks."

She looked down and picked up the spoon she'd been using to scoop out the squashes. She dug the spoon into the curve of a squash and fought through the images he'd conjured, tried to drag her attention back from her ridiculous loss of control and toward the thread of the conversation. The polite thing to do was to ask about his life. That questions about him turned the conversation away from her was a bonus.

"Where are you from?"

"East Texas. I grew up on a ranch. Sometimes I think East Texas doesn't suit my mom, being that she's an easterner," Ryan added, "but my dad will never move." He took a long draw from the glass he held. "He's a stubborn man."

A mother from Boston explained why Ryan's accent had little of Texas in it. To her ear, Ryan's speech was a refreshing mixture of melodic Southern drawl and the flatter, more articulated consonants and vowels of the Northeast. And his voice had a deep, velvety quality, almost mesmerizing. He could've been a hypnotist or a radio personality. She'd listened that night he'd bantered with Cain at the ball game and tuned in as he'd joshed with the kids. His voice seeped into her like warm, golden honey and made her want to hear more. She liked it. Maybe a little too much.

And she'd be lying if she didn't admit that more than his voice had shown up in her dreams. Now that she'd seen how hot he was and felt her blood sizzle just having him near, her dreams would likely take on a whole new dimension. *That* she could look forward to. Dreams were safe. No trouble there.

But she sure didn't want to get into a loop of questions about families; that always proved to be rocky territory.

"We'd better get back to work or Belva will have our heads," she said, angling for an ease in her tone that she didn't feel.

She picked up another of the squashes he'd cracked open and hoped the slight trembling in her hands didn't show as she began to separate the seeds from the bright orange flesh.

Ryan put his glass down on the slate path and took up the ax.

"How long have you been living out here?" he asked. He angled a perfect swing and split a squash.

Hiding her identity to preserve her freedom had proven to be a greater challenge than she'd expected. Though she longed to share the connection, the closeness that wove the people of Albion Bay into a thriving community, she had to keep her distance. Some days her deception exacted a very high price.

"Three years next month," she answered. Some questions could be more easily answered than others.

He picked up his T-shirt and mopped at the perspiration that glistened along his neck and arms. She'd never seen a man with arms like his, not up close. It was a look that movie stars worked hours in the gym to perfect, but as Ryan swung the ax again and executed a perfect severing of a squash, she knew that actors, no matter how well trained, never came close to approximating the body of a man whose strength was an integral part of his everyday life.

He shot a glance her way, his eyes sparkling in the sunlight. At least she thought the glint was from sunlight. Maybe he was one of those guys who just had lively eyes.

But to her, Ryan's eyes seemed to dance with a mysterious merriment.

"Perk told me you've been a big help on the town planning committee," he said.

"I've been to a few meetings," she responded, grateful for conversation that took her mind off the effect he was having on her.

"I'd rather face a wild pitcher with a ninety-eight-mile-an-hour fast ball than sit through a meeting," he said with a grin. "Perk said the town needs a medical clinic. You helping with that?"

"I've been trying," Cara answered honestly. "The clinic's a sore spot. Albion Bay is twenty miles from the closest medical help. Twenty long and rutted miles to a tiny clinic that's only open during the day. And closed on holidays."

"What about EMTs?"

"It takes thirty minutes for the EMTs from the Point Reyes fire station to arrive. Usually the locals have to drive to the nearest hospital, but that's a *forty*-minute drive."

Forty minutes *if* road conditions were good. Sometimes people didn't survive the drive. Belva's husband, Roy, hadn't.

Six months ago Cara had tried to convince the planning committee that maybe an interim step would help, that they could make use of one of the vacant offices in town and pay the salary of a doctor, maybe two. Though she couldn't tell them outright, she would've been able to direct some of her money through her attorney and fund a doctor's salary, pay the rent on the office and buy basic equipment and supplies.

But the committee had argued that Albion Bay needed a 24/7 clinic and they didn't want to get waylaid with interim steps.

Instead of acting on the plan she suggested, they'd

hired a consultant to help them figure out how to raise the money to fund a proper clinic. Cara's heart fell when the consultant's first effort was to put together a study to assess the feasibility of raising the money they'd need. When the consultant's study reported that the town couldn't even afford the interim doctor, the committee had fired her. Sometimes the truth wasn't what anyone wanted to hear.

Until three days ago, Cara had no way to fully fund a clinic; it was out of her league. But if she stepped up and took the reins of the Barrington Foundation, she could pay for the whole damned thing. For the past week, she'd managed to ignore her conflicted feelings. But Ryan's innocent question drove her dilemma home hard.

"Then it's ranch first aid that'll have to do," Ryan said. "I got pretty handy at stitching myself up."

Nausea waved through Cara as Ryan lifted the ax. Just the idea of stitching herself up was horrifying.

"There's talk on the council of a new bakery," she said in an attempt to brush the image out of her mind. "And suggestions for opening an ice cream fountain."

He paused and wiped sweat from his face. "*That* I'm ready for."

He split the last of the squashes and then held the length of the wooden ax handle and used it to stretch his arms above his head. She saw the wince of pain flicker in his face as he circled the ax to stretch out his shoulders.

"You okay?"

A wail ripped through the silence.

Ryan ran to the kitchen before she could get up from the ground.

When she got inside, he had Belva in his arms and was lowering her to the floor. Blood spattered her apron and across Ryan's bare chest.

"Get some clean towels and a bowl of water," he

ordered to no one in particular. "And a needle and thread." He reached up to the counter and pulled a towel off it and pressed it against Belva's hand.

"I'm fine," Belva sputtered.

"You will be," Ryan said in his gentle, easy tone.

To Cara's surprise, Belva relaxed. Maybe Ryan did have the ability to hypnotize. Cara had never seen Belva succumb to anyone's authority, not even Roy's.

Ryan pulled back the towel, and Belva yelped.

"Don't look at it," Ryan said. "Just take some deep breaths."

He took the wad of towels and basin of water one of the women brought over and washed the blood off Belva's hand. Cara couldn't see the wound from where she stood, but from the intake of breath from the women standing nearby, she knew it was serious.

"Thread," Molly said as she rushed over to Ryan and Belva.

"I'll need about a foot. Would you thread it?" He looked down to Belva. "I'm just going to stitch this up. Then we'll get you to a proper doctor."

"I won't look, but you tell me what the damage is, young man."

"Ryan."

She cast Ryan a wavering smile. "Right. You tell me the truth, Ryan."

"I'm good at the truth, ma'am."

"Belva," she said, wincing.

He pulled the blood-soaked towel away.

"Inch and a half. Clean slice. You missed the vein. But your muscle's protruding." He motioned Cara over. "Let her head rest in your lap," he instructed.

She should've mentioned that she fainted at the sight of blood. But she walked over and nestled Belva's head in her

49

lap, keeping her eyes on Belva's face and away from her bloody apron and hand. And well away from Ryan's blood-smeared chest.

"He's done this before," Cara said as she stroked Belva's forehead. "He knows what he's doing."

"Don't have much choice, do I?" Belva shut her eyes. "Laird is in the city today."

Ryan shot a questioning look at Cara.

"Laird's the local vet. He's our go-to guy for minor emergencies," Cara said.

"I called as soon as I saw the blood," Sarah said from across the room. "Left a message on his phone. I called 9-1-1 too, but they're on a fire call in the park. Said they could be here in half an hour."

"Take a breath, Belva," Ryan said. "A long, smooth one."

Cara knew he was about to stitch up the cut, but she couldn't look. Belva twitched in her arms and pressed her lips together, fighting back the pain, but she didn't let out a squeak of complaint.

Cara stroked her forehead and murmured that it was going to be okay.

Molly handed Ryan a roll of gauze. It was frayed, but he took it with a nod. Cara felt the tension ease in Belva's body as he tied off the last stitch and rolled the gauze around her hand.

The back door to the kitchen opened with a bang. Laird Benson stood in the doorway and eyed Ryan tying off the bandage.

"There goes my job security," Laird said in a tone meant to be joking but one that had worry laced under it. "Although maybe I'll try the shirtless angle."

The ladies moaned. Laird's days of being appealing *sans* shirt were well behind him.

Belva sat up and glared at him. "I thought you were in the city."

"I got a late start," Laird said. "The Diegos' mare had a breech birth this morning." He helped Ryan ease Belva to her feet. "I'll take you to the hospital; it's on my way."

"I'm *not* going to the hospital," Belva protested.

"You are," Ryan said. "Either with him or me."

Belva eyed them both. "Now *there's* a hard choice. Sarah, dear, call Dot at the fire station and tell her we've got this handled. Those boys have enough on their hands without tending to careless old ladies." She looked around at the women in the kitchen. "What are you ladies gawking at? I expect this canning to be finished and the kitchen cleaned up before I get back. We've a party to prepare for tonight, in case you've all gone daffy-brained."

She patted Cara on the arm. "And don't go thinking you're skipping out on the party, missy. A little fun will crack open that armor of yours."

Cracking open her armor was exactly what Cara was afraid of.

Cara stripped off her sweat-drenched blouse and tossed it into the woven laundry basket in the corner of her bedroom. They'd worked until five and barely finished the last jars of squash soup and canned pear butter. Without Belva's expert help, several of the batches had to be hot bathed a second time to get the jars to properly seal. Ryan had stayed to the very end, helping her and Molly make labels and pack the jars into crates.

She eyed her bed. A nap sounded better than dressing for a party.

The physical work of scooping and chopping and

stirring had exhausted her. Before she'd moved to Albion Bay, if anyone had told her that wrestling produce into cans and jars would prove a challenge, she'd never have believed them. But more than the actual canning, her efforts to keep a handle on the rush of emotions that working close beside Ryan had triggered had worn her out. His transporting laugh and easy conversation made her lose her focus and make mistakes. Simple mistakes, but mistakes all the same.

She'd nearly poured the pear butter into the pot that held the squash soup.

When he'd grasped her arm to stop her, nothing could've prepared her for the shocking rush of heated desire his touch fired.

Until that moment she'd never believed the stories of life-rocking attraction, stories of people whose lives had been altered by sensual, alluring energy they couldn't control. That was the stuff of fairy tales and myth or of deluded, unbalanced people, people who mistook sexual energy for what really mattered.

She picked up the book on her night table. For months she'd been following the exercises it prescribed, exercises for practicing turning up the good, for holding and savoring the peaceful, joyous moments in her life, ramping them up so they'd fire new patterns in her brain, patterns that could stand in the face of habitual, jittery, negative thoughts.

But she couldn't ignore the insistent, edgy energy sparking in her chest when she let her thoughts float to Ryan Rea. Like flames lapping at kindling, the unsettling feeling grew stronger with every effort she made to tamp down its power.

She wasn't in the market for having her world cracked open by a force beyond her control. Not today and not ever.

She stripped out of her jeans and stepped into her shower stall and let the hot water flow over the tired muscles of her neck and back. She closed her eyes and put her face under the blissful warmth, and images of Ryan rushed in—Ryan swinging the ax, Ryan reassuring Belva and stitching her hand, Ryan laughing and wiping away a spatter of soup that had splashed her neck. Vivid images that wouldn't be suppressed, images that seemed to live in her body, well beyond her mind's control. She poured shampoo onto her head and vigorously worked it into a lather. And tried to shove down the memory of his forearm muscles rippling with power as he lifted the heavy pots from the flames, of his steady hand as he helped her scoop the velvety liquids into jars.

But the hardest memory to ignore was the power of his gaze.

No touch could be as powerful as the arresting feeling of being held in Ryan's gaze. It was as though she'd been infiltrated by the energy flowing from him. As though some alien force had moved in and taken hold of the controls and was distorting her sense of reality.

She rinsed the shampoo from her hair and grabbed the bar of vetiver soap. But as she skimmed it down her body, she realized that was what Ryan smelled like—the scent of vetiver and lemons and man. She ran the bar of soap along her thighs and then lathered it in her hands and stroked between her legs. Ryan had amazing hands. She closed her eyes and imagined what it would feel like to have him touch her, just right, just *there*. Pleasure raced in her veins, and she leaned against the shower wall for balance. The cool wall shocked her back to reality.

What in God's name was she doing?

She sorted through her mind for an explanation for her unnerving reaction, for her driven focus on a man she'd just met, a man she knew little about...

Maybe it was because he played baseball—her brother

had told her that the near-inhuman speed the sport required selected out men whose eyes and bodies were so finely tuned they could call up reactions most normal people couldn't. That the best baseball players used their eyes in a way unlike in any other sport. That some batters could send a pitcher cowering with their eyes alone.

That made sense. She'd just never been around a ballplayer before. Her brother played polo, but that was different; the horses held the real power in that game.

She'd simply had a taste of what it was like to be around an athlete, a man who used nothing but the power of his body and a few tools to shape his world. Of course she'd feel the energy of that.

She toweled the water from her hair and felt more centered. She'd discovered the source of the power she'd felt and now her reactions didn't feel so alarming. Ryan probably had the same effect on anyone near him. After all, that power, that prowess, was what drove fans to be avid about sports, wasn't it?

Happy with her explanation, she slid open the door to her small closet.

Jeans and shirts—her everyday work clothes—filled most of the space. Tucked in the back were a few dresses, a couple of cotton ones and a few warmer, knitted wool ones for when the weather turned chilly. She'd meant to buy some new clothes that year but hadn't made the time.

She thought of her storage unit in New York, jam-packed with ball gowns and city clothes, clothes she'd never have a reason to wear in Albion Bay. Leaving those outfits behind had felt almost as freeing as leaving the trappings of her life. She didn't miss the private jets, the over-the-top, opulent parties, the posturing and preening of charity balls. She couldn't think of anything she missed except for a couple of friends she kept in touch with by phone.

She slipped into her favorite blue dress and savored the feeling of the soft cotton against her skin. Her simple clothes represented the freedom she'd fought for, the life she'd carved out for herself.

She had to stand back to see her image in the three-paneled mirror of her consignment-store vanity. The little wooden table and antique mirror had been a find she was proud of. But her dress had seen better days; the hem had come loose and needed mending. She wasn't handy with a needle and thread, much to the consternation of the Albion Bay women's quilting circle. Even Ryan had showed greater prowess with a needle. Her stomach tightened as she remembered the tender way he'd stitched up Belva. And the way he...

No, she wasn't going to start rolling thoughts about Ryan through her mind, not again.

She fumbled with a needle and was poised to attempt her first stitch when her phone rang.

"For goodness' sake, Cara, don't you *ever* check your messages?"

Her mother had entered the realm of instant messaging and texting. An unreturned phone call was nearly as great a travesty as wearing white after Labor Day.

"I got home late," Cara said, wishing she didn't feel she needed to apologize.

"We're making Thanksgiving plans. Since your father wants to go to Rome for Christmas, I thought we'd just have a simple family affair here for Thanksgiving."

Her mother's idea of a simple family affair at Barrington Manor, the family estate overlooking the Hudson River, involved hordes of houseguests, miles of food and oceans of drink. And endless imported entertainment. Last year she'd hired the Beaux Arts Trio to play for the morning-after brunch.

"I only have four days off for Thanksgiving this year," Cara said. "I have to drive the bus on the following Monday."

"Don't tell me there's no one else in that town who could drive for a couple of days. They do *drive* out there, don't they?"

That her mother hadn't gotten her head around Cara's choice to live in Albion Bay didn't surprise her. But after three years, Cara thought she'd warm to the idea or at least accept her choice. Her father was a different story. He'd never get it.

"I really can't," Cara said. "I volunteered to help with the Thanksgiving bird count this year."

"We have birds here. Loads of them."

"Mom."

"Okay, okay. But if you're not coming for a visit, I'm coming out there. It's time that I see this place that has so transfixed you. And to make sure you haven't been inhabited by an alien."

A visit from her mother was exactly what she did *not* need. There was no way to keep her mother in check for the duration of a visit.

Her mother had been a socialite for most of her life, but in her midforties she surprised everyone and decided to get a degree and start a career as a psychotherapist. She was full of the wisdom of the recently converted and shared it freely. But that wisdom hadn't yet stretched to comprehending the life choices of her children. She still saw Cara's move to Albion Bay as a back-to-the-land phase that she'd grow out of. Cara hadn't told her mother that before she'd fled New York, she'd nearly had a nervous breakdown or about the month of intensive therapy she'd slogged through after her best friend, Laci, had committed suicide. Maybe she should have. But at the time all she could think of was escaping, fleeing the world she'd watched take Laci down. The world that might've taken her down too if she hadn't fled.

She *had* tried, more than once, to explain to her mother that she'd fought a bottomless emptiness that scared the hell out of her. That the life that so suited her parents held no meaning. That moving to Albion Bay was no whim. It was her desperate attempt to restart her life.

Having her mother interacting with the people of the town would blow her cover in a heartbeat. Her mother knew it and was at that very moment leveraging Cara's life for purposes of her own. Cara considered pointing out that her mother was using emotional blackmail, but thought better of it. She wasn't in the mood to be analyzed.

"Look, I'll think about coming back East for a visit, okay?"

"Darling, I'd *like* to visit you," her mother said in a softer tone. "Bring you some of your things."

"The rains are coming," Cara said. "You know how you hate the rain."

"I might make an exception for you." Her mother paused. "Alston called with the news," she said in a lowered voice. "That's a lot of money, Cara. You can talk to me about it, you know."

Cara heard her father's voice in the background. He sounded impatient. He always was.

"I have to run. But think about Thanksgiving, darling. I could pay for a driver to take your shift. It'd be easy."

"It's not about the money, Mom."

How could she explain to her mother that driving the bus on the days following a holiday break were her favorite times? The kids were all lit up with their taste of freedom and energized by being back around their buddies and friends.

She didn't try to explain.

After she hung up she couldn't concentrate well enough to stitch up her dress. She pulled a soft white one from the back of her closet. To hell with the fact that it was well after Labor Day. She really didn't have another choice.

But as she turned to leave her bedroom, she took one last look in the mirror and frowned. She dragged the dress off and threw it across the bed, then fumbled in the drawer of her vanity and came up with a roll of transparent tape she'd stuffed in the back with some wrapping paper. Without measuring, she tore off a long piece and taped the hem of her blue dress. She slipped it on. Then she sat at her vanity and stared at the tubes of makeup she hadn't worn in weeks. A stroke of mascara and some blush-pink lipstick looked okay. As did the tiny gold earrings she added. She looked into the mirror again.

What the hell was she doing primping for a hoedown being held in Grady's old feed barn?

Maybe she had been inhabited by an alien.

CHAPTER SIX

THE SOUND OF FIDDLES AND CLAPPING MET RYAN AS he walked the potholed street that led to the feed barn. Just inside the huge open doors, long strings of Christmas lights hung above stacks of hay bales and lit the dust stirred up by dancing couples. Tables lined the perimeter, and men and women clustered around them, chatting and eating. Ryan scanned the barn, but didn't see Cara.

He nodded a greeting to Sam, who sat in a corner with a group of boys from the middle school team. The boys eyed the girls on the other side of the barn, laughing and chatting and shooting glances at them.

The music stopped, and a man walked to the mike in the middle of the plywood platform that served as a stage.

"Now I *know* you all can do better than that," he said with a laugh. "This next one's the Grapevine Twist. I'll call the figures, but Grady, get out here and show these sprouts how it's done."

A few more couples made their way to the dancing area, and the fiddlers started in on an upbeat tune. Ryan had never seen a barn dance. In Texas dances were more formal affairs that he and the other boys avoided. As soon as he was old enough, he'd joined his friends and gone off to nearby towns for concerts in arenas. He'd grown up watching other people play music. This was local people making and enjoying music of their own. No massive sound systems or towers of speakers or commercial hype, just a few townies and a whole lot of energy.

"Decided to slum it with the locals, did you?" Belva said as she sauntered up and took his arm with her unbandaged hand.

"I heard there was free food," Ryan teased back. At least he hoped she was teasing. He didn't want people in town thinking he was too good for their company. His roots were poorer than most of theirs.

"Better get at it before those boys do," Belva said. "Or before Cain gets here. The man can eat his share and that of three other men."

She looked up and smiled at something behind him. He turned and saw Cara. If a woman could look confident and awkward at the same time, she did. But it was her simple beauty that shone through and reached out to him.

She smiled at Belva, maybe at him too; he wasn't sure. His pulse picked up its pace as she walked toward them. An odd image formed in his mind as he watched her approach. It was as though the feed barn faded into a muted focus on either side of her, as if she were walking through a film set or one of those Internet videos. As if she wasn't really moved or touched by anything around her, as if she stood apart from everything happening in the barn. She smiled and nodded as she passed people, like a queen might as she moved through a crowd of her subjects.

There was no arrogance to her movements or gestures, and her smiles seemed genuine. But Ryan had the oddest sense of a woman out of place, like a tropical tree planted in a forest or a thoroughbred running in a herd of wild ponies.

She stopped to exchange a few words with a tall man wearing work clothes. The guy said something that made her laugh. Ryan felt jealousy flare, but bit it down.

"I was just telling Ryan here that he'd better get to the food before the boys do," Belva said as Cara reached them. Belva's voice brought him back to reality, and he shook off the vision.

"It's squash soup," Cara said, her eyes lighting with a mischievous smile.

Ryan groaned. "It'll be a long while before I can face another squash—pureed, on the vine or in any other form."

Belva laughed. "She's pulling your leg. I made the lasagna myself. Good thing I made it yesterday." She held out her arm. "Your doctoring beats that boy's in the hospital any day. The shot he gave to numb me hurt more than your stitches."

"Yes, but his instruments are sterile, as are his bandages."

"Yours were fine. I tried to tell him, but he wouldn't listen. He insisted on taking me through all that all over again."

Ryan was glad the doctor had been thorough; the risk of infection was nothing to toy with.

A man about Belva's age walked up behind her and winked at Ryan.

"I'm borrowing this lady for a while," he said as he tugged her away. "She's the only one who can get me through this dance."

Belva sputtered and said something about her injury, but Ryan noticed she went along with the man rather easily.

"That's Grady," Cara said as she watched them walk into the crowd of dancers. "He's loved Belva since he was ten. She's still mourning Roy, though. But Grady's patient."

"Patience is underrated," Ryan said, trying to sound casual and ignore the keyed-up feeling in his chest. Two days ago he'd gone three for three against the strongest arm in the division; standing in a barn dance talking to a school bus driver shouldn't make him nervous. But the couple of hours he'd spent away from her since the canning session hadn't diminished his hankering to know her better. Way better. He'd even driven the Bugatti to the party and now felt real silly about it. What had he expected, that she'd agree to take a spin through the night with him? But he *had* hoped. Or else he wouldn't have done it.

"Patience isn't one of my virtues," Cara said.

"I won't be much help to you in that category. I'm still working on patience myself." He liked the smile his words brought to her face. "But I find that admitting what's true makes a difference, gives a person a place to start."

Her face went still, like a pitcher refusing a sign. Then she nodded and looked down at her feet.

What he'd said hadn't had the effect he'd intended. The party was swirling around them, chatter and laughter and music, and yet he felt like he stood in a vortex, one he'd just chilled down by about ten degrees.

"The sign on that table says hard cider," he said. "Want a mug?"

She laughed then, and the sound gave him hope for the evening.

"Watch out for Grady's cider. That is if you value having a clear head in the morning." She shook her head and looked up at the twinkling lights. "I'm starting to sound like a bus driver."

"You *are* a bus driver," Ryan said. "No crime there." He put his hands over his heart. "I'll take your advice about the cider."

"In that case, I'd love some."

Maybe it was Grady's home brew, maybe it was just the spirit of the party, but she seemed to let her guard down a bit. And he was feeling pretty damn good. He shouldn't have had a second tall mug of the cider, but it had a crisp bite and tasted like apples and autumn. And he liked the buzz. It made him bold enough to ask Cara to dance.

To Ryan's relief, the caller and fiddler started in on the Texas Star. He'd danced the Star when he was a boy, when his parents had dragged him and his sister out with them for the evening. Though he'd complained, he'd always had fun. But with Cara as a partner it didn't feel like the same old dance. Every time he swung her and then spun her off to a new partner, he felt the sizzle of wanting more. More of the town, more of the music, more of her.

When the caller announced the Watermelon Crawl, even the boys joined the action. Cara got confused with the grapevine and the kicking and clapping, but he guided her through it and by the time they'd come full around, she was laughing and whooping and clapping right along with the crowd.

The musicians ended the line dance and started in on a slow tune, and couples began pairing off. He couldn't help but laugh at the collective groan from the boys fleeing the dance floor and retreating to their corner. Evidently raucous line dances held more appeal than finding a girl and holding her close. He remembered those days. Back then, hitting tennis balls off the wall of the garage to practice his swing held a stronger appeal than parties and girls. Back in the days when the gap between him and the fairer sex was an unfathomable abyss. Hell, maybe it still was.

"Water," Cara said as she let go of Ryan's hand and edged away.

"Dance," Ryan answered as he took hold of her and swung her deeper into the throng of couples.

She tilted her head, and the light of challenge sparked in her eyes. "You're rather used to getting your way, aren't you?"

One minute she seemed fragile and gentle and the next she was defiant and strong. Maybe the knife-edge tension provoked by her contrasting qualities was what whipped his desire beyond any he'd experienced.

"Only when it matters," he said, pulling her closer.

Some of the locals had stepped up to play with the musicians onstage. Ryan envied their talent. To master an instrument was on his bucket list.

And so was kissing Cara West.

She'd shot to the top, and he wasn't feeling patient, not patient at all.

He knew there was a God when the musicians started in on a country rendition of "Unforgettable."

He stroked his thumb at the small of her back and felt her tremble under his hand. As he raised his arm and turned her under it, she smiled up at him from beneath her dark lashes. When he pulled her back close, it was all he could do not to bend down and taste. But he wouldn't. Not in front of all the town. But maybe later in the shadows of the night he would taste her.

The song ended too soon. She pulled away, and they walked toward the table where ale was being sold. He bought one for her and one for himself.

"You dance like a prince," Cara said from behind the rim of her mug.

"Have you danced with princes?"

He'd meant to be teasing. She lifted the mug to her lips, and he saw the cool guardedness slip into her eyes before she averted her gaze to the foamy liquid.

"Mind if I take this lovely lady for a spin?" asked the guy she'd been talking with earlier.

There was no question in his voice, and the way he looked at Cara made Ryan want to deck him. Ryan did mind, but there wasn't much he could do about it. Of course every guy in town would be after her.

Cara turned to Ryan. "This is Adam Mitchell. He's doing my decks."

Ryan wanted to say that'd better be all the guy was doing, but that too was ridiculous. The guy didn't wait for introductions; he slid his arm to the small of Cara's back and drew her away.

As Ryan watched the guy move her onto the dance floor, he knew he had to win her. Around her, life had zing; he felt lit up in a way he rarely felt except in the ballpark. He wanted more of that feeling, and Cara was its source. He sipped and turned away. Maybe it was his imagination, but the stacks of squashes and pumpkins lined against the back wall seemed to be grinning at him, as if to say he'd just let the fox run away with the hen.

Just then Cain Bryant walked into the barn with a woman on his arm, and an idea fired in Ryan's mind. He had a pretty good idea just how to court one Cara West.

CHAPTER SEVEN

R YAN BRACED HIMSELF AGAINST THE DECK RAILING as Cain's boat slammed into the face of an oncoming wave. An early morning of deep-sea salmon fishing wasn't Ryan's idea of a perfect first date. When he'd asked Cain to set something up as a double date, at first Cain had razzed him. But by their second cup of coffee, Cain had agreed to cook something up. Between Ryan's game schedule and Cara's work driving the bus, opportunities to hook up were limited, but he figured Cain could help him get something going.

Ryan kicked himself. He should've been more specific about what constituted a good date activity. Evidently early morning outings on raging seas were Cain's idea of bliss.

"If this is your idea of an initiation ritual," Cara shouted back to Cain from the bow of the boat, "it's working. I'm gonna want to do this again."

Although Cain's date, Laurel, had gone quiet and pale as they'd motored out of sight of land, Cara seemed thrilled with the splashing water and rolling waves of the open sea.

"This is my idea of real living," Cain shouted up to Cara with a broad grin.

Laurel scooted along the flat seat cushion until she was directly beside Cain.

"It'll calm in a couple more miles," Cain said, "once we

get past the shoal."

Laurel gave a half-hearted nod and gripped the edge of the seat.

Cain sure knew how to woo a woman. *Not.* But Ryan's efforts had fared little better.

After the party at Grady's, Ryan had asked Cara to go with him for brunch at a resort in Sonoma. She said she was busy. He'd asked her to come to the Giants game the next night and join him after, and she'd said she had plants to get in the ground. When he'd pointed out that it was a night game and asked if she really planned on planting by moonlight, she'd just laughed and shook her head. When he'd texted her the next day to invite her to go fishing with him and Cain, she'd finally agreed.

Ryan made his way to the bow, where Cara stood facing the spray.

"I love it out here," she said, turning into the wind. "I feel free. Up close like this, I feel I'm a part of the sea."

The boat lurched, and she stumbled. Ryan caught her before she slid down to the deck. He tightened his arms around her and closed the space between them, felt her body mold against his. He didn't want to let her go. She tipped her head up. As if some drug was shooting through him, messing with his senses, the spray of the waves and the rumble of the engine drifted away as he tried to read the look in her eyes. Thoughts raced in her, that much he saw. But his own thoughts stilled as he flicked a glance at her lips. He bent his head, wanting to taste, but she wriggled out of his arms.

"Nice catch," she said, her cheeks coloring. "I'm not used to such small boats." The flush in her face deepened, as if she'd just admitted some great secret.

"This is the biggest boat I've ever been on." He brushed a strand of hair from her face. "Not much call for boats where I grew up."

She shivered and looked away, then turned to hold the rail, using it to move cautiously hand over hand toward the cabin. "Maybe we'd better join Cain and Laurel," she said over her shoulder. "It's rough out here."

Rough indeed. He followed her until she was safely in the cabin and then ducked back out to the bow. He needed more than a few minutes to calm the spike of desire firing in him.

As they traveled farther from shore, the waters calmed and Cain began setting out fishing poles. Laurel perked up and appeared to enjoy Cain's very hands-on instructions.

Ryan eyed his own pole and gave the reel a spin. In East Texas, fishing required a simple pole and line and patiently waiting at the edge of a man-made reservoir for a stocked bass or trout to find the bait. It required some skill, but nothing like pitting yourself against the open ocean and a wild fish that navigated thousands of miles to spawn in the creek it was born in.

"We're lucky to get out here at all," Cain said as he baited Laurel's hook and helped her feed her line down into the water. "The fishery was closed last year—no pulses."

"Fish have pulses?" Ryan had never heard of such a thing.

Cain pushed back his cap and then rearranged it low on his forehead. "I'm sure they do; I hadn't considered it. But it's water pulses that mean life and death to fish like salmon. When the snow melts, pulses of fresh water rush down from the Sierra, through the delta and out the bay to the sea. The salmon rely on the pulses to push them back to the sea. Between lack of snow and the dams, the fresh water flow isn't what it should be and the fish populations have crashed. And that's nothing to the way the spawning grounds have been screwed with."

Ryan was aware that Cara was listening intently.

"I thought the state was regulating the water flow for the spawning runs," she said.

Cain looked up from the hook he was baiting. "Been studying up on California water regulations, have you?"

Cara pressed her lips together. "I've read a bit in the papers."

Like a hermit crab retreating into its shell, she coiled in on herself. Ryan observed bodies for a living; any player who couldn't read the body language of guys on an opposing team didn't last long in the game. He wondered what he was seeing in her reaction. Maybe she was one of those women afraid of appearing too intelligent. But this was the twenty-first century and nothing about her fit the type.

"Water's a serious issue in Texas," Ryan said in an attempt to smooth things over. "If the state doesn't shepherd its groundwater, oil is about the only export we'll have."

He leaned over to help Cara bait her line, but she'd already fastened a herring firmly to the hook. She whipped the pole over her head, and her line trailed perfectly out from the boat. He cast his line out beside hers and shoved the handle of the pole into the PVC holder bolted to the side of the boat. For a moment he searched for something neutral to say that wouldn't spook her.

Cara's rod doubled over as her line whizzed out away from the boat.

"I've got it," she said as she grabbed her rod, braced her legs against the side of the boat and began to turn hard on the reel.

"You're in for a battle," Cain said as he stepped beside her. "Want me to take it?"

"Ha! No way. This guy's mine," she said, laughing.

The fish quickly peeled off about eighty yards of line, then followed that with a few magnificent leaps. Ryan saw the strain as Cara began the long process of reeling the fish in. Several minutes went by. He bit back the urge to help her and reveled in her determination.

Cara fought hard, but so did the fish. Cain stepped up to her and motioned for her to follow him.

"Walk backwards toward the front of the boat," Cain directed. When she did, he dipped the net into the water, tipped the handle straight up in the air and closed the net around the salmon.

"If I'd known you were such a hand at this, I would've brought you out here sooner," Cain said as he lowered the net and the fish to the deck. "That's a twenty-pound buck if I ever saw one."

Cara blushed

"Want to give it another go?" Cain leaned her rod against the side of the boat and reached into the bait pail.

Cara looked to where Laurel stood, watching them all. "Let's have a look at Laurel's line," Cara said.

She helped Laurel reel in her line; the bait had been eaten off the hook.

"I'm not really a fan of fishing," Laurel said. "I might be wasting your bait." She looked over to Cain, her cheeks flushed.

"There's plenty of bait," Cain said with a half-hearted grin. "But would you rather have a cup of cocoa and watch?"

Laurel's relief was matched only by Ryan's own. He hated to see anyone forced by circumstance into an activity that didn't suit them.

"I'll join you," Cara said and followed Laurel into the cabin.

"Not the cleverest invitation on my part." Cain nodded toward the boat cabin. "I should've asked Laurel if she liked fishing. I should've seen she's a woman who likes land."

"Women aren't always so easy to read," Ryan said. Especially the woman he'd begun to obsess over.

"Yeah, well, some are harder than others." He nodded again toward the boat cabin. "Cara's a puzzle."

Ryan shrugged. She was a puzzle, a puzzle he looked forward to finding the key to, even if he had to do it slowly and step by painstaking step.

He and Cain each landed a large salmon and then sat for about fifteen minutes with no strikes on their lines.

"I never like to admit it, but I'd say that's it for the day," Cain said as he reeled in. He looked out over the blue-green expanse surrounding them. "I think we got lucky."

Cara and Laurel stepped onto the deck and handed them both a steaming mug of cocoa.

"Had to share the goods," Cara said.

"Lucky me." Ryan felt his face flame. "I mean lucky us," he added, lifting his mug toward Cain.

Cara turned to Laurel, who held her mug of cocoa as if it were a life-saving device. "What do you do when you're not fishing at dawn?"

"I'm finishing a degree in natural history," Laurel said, the light returning to her eyes.

"My brother's interested in birds," Cara said.

Ryan admired the way Cara drew Laurel out, made her feel comfortable, helped her forget the misery of the morning and the rough seas closer to shore. Cara had a touch with people. She sure had a touch with him.

"I'll have to take some online courses," Laurel added. "My new job at the bakery will make it hard to get to class. I might have to put my studies on hold for a while; it might be hard to handle classes and work."

"No, better to keep at it," Ryan said. "I left college to play ball, pissed off my old man. Can't say I would've done it different now, but you're there. It's a good idea to finish."

Cain started up the engine.

"Did you go to college?" Laurel asked Cara over the chug of the motor.

"I did."

"Where?"

There it was again, Ryan observed—the drawing back. Cara obviously did not like answering questions.

"Oh, a small school back East."

"I've always wanted to go to New York," Laurel said. "I'm saving up. Have you been there?"

"Yes."

"Okay, ladies and gentleman," Cain boomed. "Places everyone. We'll be hitting a rough spot in about five minutes." He motioned to Laurel. "Sit back up here."

Laurel smiled, but Ryan saw her shoulders brace as she prepared for another bout of rough seas. She wasn't a girlfriend for an ocean hunter like Cain. He looked back to where Cara stood, braced and riding the motion of the boat with the finesse of a rodeo rider. The wind spread her hair out behind her like a chestnut-colored flag of independence.

Cain was right—she was a puzzle. A puzzle he was no closer to solving than when they'd set out.

⌒

"Looks like trouble," Cain said as they came in sight of the marina at Albion Bay.

On the short stretch of rocky beach north of the marina, Ryan could make out a woman wielding a massive pole net. At first he thought she was trying to net a dog, but as Cain maneuvered closer to the dock, Ryan saw that it was a sea lion. A very big and apparently angry sea lion.

"Grab the dock line and loop it through the cleat," Cain said to Ryan. "Jackie's going to need some help with that big boy."

The four of them jogged down the dock and over to where the woman Cain had called Jackie was trying to net the sea lion.

"Stay back," she shouted to them.

"Jackie, I've helped you do this a dozen times," Cain said, ignoring her. He turned to Ryan. "Go around to the other side, but keep your distance. I'll cut the sea lion off at the shoreline. Laurel, Cara, stay put."

Cain waded into the water and spread his jacket open. To Ryan he looked like some sort of crazed superhero from a video game. The sea lion backed away from the water and moved a few feet up the beach.

"I have it *handled*," Jackie said.

The animal snorted and lunged for Jackie. She dodged out of the way and the net she'd held fell to the pebbled beach.

"Well, almost handled," she said with a laughing English accent.

The woman was about to be charged by a four-hundred-pound sea creature and she was laughing?

Ryan grabbed the net and stretched out to hand it back to her.

"You're taller," she said to him. "See if you can get the net over him."

With a move he'd used a hundred times to rope steers, Ryan settled the net over the animal's head.

"One sea lion about to be freed from a packing strap," Jackie said.

But the sea lion fought in the net and roared its disapproval. Cain splashed out of the shoreline and helped

Ryan and Jackie steady the net against the animal's forceful bucking.

"Can you grab my case?" Jackie shouted over to where Cara stood with Laurel.

Cara dashed up the shore and grabbed what looked like an oversized tackle box.

"Open it and hand me the syringe on the right."

Cara pulled a large hypodermic needle from the case. The sea lion lunged through the net at Cara as she approached.

Jackie took the syringe and with a quick, deft move, injected the sea lion, then backed away from its snapping jaws.

"Hold the net tight," she ordered. "Maybe four or five minutes. That sedative will put him out enough for me to clip off the packing strap and see to his wound."

The sea lion stopped bucking and slumped to the beach.

"Keep the net on," Jackie said in a level voice. "I'll work through it, just in case."

Cain braced both feet on the rim of the net. "Where's your rescue crew?"

"Helping out in the Sausalito headquarters today. I was out for a walk on the beach. Lucky thing I had the net in my truck. Another couple days and this guy would've been done for. It's only a few centimeters from severing his artery." She turned to Cara. "Nice save. I've seen you around town, but we haven't met. I'm Jackie."

"Cara."

Jackie turned to Ryan. "I'm your first baseman's wife," she said with a grin.

Ryan had known that Alex Tavonesi's wife headed the Marine Mammal Center and that they'd built a small triage center and research lab just outside of Albion Bay. He actually had Alex to thank for finding his ranch; it was Alex who'd suggested that Ryan look for land up in the area. He'd just never expected to meet her like this.

"And that's Laurel," Cain said with a nod up the beach. "She's... um, she's—"

"*Crazy* to be going out with you on a day like this," Jackie finished for him. She clipped the strap and smoothed a thick ribbon of salve on the wound. "You all are."

She injected the sea lion with a hefty dose of antibiotics and asked Ryan and Cain to help her remove the net. But it had caught under the animal's front flipper and it took him, Cain, Jackie and Cara to move the sea lion enough to pull the net free.

"Normally I'd have a crew take him down to headquarters," she said. "But I think he'll do better in the wild."

She motioned for them to back away. "We'll hear if he re-strands." She put her hands on her hips and stared down at the sea lion. "That light sedative will wear off in about five minutes." She squatted down and packed up her case. "You the same Ryan that stitched up Belva?"

"Guilty," Ryan said. "Apparently this town is short of a clinic."

"We make do," Cain said.

Ryan heard the defensiveness in his voice and saw Cara brace. He hadn't meant it as a criticism, but he was an outsider. He'd have to watch his step if he wanted to be accepted into the community.

They watched from up the beach as the sea lion revived. Ryan couldn't help cheering as it waddled down to the water and swam off.

At his suggestion, the five of them celebrated over cinnamon buns and coffee at the diner. The story of the rescue had already spread around town. Several locals came up to congratulate them and to ask Cain about the best spots for fishing, but Ryan's attention was on Cara. Though he noticed that Cara asked more questions than she answered, she and Jackie seemed to hit it off. Laurel appeared fascinated by the fast banter between the two women. Jackie watched Cara with a thoughtful look in her eyes.

Before they paid their bill, Laurel offered to volunteer for Jackie's marine mammal rescue squad. As long as she didn't ever have to get on a boat, she qualified with a shy laugh.

Ryan was intent on securing another date with Cara. When she rose to leave, he walked with her out of the diner.

"I have a game tonight," he said as they stepped onto the front sidewalk. "Would you like to come?" He shoved his hands in his pockets. "I could send a driver for you," he added when she didn't reply.

She stared at him for a moment and then shook her head.

"That's kind," she said, "but I can't."

"Tomorrow's Sunday, it's a day game. We could have dinner in the city after. There's a new chef at the Ritz"—he saw her stiffen—"or we could just drive up the coast to The Blue Heron and have some oysters."

"I really can't," she said again.

Maybe she hated baseball.

"How about a hike? There are some good trails that back up to my ranch."

He was grasping at anything he could think of. Hiking was not an activity high on his list. If he'd gone out hiking on the ranch where his father worked, the hands would've thought he was nuts. But right then he would've offered up almost anything just to have another opportunity to see her. A hike was a small price to pay.

She laughed. "Okay." She crossed her arms and

shrugged, and an enchanting smile curved into her face. "I thought I'd better stop you before you threw in an offer for hang-gliding."

He laughed with her, but he felt off balance. One minute she seemed a simple country soul and the next her smooth, sophisticated manner and ability to charm him made him feel like he was dealing with a worldly Cleopatra. She had a damned disturbing way of shifting her behavior and his expectations.

CHAPTER EIGHT

C ARA PULLED UP TO THE GATE AT RYAN'S RANCH. ALL week she'd considered calling and canceling their date to hike.

It'd been a week from hell.

The school bus blew a tire and scared the daylights out of her, to the delight of Sam Rivers and his friends. If they'd been on anything but a straight stretch of road... Well, she didn't want to think about what could've happened.

Her mother was still insisting on coming out to Albion Bay. Cara had put her off again, but the deferment wouldn't last.

The details and bother of dealing with her financial life had mushroomed beyond belief. She'd bought herself a reprieve by stalling her decisions, but it was just that, a stall.

And hiding her business was becoming more difficult. Although she'd wisely opened a post office box in a neighboring town, the clerk had eyed the pile of registered letters when she'd gone in to collect her mail. She hoped he wasn't a talker.

She had few choices for dealing with the mountains of paperwork that settling her grandfather's estate had generated. When there was that much money to deal with, electronic signatures just wouldn't cut it. Alston offered to hold her mail and have it delivered twice a week, but the idea of having a convoy of special delivery trucks hauling in and out of her place was appalling. Already that week she'd had to drive into the city twice to meet with Alston and her financial advisor and sign papers that Alston hadn't felt comfortable sending by mail.

And she hadn't been sleeping well. Adam Mitchell had started on her decks, and the fumes of the deck stain had given her headaches, keeping her tossing and turning.

But worse than all that, she couldn't keep her mind off Ryan Rea.

Before he'd shown up in Albion Bay, she'd been fine. *Fine.* Going about her life and living as she chose.

If she were honest, she'd have to admit that it wasn't the deck fumes keeping her awake. When she'd given up trying to sleep in her bedroom and dragged her duvet outside to her hammock, sleep was far less appealing than remembering the delicious feeling Ryan had fired in her body, than imagining what it might feel like to kiss him or be held in his arms.

But she wasn't being honest, and it was starting to get to her. For the past three years she'd imagined that she could continue to live quietly and keep the world at bay. More than imagined, she'd done it. But now everything was fraying. The last thing she needed was to complicate her life by getting involved with a flashy guy like Ryan.

But her heart wasn't as easily put off as attorneys, decisions and family pressure. Though she'd made a life for herself in the sleepy little town, she'd be lying if she didn't admit she was lonely. She'd thought that developing a community of friends—friends who cared for her, for what she did and not who she was—would be enough.

But every encounter with Ryan told her she was fooling herself.

Somehow he'd stormed her boundaries and thrown

open the gates to a place she had no idea how to navigate, a place where a deep yearning held more power than rational thought and her carefully charted plans. The yearning had spread through her like the opposite of a magic spell. Instead of turning everything into sparkling clarity, the feelings muddled her every thought—and drew her deeper in spite of her mind's objections.

She pressed the buzzer on Ryan's gate. He ran out of his house and down the drive, flashing his easy smile and moving with the grace and power of a panther. The bolt of desire that flamed through her and the catch of her breath sent her senses into high alert and warned her that Ryan Rea might be damned hard to keep in perspective.

"I thought you might not come," he said as he opened the gate.

"I got lost," she said out the window as she drove through.

To his credit, he laughed.

She sure wasn't going to tell him she'd started out from her cabin and turned back three times.

"Would you like a coffee?" He offered his hand to help her from the car.

Guided by the power of his strong grip, she nearly sprang out of her seat. Nothing about her world seemed normal when she was around him. But normal was beginning to lose its appeal.

"Coffee?" he repeated.

His eyes crinkled at the corners. He had a way of looking at her that made thoughts flee. Finding herself in an oasis, an oasis she hadn't had to carve out with her wits, was perhaps part of what she loved about being around him. Even if the power and pleasure of it scared the hell out of her.

"I have a new espresso machine." He offered the crook

of his arm in a disarmingly sweet and old-fashioned gesture. She looped her arm through his and felt the steel-hard muscles of his forearm under her palm. "You'll never want to drink the diner coffee again."

"How could I refuse?"

They walked toward his house. His steps and hers felt oddly matched, almost dancelike. Still, while her steps might be steady, the surge of her pulse made her feel anything but stable.

"You've done so much here in such a short time," she said, dragging herself back to reality. Maybe it was lack of sleep, but she felt strange, as if she'd drunk some potion marked "bliss" and her body wasn't used to handling its effects.

"I'm turning this place into a rescue ranch for abused and neglected donkeys. When I was eleven my mom pried me away from baseball for a week and sent me off to a camp on a rescue ranch. I fell in love with the donkeys on the first day." He shrugged. "My dad will think I'm nuts, but he already does."

His plans stunned her as much as the steady hammering of her pulse did. People in town had speculated and gossiped about what Ryan might do with the dilapidated Smith place, but no one had guessed anything even close. She'd given a grant just last year to an organization in Nevada that rescued abused donkeys, never imagining such an effort might start up so close to home. Nothing about Ryan fit with the flashy image she'd formed that first day she'd seen him alongside his Bugatti.

"I understand donkeys are very curious," she said, hoping the flush of heat rising in her face wasn't too obvious.

"They're also independent thinkers. And did you know they can live to be over fifty years old?"

She shook her head.

"They'll be here in a few weeks. Most of the fencing and paddocks are in." He gestured toward the back pasture. She gawked, couldn't help it. If he were to extend both arms, they'd reach wider than she was tall. Yet there was a tensile grace to his every move. And, standing near him, she felt as if her own body was caught up in an energy field, energy that sparked with life and mystery. Her reaction confounded her. *He* confounded her.

"The barn still needs work, and some sections of fencing along the perimeter need repair," he added.

She heard his words and forced herself to snap to. Daydreaming and fantasizing weren't usually her style.

"Adam is good with old barns," she said as they stepped up on the porch. "He's doing some more work at my place."

His eyes clouded. "Then he's a clever man."

He pulled his arm away to hold the screen door open for her.

"Watch your step," he said as he came up behind her and grabbed her arm, just in time to keep her from falling into a hole next to the stove. She danced around the hole, but he didn't release his grip on her elbow. Firm. All encompassing. Warm. She rather liked the feeling.

"Sorry. I'd planned on having the kitchen finished up before I had guests."

He caught her in his gaze. There was no way the flush she felt wasn't obvious. She looked down to where he still held her arm.

He released her and stepped back. His slow smile built to a full-on grin. "But the wine cooler works and the grill fires up, so I can't complain."

He crossed the kitchen in two long strides. Maybe the pulse she felt was a one-way thing. She didn't think so, but it'd been so long—no, it had been *never*—that she'd felt the surges of desire that she felt around Ryan.

He tapped coffee into the levered receptacle on the espresso machine. Its sleek stainless steel shape made it look more like a rocket ship for elves than a machine to make breakfast beverages. He fiddled with some knobs and stood back.

"That should do it."

The machine hissed and hummed and sent a dark spatter of coffee across the room. They both jumped back, laughing.

"Maybe I should've read the directions," he said as he dabbed at the coffee splayed across his shirt. "At least it missed you. The machine must have respect for guests."

"I have some experience with these," she said as she stepped closer.

He looked at her oddly.

Right. Where would a bus driver get experience with an exquisite two-thousand-dollar espresso machine? Her dad had a fetish: he owned nearly every high-end espresso machine known to man. Next to collecting impressionist art, coffee and its accoutrements were his passion.

"I saw one demoed at a kitchen store," she said, backpedaling. And it was true—she had seen the demo. And her dad had bought three of the machines, one for each of his houses. "Mind if I give it a go?"

He nodded, and she unplugged the machine. She took the towel from him and levered the filter off the machine. He'd put it on crooked, but she wasn't about to tell him that. She emptied it, tamped in fresh coffee and snugged the filter back on.

Ryan handed her two large mugs. "I'll need that much after all this. And you'll need your strength for the back forty."

She drew out two steaming half mugs of coffee.

"Milk?" She pointed to the steam wand.

"Way too dangerous." He grinned. "Besides, I like mine black."

She didn't, but she decided not to fuss with the steamer. One cup of black coffee wasn't going to kill her.

She handed him the mug, and her fingers brushed his. A brief touch like that shouldn't send a ripple of want deep into her. But it did. If she didn't get out of the kitchen and put some space between them, she just might throw her arms around his neck and kiss him. And probably make a total fool of herself.

"Let's have that hike you promised." She pulled her mug to her chest like a shield.

"Want to see the barns?" He said it like a kid wanting to show off a new toy. His enthusiasm for the ranch charmed her.

They walked across the gravel drive. Though they didn't touch, she was aware of his every move beside her. An energy arced between them, an energy that she didn't, couldn't, trust. How could she when she'd never even known such power was possible? But already the fluttering in her chest warned that she might fall into the spell that filtered through her whenever he was near, and never come out again.

Suddenly the folly of accepting his invitation weighed on her. Allowing herself to be carried away would be the worst possible move she could make at a time like this. He was a star, a public figure. If word got out, the press would be all over them both.

She stopped and sipped her coffee. And tried to think. He stopped too. And smiled at her before sipping from his mug. His smile trumped her urge for self-protection; it was too late to turn back. But she'd be cautious as she moved ahead.

"You make a fine cup of coffee, Cara West."

His voice caressed her, whether he'd intended it to or not.

She smiled her thanks, not trusting her voice.

He threw open the doors to the *smaller* barn, smaller being a matter of perspective. Inside, just beyond the gleaming Bugatti, was a pool table and beyond that a net cage suspended from steel pipes that stretched the length of the back wall.

"The pool table's an antique from the eighteen hundreds. The guy who sold it to me said maybe it had been used in one of the gaming halls during the Gold Rush. The cue sticks are hand carved."

This was the Ryan she'd expected. Though he wasn't throwing dollar signs around, he was trying to impress her. The effort was wasted on her, but he couldn't know that. She'd seen far too many people get caught up in the drive to acquire things, as if they could fill a gap that would make them feel whole, make them feel worthy, attractive and successful, make them feel that they'd arrived or that their lives had meaning. She'd watched Laci fight that battle and lose. And she'd nearly bottomed out in that world herself.

"And that's a state-of-the-art batting cage," he said with a touch of pride as he pointed to the massive structure at the back of the barn. "It'll help me stay in shape during the off-season, but I'm hoping I can get the kids from the team in here over the winter. See if we can ramp up their game."

And *that* was the Ryan who confounded her. The man who was genuinely interested in mentoring kids and helping abused donkeys, the man who in spite of his superstar status wanted to live in a small town and have a life. She could relate. Maybe too well.

He nodded to the cage. "Want to see how it works?"

Fascination blossomed in her. When would she have

another chance to experience his world up close? She nodded back.

He took her mug from her hands and set both mugs on a low table. Then he opened the gate and motioned her inside.

"You'll need a helmet."

"Oh, no." Instinctively she backed against the netting. "I was just hoping to see you demonstrate."

"No way. Here." He handed her a bat and a helmet. "That's one of the helmets I got for the kids on the middle school team."

She plopped the helmet on her head. He leaned in close to check the fit. His hands closed around the helmet and as he wriggled it, she felt his breath against her neck. Caught between his arms—her head held in his hands and weighted by the helmet, her heart thumping, erratic and excited, surrounded by the cage around her and over her head—she felt trapped. Maybe it was the sound of his breathing so close to her face and the heat from his body that had her feeling off kilter. She backed away.

"I don't really think—"

"Don't think. Just step into it. I'll set it on the lowest speed. It's an Iron Mike."

He must've seen the puzzlement in her face.

"An arm-style machine is the only type of pitching machine that gives the same sense of timing as watching a pitcher. With each pitch you'll see the machine's arm wind up and release the ball. You'll see the ball coming."

He saw her hesitate.

"It won't hurt you."

The pitching machine was the least of her worries. She wiped her sweating palm against her hip and grasped the bat.

He crossed his arms and studied her for a moment. Then he shook his head and took the bat from her hands.

"I'll take a couple swings, show you the rhythm. Then you can try it." He walked to the side of the cage. "And here's the emergency switch. Big, red and effective. It stops everything."

Everything but the pounding of her heart.

"Maybe I'll just watch from outside the net." She headed for the gate.

"You sure someone didn't abduct the woman who reeled in a humongous salmon through wild waves and replace her with a body double?"

She laughed. And reconsidered. If the kids in middle school could handle Iron Mike, maybe she could.

"Okay, but you go first. And I didn't reel that fish in by myself—Cain helped, or I would've lost it."

"A stickler for the truth," he said with a nod. "I like that."

Her stomach lurched. He couldn't know her secret, and she wished that she could tell him. Maybe someday she could. But the thought didn't ease her conscience, nor did it stop the surges of desire flooding her as she watched him stride to the side of the cage and flick a switch. Or the tingling of unabashed lust that danced in her core as he took his stance beside the white home plate.

The machine spit the ball so fast she didn't see it. But Ryan smacked it into the opposite end of the net.

She backed into the netting of the cage. "Now I'm *sure* I don't want to stand in front of that thing."

"I'll set it on the lowest speed for you." He handed her the bat and smiled when she took it. His smile coaxed warmth through her, but it was a warmth in no way soothing.

"Atta girl."

She walked to stand beside the plate. She tried to focus, tried to mimic his stance.

"Hitting's all about rhythm and timing," he said as he joined her. He put his hands on his hips. "Trust me, you have plenty of both."

She heard the flirtation in his voice; it called to a region of her brain that wouldn't be governed by plans and pre-made decisions.

She lowered the bat and stepped away from the plate. Took a deep breath and tried to concentrate. It was even harder now.

He took the bat from her.

"Just hold it like this." He wrapped his hands around the base of the bat and held it out in front of her. "Pretend you have rings on and that you're lining them up. And keep your top hand loose."

He held the bat back out to her. She nodded and tried to copy the handhold he showed her. Suddenly the bat felt heavy. And she felt heavy, as though some force of nature had swept into her and anchored her midmotion.

He tilted his head and swept a hand though his hair. She stared, seeing the full-on power of his maleness for the first time. Nothing in her knew how to react. When she didn't move to swing, he took the bat from her again.

"Here, I'll help you through a couple swings, give you the sense of the weight shift."

He stepped behind her and reached around her hips to place his hands on hers and lifted the bat.

Her pulse flared, and she lost her balance. He steadied her with his arm and then, to her surprise, he dropped his hands.

"Maybe if you hold my hips while I swing, it'll give you a better idea." He turned and took the bat from her, stepped in front of her and took his stance. When she didn't move, he looked over his shoulder. "Just put your hands on my hips."

Maybe he knew he was torturing her. He must know. She wrapped her fingers tentatively around his waist.

"Lower," he said. "You need to feel how my body moves."

His voice had changed; there was nothing flirtatious in his words. He could have been teaching the kids for all the innuendo he put in his voice.

She inched her hands lower and gripped him at his hipbones.

"Perfect," he said. "I'll go through it slowly." He glanced over his shoulder. "Wouldn't want to bean you with the bat."

Her body sizzled with sexual tension, but he was all earnest batting coach.

He stepped and pivoted his hips, and she felt the power of his body in her hands. She also swallowed down the flush of heat threatening to engulf her.

"It's stance—which I'll help you with in a minute," he said over his shoulder, "then coil—that's your weight shift or stride—and *then* swing."

He demonstrated again and in spite of the flush of hormones revving through her, she began to get a sense of the rhythm he was talking about. Yet though she concentrated, she couldn't ignore the desire that touching him ignited. It had been too long since she'd felt such a connection. Such a want. She wasn't even sure she'd ever wanted a man as much as she wanted Ryan.

He pulled away from her hands and turned to face her. A smile lit his eyes, but she was pretty sure he was fighting to bite it back.

"You try it. Keep your hips in line with the pitcher. Well, in this case, with the machine."

She adjusted her grip, lining up the imaginary rings, and raised the bat over her head. If he knew the effect he had on her and how difficult her rushing pulse made concentrating, he was a hard-hearted man. A very hard-hearted man.

She peeked back at him and saw the absorbed look on his face. He was focused on teaching her to swing a bat. Caught in the keen web of his attention, the tremor of want surged deeper into her. She bit at her bottom lip and called up what control she could muster.

"Keep your knees bent, your feet flat, and then step into it. Just pick up your front leg and shift forward, making a slight inward coil as you do."

She picked up her leg and stepped forward, did everything she could remember.

The swing she took felt fabulous.

"Try it again." He picked up a bat leaning against the net. "But this time let your elbow go up and back."

She made the motion he demonstrated.

"No, not quite so far back; your thumb shouldn't touch your shoulder."

She swung again.

"Good."

She felt more than good. At that moment the energy zipping in her could've burned down the barn.

"Now, this time as you swing, start driving your back shoulder and back elbow down toward your hip as you rotate."

He demonstrated. Her eyes followed the movement of his body, but her mind was taking a ride in another realm. No one man should be allowed to have all the sensual, sexy, powerful attributes that he did.

But it was his earnestness that wiggled its way into her heart. He loved what he did, and seeing his sincere enthusiasm was like breathing mountain air on a spring day. She'd felt it that first evening as she'd watched him working with the boys, then again on their fishing adventure with

Cain. And though he might have quirks and foibles—who didn't?—he was a man with a good heart, the sort of man she'd never imagined meeting.

"Your back hip should move toward the ball," he continued in his level, coaching voice. "Move your hips at the same pace as your back shoulder."

"I'll never remember all that." And not just because it was an overwhelming sequence of details.

"That's why they call it practice."

He demonstrated again, and she managed to copy him.

What she'd rather have done was sit at the side of the cage and watch him move. She was beginning to grasp the allure of professional sports. Where else could anyone see such power, such grace, such excellence—such downright world-rocking physicality?

He walked over to and fiddled with the machine, and then returned to her. "Ready?"

"Maybe."

He pressed the black button at the top of the emergency switch box. "Don't think too much. Try to enjoy it. It's a game, remember."

The ball fired past her before she could move the bat.

"That's the *lowest* speed?"

"Yup. Take your stance." He was ordering her now, the sterner voice of the coach. It'd been years since she'd heard that voice. She'd played intramural soccer at Harvard, had been a decent halfback. But her coach never fired up the sorts of images that she fought to keep at bay listening to Ryan.

She connected with the next ball, but it rolled across the top of the bat and into the net behind her.

"There's no way—"

"Don't talk. Just focus and swing."

She hit the next ball halfway down the cage and leaped with joy.

"This is great, this is—"

The next ball nearly hit her in the stomach.

She flipped back around to face Iron Mike. "Okay, I'm concentrating."

"Think of it as a dance," he said.

It was one hell of a dance.

By the time he turned the machine off, her arms, back and legs ached.

"Could I see what it's like when it goes at the speed you hit? The ninety-mile-an-hour sort?"

She wanted to enter his world, to know more of this man who had opened her to a realm within herself she'd never explored. Someday she might curse him for opening the door to that world, but not today. Today she felt strong. Today she felt whole. Today she could almost imagine facing down and casting away forever the demons that had claimed Laci and had threatened to claim her.

She pulled off the batting helmet and shook out her hair. And caught him staring. He didn't look away, just smiled that devastating smile that made her insides turn to molten gold and sent shocks of delicious desire through her. These were feelings she wanted to remember; feelings she wanted to soak in and call up to counter the darkness when it threatened.

"Okay." He picked up the bat. "But you stand to my right, just in case." He pointed to a spot about three feet from him. "And put your helmet back on."

She saluted and then felt ridiculous for doing it. But he was so earnest, so focused, she couldn't help it. She plopped the helmet back on her head.

He fiddled with the machine again.

"Ready?" He stepped into position beside the plate. "Do *not* move."

She saw the arm of the pitching machine go back and

felt the ball more than saw it, as if it cleaved the molecules in the air. The crack of Ryan's bat made her jump. The ball ricocheted off the machine and flew back at her, missing her by less than a foot.

He dashed to the wall and pushed the red emergency switch.

"You asked for it."

"I did." Her blood pounded in her ears.

"You'll be sore tomorrow," he said as he turned to her. "In places you didn't even know you have."

The gentle smile creasing his eyes teased at her rational reasons for fighting her feelings and keeping her distance. He opened the gate and ushered her out, which was a good thing. If she'd spent a few more minutes inside the cage with him, she might've leaped into his arms.

He put his hand on her shoulder. He couldn't know it branded heat into her core.

"Not bad for a first time out. You have a good sense of movement."

No other compliment would have meant as much.

But now that she'd seen what it was like to stand in front of a speeding ball, she wondered why players didn't suffer from nervous overload. She'd stood well away and still it had scared the hell out of her.

"Don't you ever feel fear?"

He pulled his hand away. "Any guy who can't transform fear into a functioning, healthy respect doesn't last a week in the majors." He shot her a too-quick smile, a smile that told her she'd touched a nerve.

He turned away from her and secured the gate to the batting cage, every movement precise, measured, sure. Her own nerves hovered near overload, but not from standing in front of the speeding ball. She could still feel his hands on her—guiding her, coaching, coaxing. *Arousing.*

"I'll give you a quick tour of the animal barn," he said, "but then let's get outside. It's too nice to spend a day like this surrounded by walls."

She followed him into the light, knowing that the walls blocking her were of her own making.

CHAPTER NINE

THE ANIMAL BARN HAD BEEN METICULOUSLY RENOVATED. Paved flooring sloped down to midfloor drains, and the stalls were spacious, with high arched windows. Each stall had a hand-built feed rack and plumbed-in water troughs. It reminded Cara of the stalls her brother had built for his prized polo horses. That Ryan had invested such money and care into housing homeless donkeys touched her, made her want to thank him on their behalf.

She ran her hand along the curve of a carved stone water trough. "Lucky donkeys," she said.

"Not so far. Their lives have been pretty gruesome."

"They're likely to perk up after a week or two here. I've seen spas that don't look this good."

He turned and raised a brow. "Haven't been to a spa myself, but I'll take your word for it."

Spas. What a stupid thing to say. It was as though her secret pushed at her, determined to leak out in any way it could.

"Are there spas around here?"

Right—she'd opened the box and now had to close it.

"A few. People go on special occasions. Girls' nights, that sort of thing."

"Sounds like an invitation I'd like to wrangle."

Imagining Ryan with her in a hot tub under the stars

was more than her self-restraint could bear. "Is there much left to do?" she asked, trying to turn the conversation.

"It's nearly ready. I have a man from a nearby town coming to interview for the job of daily maintenance while I'm on the road, but the guy I had finishing up the carpentry works for my contractor, and he got pulled to a bigger job in the city. Put a real kink in my timing."

She took a breath and again pushed back the image of Ryan in a hot tub, all muscles and heat and man. "Like I said, Adam Mitchell does good work."

Ryan shot her a look as if he were taking her measure. "If you're recommending him, then I'd like to have his number."

He closed the barn door and headed her to a path that ran toward the back of his property.

"C'mon," he said with a grin bordering on boyish, "I'll show you where I'm going to put in their outdoor spa."

After seeing the exquisite work he'd had done in the barn, she wasn't sure he was kidding.

"This water trough is self-cleaning," he said with a touch of pride.

Calling the structure a trough didn't do it justice. The three-tiered water station had smiling gargoyles for spouts. The bottom tier was wide enough to swim in.

"It's nice enough to put beside the Trevi Fountain."

He looked at her, puzzled.

"The Trevi is a lovely fountain in Rome. I meant it as a compliment."

He raked a hand through his hair, then fisted both hands to his hips and studied the fountain.

"I know it's a bit over the top. I bought it online. Some lady's husband wanted to go with the southwest adobe look, and he gave me a good deal. The guy was so happy to get rid of it, he had it delivered himself."

The gleam had gone out of his eyes. She'd made him uncomfortable and was sorry. Justifying choices was no fun, she knew that too well.

"Is that a stream?" She pointed to a winding swath of willows at the bottom of a swale in the distance.

"Spring fed. Good thing since they're predicting late and lower-than-average rainfall this year."

He followed her as she picked her way along a rutted path down to the trickling stream. Bay trees and a few oaks were dotted among the willows. The deep cut of the bank told her that water would rush furiously when the rains did come.

"I love it here," she said, turning to him. His pleased smile warmed her. "I can focus on the simple pleasures when I'm outdoors."

He knelt at the side of the stream and picked up a fist-sized rock, turned it in his hand, then tossed it upstream with the ease of a child throwing a hollow ball.

"Even out here I sometimes can't leave all my negative mind chatter behind," he said.

She wanted to wrap her arms around him, hold him. Like everyone, he had troubles, but she'd been far too focused on her own to consider what shape his might take. She bit back her urge to go to him and found herself chattering instead.

"It's not our fault that the negative has such power," she said. "Human survival forced our brains to develop a negativity bias, a strong bias that makes the brain sort of like Velcro for bad experiences and Teflon, no stick, for good. If we don't focus on and hold the good, it rolls right off."

"That would explain why at the end of the day I remember what didn't go right better than what did." He tossed another rock upstream.

If anyone had told her that watching a man do

something as simple as tossing a rock could send shots of unprecedented wanting through her, she'd have told them to get their realities checked.

She knelt and fingered a fallen willow leaf that lay golden against the grass at the side of the stream. When she looked back up, the tender, thoughtful look in his eyes made her want to share more of what she'd learned, what had helped her find happiness.

"Holding tight to the negative is our worst habit, but it's understandable. After all, any of our ancestors who didn't pay attention to warning signals—signals that said tigers lurked nearby—and instead went blithely along enjoying the bliss of their day were eaten."

He laughed. "Higher stakes than calling for Chinese takeout."

"So we're their legacy." Talking allowed her to keep the urge to fold into his arms at bay. "We learned to pay attention to danger, to the negative, learned to run around and around our tracks until the furrows cut deep and it became impossible to see out."

He sat back on his haunches and rested his elbows on his knees.

"Reprogramming our b-brains is possible." Her carefully formed conversation began to dissolve as his eyes lit with the same slow smile curving his lips.

"Yours, maybe. Mine's pretty entrenched."

"No, really." She looked away, forced herself to concentrate. "You can lay down new patterns. I was shocked at how simple it is. You just have to savor good experiences and take them deep into your body—*feel* them, not just think them."

"I like anything I can practice," he said as he threw another rock upstream.

She watched the ripples spread out, lit by the rays of

the sun. "The book I'm reading says there are three things—easy things—anyone can do."

He walked to her. His thighs bulged under the fabric of his jeans when he crouched beside her. It wasn't the late morning sun blazing a path of heat through her body, it was Ryan. She looked into his eyes and saw something she couldn't name, but it seared her to her core. Her heart thrummed in her chest, and she couldn't remember even one of the three steps recommended by the author. How could she think when she was so caught up with feeling?

She was pretty sure he was going to kiss her. If he kissed her, she knew she wouldn't stop there. Not with just a kiss. She scooted back a few feet.

He followed.

"Don't you ever feel like your brain is playing tricks on you?" She was ad-libbing, scrambling. "I mean, it's important to focus on the future, to have goals, but sometimes I think my brain tricks me into thinking that the future is a real thing, something solid. But it's not." Her statement was strong, but she heard the tremor in her voice. "It's not. The future never comes. There's always only now."

"As in *this* now?" He wrapped his hands around her, the heat of his palms searing her shoulder blades as he drew her to him and pressed his lips to hers.

His kiss reached her soul in such a flash that she had no time to put up a defense, its power almost laughing at the suggestion that she could've deflected it.

Sounds dropped away. The gentle tease of his tongue against hers fired heat through her, and she fell into the spell cast by the meeting of her lips and his.

He tasted like lust, like need and desire and rich passion. But he also tasted like joy, sweet and refreshing. And she wanted more, another taste of the heady combination.

They separated but not far and not for long. Then they were tasting one another again and then again.

How could a kiss make her feel as if he'd entered every part of her? As if she flowed into him and he into her and there was no boundary between them? His heart beat against hers, so fast, so strong. She had to stop him, stop herself, before she lost all control, before she—

His fingers laced into her hair, and he tugged her closer, his mouth tasting, then plundering, banishing all thought from her mind.

He pressed her back against the soft grass and traced kisses along her neck. She twined her fingers in his hair and pulled his mouth back to hers. He skimmed his tongue over her lips. She opened her eyes and saw passion in his, passion and hunger that matched her own. But it was the tender look he gave her that made her pause. This was no game. Not for her. And now she knew, not for him.

But the craving he'd awakened—the yearning for joining, for mating, for a man to share her life—was new to her. She'd heard, read, that bodies were wired for love. She'd read and believed, but never felt the truth of it. Desire opened a realm she couldn't explain, but at that moment it didn't matter.

Ryan pulled back and searched her face. Then he brushed his fingertips against her cheek. His breaths came quickly, though she noted that he tried to control them.

"You're unlike any woman I've ever met." His voice was velvet. She could slide along the nap of it and into bliss. "So straightforward. So happy in your life. So beautiful."

Straightforward.

The word cut into her and, like a genie returning to its bottle, thought rushed back in. He was looking for someone to share his life, she could feel it. With all her heart she wished she could be that woman.

He lifted her hand to his lips and kissed her fingertips.

She pushed up onto her elbows and wiggled back, away from him and sat up. He reached out and circled his fingers around both wrists.

"I have to get back." Those were certainly the hardest five words she'd ever uttered. But they were necessary words.

He didn't release her, but his grip softened.

"Really. I have to... "

She couldn't come up with an excuse and didn't feel like lying. She moved to him. He wrapped his arms around her. She laid her head against his chest and felt the pounding of his heart under her cheek. And wished she could stay right there, held by him, and forget the world.

He tracked his hand to the small of her back and then up to her shoulder blade, rested it there, held her.

"Hey," he said quietly, "I can't say I want you to go, but I understand if that's what you want to do."

She nodded against his chest, then closed her eyes and let herself feel the warmth of him, the strength of him. She wasn't sure what she wanted. She wanted him, but the timing was all wrong.

Timing? No, what stood between them was more than timing. She braced herself and pulled away. If circumstances were different, he'd be the sort of man she could love. But she needed to put those thoughts out of her mind. She might be able to have a taste, but that was all. The memory of their time together would generate many good feelings she wouldn't have to work very hard at sinking into, holding on to, calling up. But at the edge of her awareness she knew there would be pain. Pain for what wasn't, for what wouldn't be allowed to grow. She cursed the fates that brought her such a man, a man looking for the woman she fought to be, wanted to be, but wasn't.

She'd cut it off now, before either of them got too involved.

He held her hand as they walked back to her car. She was relieved that he didn't force any explanation. Perhaps he was more patient than he'd admitted. Whatever the reason, she was grateful. What she would've said, she had no idea. And what she wanted to say, she couldn't.

He opened her car door and held it as she slid behind the wheel. He draped his arm along the roof of the car and leaned in—close, but not too close. The man was a good judge of distance.

She tilted her head and studied him. Perhaps she wasn't at the helm, as she'd thought she was. It occurred to her that Ryan Rea could be a formidable force if he set his mind to it.

"Maybe I can come over and see the work that guy has done on your place," he said with a slow, curving smile. "We can watch a game. I have a night off and don't have to travel."

Could any woman resist him? Could she?

"I don't have a TV," she said. She should've said no outright, but didn't want to. And as she watched his smile widen, as if he hid a delightful secret, she couldn't have said no anyway.

"That's no deal breaker. Monday evening, around six?" he said. "You can tell me more about this *ramping up the good practice* of yours."

She nodded.

She should absolutely be saying no, but there was no way she was going to. Not yet. Not when she knew the pulse of energy, the carried-away feeling that she'd heard and read about, the feeling of falling for someone beyond her wildest imagination. She wasn't going to cut it off. Not just yet. She had time.

He lifted her hand from where it rested on the steering

102

wheel and brushed a kiss to it.

"I'll bring dinner," he said. "And just in case your schedule frees up, I'll send tickets for the game on Sunday."

"No, I really can't," she said in as firm a voice as she could muster.

Her father's golf partner was a part owner of the Giants. With her luck, she'd run smack into him or another of her father's clubby friends before she found her seat in the stadium. Word of her presence would spread and fast. Her father's cronies in the Bay area would pelt him with questions and try to locate her to match her up with their playboy sons and get their hooks into her fortune. Her father never saw it that way. To him they were all Good Prospects. Stand-Up Young Men. He was beyond oblivious.

Nope. Public events in the city were strictly off her list.

"I'll send them anyway," Ryan countered.

No guy should be allowed to have a grin like that. It melted what little resistance she held on to.

He closed her car door, and then patted the side of the car and stepped back. "Just in case," he added.

In her rearview mirror she saw him watch as she drove out of the gate.

The buzz of adrenaline and jitters and outright delight moving through her—each wave a stronger pulse than the last—told her Ryan Rea was indeed more than her defenses could handle, more than her well-planned-out life would bear.

She couldn't do it. She couldn't handle trying to make a relationship work when she had to hide herself. She wanted to be free and open with Ryan, but she couldn't. Not if she wanted to maintain her anonymity. Not if she wanted to continue the life she loved in Albion Bay.

So not only would she skip the game, she'd call him and tell him not to come on Monday.

He waved as she pulled out onto Highway One.

And she waved back.

Though she didn't feel like smiling, the smile came of its own accord.

Calling him would be too risky; she'd fall prey to his charming ways. And it wouldn't take much for her heart to leap across her careful boundaries on a mission of its own.

She'd text him.

A coward's way out, but a way out all the same.

CHAPTER TEN

RYAN STOOD IN CENTER FIELD AND TOOK IN THE stunning September afternoon. On days like this, the stadium was a little piece of paradise. Light reflected up off the Bay into the sky, the chilling fog parked miles out at sea and the energy of forty thousand people, all happy to be out for the game, rippled so strong in the air he could almost touch it.

He turned his attention back to the game.

Scotty had struck out the first two Padres batters, but their slugger, Vincente, was at the plate.

Vincente took the first pitch, and Ryan smiled to himself. It'd been a perfect pitch to hit.

But the sound as the guy hit into the heart of the ball on the next pitch was one Ryan preferred not to hear. He'd dubbed it the "Home Run Anthem." Every batter liked to hear it when they were at the plate, but to a fielder, that sound meant trouble.

Ryan traced the arc of the ball as he raced back toward the center field wall and leaped. He closed his glove around the ball as his shoulder slammed into the wall, knocking the breath out of him.

He slid down the wall, ignoring the pain and gripping the ball. The Giants needed to win this game if they were to keep their lead in the division.

Pain was part of the price of winning.

The roar of the crowd as he stood and fired the ball to Matt Darrington, their shortstop, took his mind off the searing pulse in his shoulder.

He jogged to the dugout, grabbed his batting helmet and walked to the on-deck circle. Aderro stood ready in the batter's box, eyeing the pitcher.

Ryan took a couple of cautious swings and felt the pull in his shoulder and ribs. Still functioning, but he'd be mighty sore in the morning. He took the doughnut off his bat and hacked a couple of swings without it. Better, but still not right. Good thing tomorrow was an off day.

A day off that included a night with Cara West.

He took another swing and glanced over to the section he'd sent her tickets for. The two seats were empty. He should've known; she'd been pretty clear about not making the game.

But he'd hoped.

Funny thing about her, she whipped up his hope. Hell, she whipped up more than his hope.

Kissing Cara had rocked him. She'd pulled away, but there'd been no ambivalence in her kiss. He'd heard that if anything predicted the destiny of a relationship, it was the kiss. A man could tell worlds about a woman from kissing her. The vibe that pulsed between him and Cara told him he wanted more. After their kisses yesterday, he'd had to walk the perimeter of the ranch just to calm the hard-on that kissing her had fired. But the walk on his ranch hadn't dissolved the images he'd had late into the night of getting her under him in his bed.

He'd have to be patient.

And careful.

At this point in his life he wanted more than a cautious fling. And though he was pretty sure she wasn't interested in him for his money, he had to play that line with caution too.

He cursed the black claws of cynicism that tore at his thoughts and made him distrust. But he couldn't deny the power of the lens it forced him to look through, a lens that made him second-guess motivations, friendships, even business transactions. And women.

But Cara was a straight shooter, the kind of person who'd say what was on her mind. And her simplicity was a welcome contrast to the world he navigated every day.

And she was damn gorgeous, in spite of the fact she didn't do much to show off her beauty. He liked that too. No pretense with a woman like her; he could be himself around her. Some things about her had fired off a few fleeting warning signals, but that was just part of getting to know someone; sometimes the surprises made unwrapping the package more enticing.

And he really liked what she'd told him about her practice of ramping up the good. It made sense, he'd just never thought about it before.

The idea that he might improve his game *and* his life by trying to hold on to good experiences was like a light dawning on a distant horizon.

He shut his eyes and closed out the sounds of the stadium, focused on calling up a good experience. He leaned in to kiss her, to taste her lips and—

The guttural call of the umpire as he called a third strike on Aderro snapped Ryan back to the game. Aderro cursed under his breath and stormed to the dugout. Catchers didn't like to go down looking. Hell, nobody did.

That'd be an experience in the negative column.

Ryan stepped into the batter's box. He watched a clean strike go by him. He wasn't one to go after the first pitch; he liked to see what the guy on the mound had. The pitcher wound up, and Ryan felt power surge through him as he connected and hooked the ball down the left-field line.

Though Johnson dug the ball out of the corner and made a good throw to second, Ryan beat it out without having to slide. He liked a good solid double. But he liked triples and home runs even better.

He caught his breath. And thanked the heavens that the drive for excellence didn't have to always be a fight—a discipline, yes, and a struggle and a balancing act, but not always a fight. Since he'd met Cara West, his game had improved and the nightmares had vanished. He didn't need a psychic to tell him it wasn't a coincidence.

After the game, which they won, the locker room was full of raucous celebrating. They were one step closer to the playoffs.

"Good blast," Alex Tavonesi said as he walked past Ryan and headed for his own locker.

Ryan's triple in the seventh had given the Giants the lead. And maybe put the icing on the contract his agent was negotiating for his future with the team. Now that he had the ranch, had plans for it, he wanted to land the six-year deal. He needed the funds if he was going to maintain the ranch as the sanctuary he dreamed of. A fifty-million-dollar contract would do just fine.

Having the ranch in his life had put solid ground under his feet and had given him a focus outside the game. And creating the donkey sanctuary made him feel he was contributing. Not that playing a good game wasn't giving back, but all he had to do was look around him to know that the guys who had something to fall back on after they left the game were the happiest. And he wasn't the sort to open a sports bar in some midwestern town and surround himself with memorabilia and stories of glory days.

"It would've taken more than a triple to close out the game if those runs you stole from them had scored," Ryan countered over the bark and buzz of his still-celebrating teammates.

Alex just nodded. In addition to being a slugger and having achieved the coveted Triple Crown, Alex had four Gold Gloves. Top performance and good grabs were what they both were paid to execute. But the expectation of excellence didn't take anything away from Alex's stunning play.

"I heard from Jackie that you and your girlfriend helped her deal with an injured sea lion last week."

Ryan ignored the girlfriend comment. He stripped out of his uniform and tossed it into the bin near his locker. "Has anyone mentioned that your wife doesn't have any fear?"

Alex grimaced. "Don't remind me. I try to pretend she spends her days doing research, safely tucked behind a microscope."

"If she did that, the evening news would have to find another poster girl," Ryan ribbed.

Jackie's exploits rescuing seals and whales made great press. Ryan had looked her up on the Internet. He couldn't imagine being married to such a whirlwind of a woman.

"I'd like to see your place," Alex said as he wrapped a towel around his waist. "And meet your intrepid girlfriend. Jackie liked her. In fact she thought she might have met her before, but couldn't place where." He headed for the showers.

Ryan didn't correct him. Cara wasn't his. But with a little luck maybe he'd find out if she should be.

The subtly painted walls of Dr. Garret's office did nothing to calm Ryan's nerves. He'd been wrong when he'd thought that the trainer's table was his least favorite place to be. Sitting in a doctor's office waiting for a cheek swab, listening to the muted sounds of the staff moving in the halls and the ring of phones in the distance, ratcheted his nerves into high gear. But he wanted to clear the slate. If the DNA test proved he wasn't the father of Elaine's child, maybe he could. Tom was persuasive; he saw now why the guy was one of the hottest attorneys in the country. He had a way of leveraging reason and facts. And he'd convinced Ryan that the fact the test would reveal was an important piece of information if Ryan was going to get a grip on his life going forward.

What Ryan hadn't told Tom was that the main reason he was submitting to the humiliation of the DNA test was Cara.

He didn't want to enter a relationship with her with any baggage he'd have to conceal. He didn't want any baggage at all. A sensitive woman like her wouldn't want to start a relationship with a guy who had a kid—a kid he wasn't allowed to see, a kid that he'd signed away all rights to.

He'd left a message on her machine telling her he needed to move their date. And just to stack the odds in his favor, he'd said that if she didn't call back, he'd be at her place at eight Sunday night. He'd just have to hope that the day game didn't run into extra innings.

Tom had arranged an agreement and payoff with the judge: if the DNA test proved that the kid wasn't Ryan's, he'd pay out a lump sum and Elaine would have to sign a gag order. A gag order that would keep Ryan from becoming the center of a feeding frenzy for the press. Ryan said a silent prayer for the timing of the season—fans were more interested in the playoffs than they were in vague rumors about players' lives.

The door opened and Dr. Garret came in.

He wasted no time in swabbing Ryan's cheek. Ryan said another prayer of thanks when all the doctor asked about was whether Ryan thought the Giants could go all the way this year. A true fan was a blessing Ryan hadn't counted on. He suspected that Tom had prepped the good doctor, told him of Ryan's reluctance to submit to the test in the first place. How things had changed in a couple of weeks. Meeting Cara had made him want a life he'd never imagined. A life with roots, a fresh start in a community he was growing to love. But first he'd have to wait for the test results. It would be a very long four days.

When Tom's number flashed on Ryan's phone on Friday, Ryan's muscles tightened from head to toe. He'd had four days to consider the possibility that the kid was his. Possible, but not likely. Still, even with the odds in his favor, the possibility left a sour feeling in his stomach. He'd wrestled with what he'd tell Cara if the unlikely chance morphed into a hard-core reality. Signing his rights away was the real kicker. What woman could love a man who'd turned his back on a kid? It didn't matter that Elaine hadn't offered him a choice. He hadn't fought, he hadn't tried. He hadn't thought.

"I had them put a rush on your test like you asked," Tom said. "No match. Not even close. The kid's not yours."

Tom's words boomeranged in his head. He stared out his living room window, eyes fixed on the line of fencing across the back acreage. The light feeling he'd imagined didn't come.

"This is good news, Ryan. I'm sending the sign-off papers over by courier." He paused. "You there?"

"Just getting my head around it." He paced to the window. "Thank you, Tom. For believing me."

"It's not about belief, buddy. This is about the truth."

There was glee in Tom's tone. And pride. Ryan didn't feel either.

"Well, maybe this news will cheer you up—a minor league player stepped up to claim the child as his—he was a perfect DNA match. He has rights, Ryan, and he intends to exercise them. And he has a good attorney; I checked the guy out." He paused again, perhaps sensing Ryan's disbelief. "The father's not rolling in bucks, but he's a decent guy. The kid will have a dad. And maybe it'll all work out for the three of them."

Relief swept Ryan then, coursing into knotted spaces he hadn't known he'd tied off. His relief was more for the kid than for himself. He would have worried about that kid for the rest of his life.

"You're free." Tom's voice drilled into Ryan as the truth he'd known all along bloomed back to life.

"Go win us some games," Tom said in a jovial tone. "I want to see one of those Series rings up close." He chuckled and then added, "But be careful with the ladies. The Internet's buzzing after that triple you blasted."

He didn't need Tom to caution him, but he appreciated his enthusiasm. And his excellence. He'd never have been free without Tom on his team. He had a night with Cara ahead, a night that he'd looked forward to more than he wanted to admit. And he could enter her world with a clear conscience, thanks to Tom's dogged pursuit of the truth.

CHAPTER ELEVEN

S TRAIGHT UP, ALSTON. I NEED THE NUMBERS AND timing straight up." Cara didn't mean to sound short with her attorney—no aspect of the hornet's nest she was in was his fault. She tempered her voice when she asked, "How much do I have left out of my own funds that could go to the Albion Bay clinic project?"

"Maybe a hundred thousand, but more like fifty. You have several large three-year obligations to pay out, most from long-term grants you made before you moved to Albion Bay. The women's shelter in the Bronx eats up most of your allocation."

"The town council is determined to build out the whole project, all at once. Not do it piecemeal." She didn't succeed in hiding the exasperation in her voice.

"One could admire them for their vision."

"In the meantime someone could *die* out here without better emergency access. It's nuts. We're talking bake sales, Alston. Do you know how long it will take for them to raise money with that sort of effort?"

"You never were much of a cook."

She ignored his attempt at humor. "They rely on the local vet for emergencies," she added.

"I shudder at the thought."

"*My* side, Alston. You're supposed to be on my side."

She flipped through her notes from the community meeting. "The way the town has set things up, there's not even a way for me to have you anonymously funnel funds to an on-call doc. It's absurd."

He didn't repeat his earlier argument that she could choose to step into her role as president of the Barrington Foundation and in a few months fund almost anything she wanted. For all his strait-laced manner, Alston was the one person who understood why she'd chosen to live a quiet life in Albion Bay.

He was the one person besides Quinn that she'd told about her near breakdown three years before. After Laci's body had been found in the surging surf near a remote beach resort, she'd had to talk to someone. She'd tried to talk to Quinn. He was her twin, and they shared secrets and hopes, but Quinn didn't get how deeply Laci's death had shaken her. And her therapist had been on vacation in a remote village in Africa; and there was no way she was going to phone some on-call therapist she didn't know and didn't trust.

Alston had listened. Alston knew Laci's family, knew that the family and Cara had tried for years to get Laci to go into rehab, had tried to help her escape the drugs and the vampires of the underbelly of the New York social scene. Twice Cara had driven Laci to a rehab center. And twice Laci had left before the first week was out.

When Laci had run off to Barbados with a guy she'd met in a club, Alston had helped Cara track her down. But they'd found her too late. The guy had dumped Laci for another partying heiress, an heiress who put out for him. Laci, unstable and abandoned, had taken her life. For almost a month, her sweet friend's face had been plastered across the tabloids. Every tidbit about Laci's life was fodder for the front covers of *Us Weekly* and *People*. A jilted, beautiful, jet-setting heiress taking her own life was the perfect story for media hype.

Cara made a decision the day the news broke. Laci's death cemented her resolve to pry herself free and find a way to live the life she'd always dreamed of, a life where she would be appreciated for herself and not for her money. A life in a town where she could trust others because they wouldn't have ulterior motives for being her friend.

No one knew how much time there was to live. She wasn't willing to bet the odds.

But she hadn't counted on the crushing guilt and fear that threatened to engulf her. For months she'd turned every conversation with Laci over in her mind. The if-onlys and the maybes and the what-ifs rushed at her until she could barely find the strength to dress and go to see her therapist.

Few people understood that she'd felt caged—forced to live in a world that didn't suit her in any way. Her close friends would smile and nod, but no one really believed that she wanted out. That she wanted to live like a normal person, away from the hype. To live in a world where what she did mattered.

Leaving and starting over had been her road to sanity.

Settling into Albion Bay, wrapping the routines of a simple life around her, had helped her heal, helped her find her feet. Helped her carve out a life that had meaning.

Without Alston's help, she never could've pulled it off.

But he was right, she faced a dilemma and there was nothing simple about it. It was one thing to turn her back on the hype, the lifestyle, the preconceived expectations that came with being born into privilege and wealth, and another entirely to deny that now that she'd seen up close what the foundation's funds could do, how the money could be put to use, that she didn't care.

She gripped the phone and rubbed at her throbbing

temple with her other hand. Her chest tightened, constricting her breath. She'd fought for her freedom, and now the fight had turned on her. The community that had saved her, that had healed her, needed help for itself, a kind of help she could provide. But that help would come at a very dear price.

"Cara?" Alston's voice pulled her back from her thoughts.

"I'm here. I was just thinking. What about submitting funding for the clinic as a discretionary grant?" She knew the idea was a dead end before the words left her mouth.

"If you don't accept the presidency," he said in a level voice, "you'd have to be voted on to the board. The next round of nominations comes up in a year. But even then, discretionary grants are limited to ten thousand dollars per member."

"What about using capital from my personal foundation to fund the clinic?"

"We've been over this, Cara. Your foundation allows you to only spend interest; there's no way around that. And as I said, the majority of your funds are already committed."

"What if I sell my place in Southampton?" It was the one thing from her former life she hadn't let go of. Too many good memories. And her brother still used it as a summer retreat.

"That would take time. Your parents would have to sign off on their share."

"Theirs is a ten percent share, for goodness' sake! I could buy them out tomorrow."

"*If* they agreed. Let's wait on thinking about the Southampton place—see what you do."

"I'm not *doing* anything, Alston. We have to figure out a way around this." She hated the petulant sound of her voice. But maybe petulance was always the sound made by creatures cornered by forces they couldn't wrangle.

"What about the money he left to me directly, the money not in the foundation? You said it's more than a billion dollars. Couldn't I take a loan against it?"

"It's not yours until you're twenty-five."

"Alston, there must be *something* you can do."

The silence on the other end of the phone told her more than she wanted to know.

"Maybe Dray Bender would fund a grant for the clinic, pass it through?" Now she really was reaching.

Alston let out a sharp breath. "I'm pretty sure he wouldn't. I suspect he's funneling funds to people he owes favors. Besides, I have no leverage over him and neither do you, unless you're at the helm. And if he sees the name of your town on a grant request, he'll know where you are. It won't take long for him to figure out your situation and play it to his advantage. And though your father has honored his promise to keep you under the radar, Bender is aware that you have high stakes in maintaining your anonymity. There's nothing about the man to trust. He played your father, or he wouldn't be heading the foundation."

Cara rubbed at her forehead. When she'd set up her home in Albion Bay, she'd never expected to hit a wall like this. Sitting on the sidelines at town council meetings, knowing full well she could help, was torture. But did she have the strength to face reentering the world she'd fought to leave behind? The world that had crashed in on Laci?

She didn't want to imagine how her relationships with people in town would change once word got out. People who weren't outright angry at her deception would likely be polite—but she knew too darn well the gap that big money created. She'd faced that gap in boarding school with the scholarship girls and she'd faced it at nearly every non-profit she'd given grants to. The deference during site visits she couldn't wriggle out of, the careful words and gestures by well-meaning staffers as they attempted to pretend that she was just like them. The people who tried to pretend there was no difference were almost worse than the ones who were awed by it. She hated it. *Hated* it.

No, that wasn't exactly right; she cut those thoughts off.

She wasn't going to hide behind the half-truths any longer. She'd been gone long enough, had learned enough about herself and about other people, that she could face the true problem head on. What she'd really hated back then was that most people hadn't known her. Hadn't seen her. Even those she'd helped. They saw the family name or the foundation's reputation. They certainly saw the dollar signs.

But they didn't see the woman. Just as those in school hadn't seen the girl. The only value she'd had was because of her family connections and the family's very great success with making money.

She'd left her privileged world not because of what she was, but because of what she wasn't.

She was rich, but she had no value. And that damning reality carved a hole that yawned wide. That dark place had swallowed not only Laci but many of their friends. They hadn't died, but every day they fought the destructive power of the drugs they used to keep from facing the truth, to keep from facing their fear, to keep from falling into the black hole that fear called home. Cara was lucky that she wasn't into drugs, but she knew the fight, she knew the fear. If life didn't feel meaningful, even in some small way, it was a slippery incline into the jaws of self-destruction.

She didn't want to be loved, or even just tolerated, for her bank balance. She wanted to be someone's friend because her friendship was appreciated. Because she, just herself, no money or reputation, was valuable to someone else.

She rubbed her forehead again. Why was she even thinking about those things? She had friends in Albion Bay, friends who did appreciate her. And she was supposed to be trying to find a way to help them.

"I can't believe my grandfather set things up this way. Two months"—she tried to regulate the exasperation in her voice—"why would he give me only two months to decide?"

"He may have suspected your father would try to stack the board in the interim. And your grandfather liked deadlines; he thought they made a person focus on what's important."

"He got that right."

But the part he hadn't gotten was what she wanted. What she *needed*. Placing her in an impossible situation was no gift.

Before she'd escaped her old life she could help plenty of people, but she couldn't have friends. Now she had friends that she couldn't help.

"Cara, let's talk this over when you come into town next week. I think so much better face-to-face." He paused. "We'll come up with something. Maybe even something that might work."

Cara's warring thoughts didn't let up as she drove her afternoon bus round. Each time she let herself imagine taking even the smallest step back into the world of privilege and big philanthropy, into the world where the force of the money itself held a power that could sweep even the most resolved person along with it, her throat squeezed shut and she felt like she couldn't breathe. The very things that made her love her life here were the things that made her situation excruciating. She loved these people. She wanted to be able to help the community in a real way.

And deep down, she didn't want to hide. Not anymore.

But stronger than all of those was her love of freedom. No amount of therapy was going to change that fact. Within weeks of finding her cabin, landing the bus-driving job and beginning to work in the garden, she'd realized that she'd been wrong about how much she craved a change. She'd thought that wrapping a life of her choosing around her would buoy her, help her push back at the dark cloud that Laci's death had hung over her life. But living and working with the people of Albion Bay had done much more than that. Life in the town had revived her soul.

She parked the bus in the school lot and walked to her car. Before she stepped in she looked out over the hills toward the coast. A pair of hawks sailed above her, riding the currents of the afternoon winds. Dave Jenkins waved as he strode out toward the baseball practice diamond, carrying an overstuffed equipment bag. Cara felt the familiar warmth of belonging wash through her as she waved back.

Some days, when she went to Grady's to buy seeds for her garden and talked with the locals about their hopes and plans, she felt like she'd been airlifted into a Norman Rockwell painting. There was a reason screenwriters and novelists wrote about small-town life. But Albion Bay was no idealized figment of a writer's imagination—the community had a spine to go with its heart. Democracy wasn't easy; like any place where individuals came together, there were problems and conflicts to be solved. But in this town and, she suspected, in many others, people wanted to solve the problems facing them. They drew together and worked at creating a place where they could maintain their diversity and yet still have heart.

She watched as Dave unloaded bats from his equipment bag and lined them up like sentinels waiting for the boys to come and bring them to life. And wished that she really was the person she was pretending to be.

She swallowed down the anxiety tightening her throat. Deception wasn't a tool of community or of democracy. One wrong step and her peaceful life in the town might all whoosh away.

It hadn't helped that a couple of her friends who were also heiresses had done those damned reality shows. They'd made heiress-watching a national sport. One tabloid picture, one suspicious reporter, and her life would change faster than she could say abracadabra. One reporter or *one nasty-ass foundation president blackmailing her father*. One likely to do anything in his power to bully her as well.

Wasn't that a twist? If she played along and didn't rock Bender's boat, her secret was safe. She'd just watch the guy squander the money her grandfather had given his life to make and save. Money intended to do good and now used to curry favor and maybe get kickbacks. She found herself wanting to wield the power she'd been offered and trounce the guy. Her knuckles were white where she gripped the steering wheel, and the force of her feelings surprised her. A hell of a lot was surprising her these days.

When Cara arrived home, loud banging from her back deck told her that Adam hadn't finished for the day. The blows of his hammer and the loud country music blaring from his radio ramped up the pounding in her head.

She should've texted Ryan and canceled their date. She'd started to. Twice. But seeing him was the one positive she'd looked forward to.

Adam cursed above the blare of the banging and the music. She wasn't up for a long conversation with him about the sad state of her cabin. Or for finding a way to gently maneuver away from his sweet overtures. Adam was related to half the people in town, so dating him would be another disaster. She hung her jacket on a hook inside her front door and tiptoed upstairs.

Steam rose from the tub as she sank neck deep into the balm of hot water. For the first moment since Alston's call, she felt the muscles banded tightly around her head relax. The goat's-milk soap that Belva had given her lathered into a bubbling froth on her washcloth. She shut her eyes and ran the cloth down her leg. *Donkeys*. Ryan Rea loved donkeys. Who could've conjured a man with his charm and excellence, a man with such body-rocking handsomeness, a man who moved to the country to make a haven for animals most people might not even consider of any value?

She dipped the washcloth into the water, watched the bubbles disperse along the surface. Who was she kidding? It wasn't just his charm and excellence and stunning good looks. The feelings he'd roused had driven her to agree to spend more time with him, a move she knew deep down wasn't wise.

She hadn't finished dressing when she heard Ryan's car in her drive. His early arrival kept her from fussing over what she would wear. It also kept her from texting him and telling him at the last minute not to come. Twice she'd fingered her phone, had tapped out a message, but hadn't pressed Send.

She dragged on her jeans and a sweater and ran down to answer the door.

"Didn't know you liked country music," Ryan said. His easy grin shot heat through her like wildfire through a parched field. His biceps bulged with the weight of the massive box in his arms. A white takeout bag dangled in the crook of his elbow.

She tried not to stare at his biceps and wished she didn't feel the blush of heat creeping into her face. "Adam's finishing up some work on my deck." She didn't like the waver in her voice. "But I do like it. Among other music."

Slanting sunlight lit his face and danced in his eyes. Magic hour, her brother called the hour before twilight. Perhaps there was magic in it. When a grin curved Ryan's mouth, she was sure of it.

"I'd love to discuss your taste in music, but right now I'd like to put this down someplace." He nodded toward her living room. "Think I might come in?"

"Oh, sorry. That looks heavy. I mean, sure."

Since when did the English language and her manners fail her?

She stepped back and he set the box onto the floor, nearly spilling the contents of the bag as he did. He slid the bag from his arm and held it out.

"Soup. From Millenia in the city. Not squash," he said with a laugh.

He saw her glance down at the box.

"It's a TV. We can watch the game."

Surprises used to delight her, not make her nerves fire and send bees dancing through her bloodstream.

She took the bag from him. He smelled like vetiver and lemongrass and like something she had far more interest in than soup or watching a game. But that something would just lead to trouble and heaven knew she didn't need to tempt the fates. Soup and a game would have to do.

"I'll just put this on to heat," she said. Her hands were trembling, ever so slightly, but trembling all the same. "I don't have cable," she managed to stammer.

"It's wireless. Works off my phone." He nodded toward her coffee table carved from a recycled redwood slab. It was one of her few indulgences. "How about I just put it over there?"

"Sure."

She wheeled around and headed for the kitchen. The plastic of the bag crinkled as she pulled the soup container

123

out and set it on the counter. She leaned her palms against the cool Formica and took a breath to calm the trembling in her belly. Never in her life had a man had such an effect on her. If she didn't know better, she'd think she was coming down with the flu.

With a flick of her wrist, she turned on the gas and then pulled a pot from the shelf above her stove. As she poured the velvet red soup into the pan, the scent of coriander and a spice she couldn't place wafted up. She stirred, willing her hands to stop shaking and her tummy to settle down. Maybe it was just a delayed effect of the shock of the day's news settling in.

She watched the spoon as she twirled it in the thick soup and then shut her eyes. Whispering, she repeated the mantra her therapist had given her to calm herself. Though it had seemed silly when she'd first heard the phrase, she repeated it now for all she was worth. In a few minutes her pulse calmed. She tapped the spoon on the edge of the pot and laid it on the silver spoon rest on the counter. Smoothing her hands on her jeans, she took a breath and headed back to her living room.

Ryan had the TV uncrated and set up on the table. Muted sports announcers gestured across the screen.

"Gotta love technology," he said as he fiddled with the back of the TV. "The game starts in five minutes."

"Then we can eat in here." Instead of coming out with a breezy casual tone, her voice sounded throaty, as if the desire that wove through her wouldn't be wrangled.

The country music switched off outside, and the door banged behind Adam as he strode into the room.

"Not quite finished," Adam said to Cara with a shrug and a smile. Then he saw Ryan. If a man could grow three inches by pulling himself up, Adam did it.

Ryan rose from where he crouched by the TV and

towered a good four inches above Adam.

"Adam, this is Ryan. He's fixing up the old Smith place."

"We've met," Ryan said in a gravelly voice.

The two men practically growled their greetings as they shook hands. Back East, she'd had men vying to win her, men who she suspected wanted more of what came along with her—to be part of the Barrington family and the perks such a liaison offered—more than they wanted her. Ryan and Adam were squaring off for her, for Cara the bus driver.

Any delight she felt was muted by the ratcheting tightness in her belly. The energy sparking in the room and in her was nothing to toy with. Movies and stories might attempt to portray the power of primal attraction, but she knew there was a potent quality to real attraction; its alluring power called for nothing less than being stripped down to the bone. It was power with an edge.

"Cara says you've done the place up well," Adam said as he stepped back.

"Just getting started," Ryan said. He hadn't done anything specific, but she felt that he'd cast a glass shield around her, a shield he wasn't about to let Adam penetrate.

"Well, I was just leaving," Adam said to Ryan. He turned a challenging smile to Cara. "See you tomorrow." He walked out the door.

Was it her imagination or did Ryan gloat as he sat on her small couch?

"Here," he said as he patted the cushion beside him. "I'll show you how to work it." He waved a gray remote. "I love this. One remote works everything." He glanced around the room. "You do have a cellphone, don't you?"

"It's Northern California, not the Serengeti," she said in a teasing tone. "We even have running water."

He laughed.

She would never tire of the sound of his laugh. It lifted her in places she didn't even know needed lifting. She felt some of the tension that had grabbed her in the kitchen ease.

"That's good, because it works off the cell signal. Until you get a satellite dish."

"I'm not getting a satellite dish," she protested. He raised a brow. "And don't go getting any ideas."

She sat beside him and took the remote he held out to her. He was right. It was easy to work the controls. And it was evident the TV was a gift. But it was vastly easier to control the TV than it was to temper the flutter of her nerves. Just sitting near him made her feel light-headed.

"You ever watch baseball?"

His tone was easy, casual. She tried to tune into it as if she could align her body and relax. Fat chance.

"A little," she answered. "I went to a few Yankees games with my grandfather."

"Now there's a tough stadium to hit in. How long did you live in New York?"

"Oh, off and on maybe... " Maybe all her life. She'd had three years to perfect answers to these questions, had even practiced some, but Ryan threw her off her game. "Off and on until I went to college."

This was going to be a tougher evening than she'd imagined. His open manner once again made her want to abandon her defenses and bare her soul. She was sure he was going to continue his questions and only hoped she wouldn't have to lie outright. She straightened her spine, preparing to dodge and wishing she didn't have to.

But then he reached over and took her hand.

"Is it okay if I kiss you?"

She froze.

A hundred reasons that it wasn't okay raced through her mind, like debris flying in a wild wind.

He moved his hand up her arm and pulled her closer.

Inches from him, all she could feel was heat. It must've melted her brain because she found herself nodding yes.

He reached his hand to the nape of her neck, never taking his eyes off hers. He wasn't smiling. How a man could appear gentle and yet searing at the same time, she didn't know. Before she could put another thought together, he dipped his lips to hers.

Tumbling. Falling, lost... And yet a voice inside her whispered *home*. But when her tongue met his, even that voice drifted away as desire melted the hard edges of her wariness and she gave over to the power his kiss fired. It felt so good, tasting him, testing herself, joining their mouths and tongues. She'd missed him. Missed this. It was as if the boundary of her body and his had disappeared and she floated with him in a radiant, enveloping pulse of light and heat and pure sensation. When he pulled away, she felt like she'd been unplugged from the source of life itself.

"I smell something burning," he said.

He stroked his thumb along the curve of her jaw. She fought her desire to feel his lips against hers, to rejoin the blissful, disorienting journey once again. But she didn't, couldn't, move.

"Maybe we should do something about it?" he whispered against her cheek.

Snapped back into the room, back into her brain, she jumped up.

"The soup!"

Her legs were rubbery as she dashed into the kitchen. Her hands still trembled as she flicked off the flame and grabbed the wooden spoon. The spoon dragged at the crusted bottom of the pot.

"I think it's salvageable," she shouted from the kitchen. Her voice sounded foreign to her. The world she'd visited while lost in his kiss hadn't fully released its grip.

She spooned the soup into bowls, slid a spoon into each bowl and walked with still unsteady steps back into her living room. Her brain tattooed messages into her, reminding her of the reasons an affair with Ryan Rea was a bad idea. A very, very bad idea. Terrifically poor timing, exactly what she did not need. If she was going to put the brakes on, she'd better do it now.

He stood and took the bowls from her and set them on the table near the base of the TV.

Then he turned and grasped her by her forearms and held her in his gaze as he drew her to him. She saw the force of his wanting and felt her own and fought both.

"It'll get cold," she stammered, backing up a step.

"Reheating is a guy's best friend." He curved his hands around her waist and tugged her back to him.

"But the game—"

"There are more than a dozen games left in the season."

Before she could come up with a response, his lips met hers.

Her body took over and shut down the voice saying no. As his hands slid up under her sweater, her body arched to meet him. She tore at his shirt and slid her palms up the hard planes of his chest. A groan escaped him as she bit at his lips. He grabbed the hem of her sweater and pulled it over her head.

"You're beautiful, Cara."

She heard his words but more astonishing, she felt them. A shiver ran through her as he curved his palms under her breasts. Her nipples puckered in the cool room, and he bent down and closed his mouth over her breast, teasing her already hard nipple with his teeth. She shuddered, and her legs began to buckle under her.

With unsteady hands she held his shoulders, pressing into them as she fought for balance. He nipped at her again and cradled her other breast in his palm. She threw her head back and swayed with the delight of rushing pleasure. He caught her around her waist and lifted her in his arms, his mouth finding hers as he lowered her to the couch. It was more than a kiss; his lips crushed hers. She arched up as liquid heat and want fired with near painful intensity.

But then he pulled away.

Cool air rushed against her breasts. She lifted up, reaching for the button at the waist of his jeans, but he put his palm to her shoulder and pressed her back against the couch. He held her in a penetrating gaze as he pulled her jeans down her hips. She saw the question in his eyes, and she nodded. Nothing would keep her from sating the want he'd ignited. His breath came quick, hers came quicker. He tossed her jeans to the floor and slid his hands beneath her. Her breath caught in her chest as he cupped her bottom. She arched up, his hands following her bucking, and lifting her higher. His lips brushed against her thighs. He lowered her hips and pulled her panties down her legs and tossed them away. As his mouth reached her sex and his tongue circled her already throbbing peak, sensation shut down thought, and Cara lost herself to pleasure.

CHAPTER TWELVE

CLUTCHING HER CLOTHES, CARA HURRIED UP THE stairs to her bedroom. In the breathless aftermath of world-rocking sex, dressing in front of him was more than she could handle. She needed a few moments alone to get her bearings. Wordlessly she had wrapped her sweater around her bare hips, grabbed her jeans and headed for the stairs.

As she'd walked out of the room, she'd felt his eyes on her and felt strangely self-conscious. No, more than self-conscious. She was off kilter. Sex with Ryan had shocked her. Not the frenzied movements, not the almost violent way they'd ripped at each other's clothes as if there were only seconds of time left to live, not the urgent arching, the primal thrusting or the loss of control. What shocked her was the realization that until the moment their bodies joined, until he'd filled her, rocked her, pleasured her, she hadn't known what she'd been missing. The recognition that her body was designed to harness the power the meeting of their bodies ignited stripped her bearings from her. It was as if the language of their touch had given her the magic words to enter a portal of an unknown universe and she was a new creature, foreign to herself. As if her inner and outer realities were no longer distinguishable.

Never had she felt such a loss of control. Never had

she been swept into a vortex of pleasure beyond imagining. Never had she felt so close to a person that she'd become a part of him and he a part of her.

She dropped down on the edge of her bed and took a breath. And a resonant peace washed through her. She squeezed her eyes shut, wanting to hold on to the bliss, knowing that any moment thoughts would rush in and tear it away.

She wrapped her arms around herself and rocked slowly. Rhythmically. And said another silent thanks that he'd maintained enough control to slip on a condom. She hadn't been in any frame of mind to remember that. It occurred to her that perhaps he hadn't been as carried away as she'd been; she had little experience with passion. She dropped her chin, her face heating, wondering if he thought she'd gotten too carried away. If so, how could she face him again?

But as she remembered the look in his eyes as he'd kissed her afterward, she was pretty sure he'd been in pretty deep too. And then she grinned. Yeah, he'd been rocked.

She rose from the bed and slipped on her robe, then turned to look in her mirror. And immediately she knew that the silken robe would send the wrong signal. Well, it would send the right signal, but she couldn't imagine surviving another rush of passion so soon.

She needed to think, get her wits back about her. There were many forces at work unraveling her carefully laid out life plan, but what truly scared her was a dawning realization that she might have to choose between freedom and love.

And perhaps what scared her most was her lack of fear at the dissolving of her established boundaries.

When she'd moved to Albion Bay she'd learned to rope in her impulses, learned to be resolute about what she could and couldn't say. Learned the forces at work in the town and come to find her place within them. So she *could* be resolute. Usually. But the power he'd freed was like a nourishing force, filling her until she felt it not only inside but outside, as if it pulsed from within her. It wasn't a power at her command.

She slipped her sweater and jeans back on and headed down the stairs.

When she returned to her living room, he had reheated the soup and had napkins set out beside the bowls.

He shook out a napkin and handed it to her, his eyes searching her face. "Told you reheating was a guy's best friend."

She took the napkin and forced a smile.

"The Braves are ahead," he said, nodding toward the TV.

It was as if he knew she felt awkward. Maybe he did too, but he didn't show it. Or maybe he did this sort of thing all the time. He was a rich, handsome, single, sexy man living in the fast lane; women probably threw themselves at him. The thought dismayed her, and doubt flooded in.

She sipped from her spoon. Though she was aware of being hungry, she could barely swallow. Trying to relax, she spooned in a few more bites. The simple red pepper soup warmed a path in her, easing her. But her pulse hadn't settled down one bit. The game was just a hum in the background; he'd turned the sound down low. To her surprise, the murmur of the announcers was almost soothing.

He set his bowl on the table and turned to her. "I won't apologize for how this went down," he said, gesturing to the couch. "But next time—*if* you'll give me a next time—I want to love you properly, in a bed. To go slow and give you the pleasure you deserve."

His eyes scanned her face, and she looked away, not

ready to reveal the conflicting feelings warring in her.

He took her bowl from her, then took both her hands in his.

"I want to know you, Cara. Everything. Your favorite color. What you did as a kid. What fantasies and fascinations you keep locked up in here." He tapped a finger against her heart.

Something snapped in her. He wanted to know more about the person she'd fought so hard to become, the person she was under all the trappings she'd thrown off with such effort. But what she presented wasn't the whole picture. It wasn't pretense, but it was exclusion.

Yet keeping details of her life from him was more than an exclusion. No matter how much she wished it otherwise, deception lived at the heart of her life. And now guilt swept her like an insistent tide that wouldn't be turned back. She could imagine how she would feel if she were him, if he kept such a secret from her. Before tonight, before he'd cracked her world open, she'd imagined they'd date, have fun, enjoy one another's company.

But that was a lie she couldn't go on telling herself.

When he'd kissed her by the stream, when she'd felt the answering energy coursing from him, she'd known then that he wanted more than to date her. The realization had buoyed and sunk her at the same time.

And she hadn't fathomed the way connecting her body with his would tip the balance and throw everything off. She hadn't thought past the driving force of her desire. She simply hadn't thought.

"I'm partial to blue," he said with a grin.

Blue.

The word barely registered. His eyes searched her face when she didn't respond.

"I'm fond of green," she said, grasping to fill the

133

silence. Green was her favorite color—at least she could be honest about that. Her brain was kicking in, whizzing out scenarios, none of them happy.

"All sorts of greens," she added as she pulled her hands from his.

She couldn't think right when he touched her.

"The greens of early spring leaves, the faded green of the late-summer grasses." She pressed her palms to the knees of her jeans, wiping away the evidence of her surging heart. "There are so many shades of green."

Her voice was shaky. And though he cast a half smile, she saw the puzzlement in his eyes. He was a perceptive man, she knew that. This was more than a conversation about favorite colors. He was testing her for trust.

Trusting a person was her number one need.

The irony of her own untrustworthiness hit her hard.

It wasn't fair to Ryan to take the relationship deeper, not if she wasn't ready to come clean. And she wasn't ready to give up the life she'd fought so hard to carve out, not yet, maybe not ever. Giving up getting to know him was one more sacrifice she might have to make if she wanted to keep her life on track.

That she'd trade the shaky prospect of love for the very real state of freedom didn't surprise her.

What surprised her was that in such a short time she'd become more than fond of him; the force of her feelings shocked her. And though she'd shoved down the voice that said he was a key to her happiness, she hadn't shut it off completely. That insistent voice felt like a lifeline to her future, like a harmony of words that, if she tiptoed across them, sounding them out as she went, would show her the way. It would've been easier to ignore the voice, to simply tell herself that she'd had an amazing experience, that he'd shown her not only a world but a way of being that maybe someday she'd know again. But she didn't believe that; fate likely didn't give people second chances, not if they turned their back on its generosity.

"The field in every stadium has a different color of green," Ryan said, picking up on the thread of the conversation and still watching her face. "The grasses, even AstroTurf, come in different shades." He lifted his spoon and swallowed down some soup. "I hate AstroTurf. It's a conspiracy to keep the trainers in business."

The muted roar of a crowd sounded from the TV.

"Now there's a sound I like." He shot her an impish grin. "*If* it's for the team I'm playing for."

He turned up the sound on the TV. She picked up her bowl again, lifted a tepid spoonful of soup to her lips. The chattering of the sports announcers flooded into her living room.

He took a sip from his soup spoon. "This is good." He grinned over at her. "A bit cold now, but good."

Out of reflex, she started to jump up. He grabbed her wrist.

"It's fine. Stay. Eat, Cara." He twinkled a devastating smile. "You might be needing your strength."

She tried to suppress a nervous laugh, but it tripped out of her.

He waved his spoon toward the TV.

"People in the Bay Area are spoiled, you know."

She knitted her brows, unsure what he meant.

"Well, maybe you don't. Take my word for it: the local announcers here are the best. They have the right combination of details and color. These two"—he pointed again to the TV—"they're okay. But there's a difference when a guy really knows the game. Of course I never get to hear the local guys since I'm always on the field. You'll have to keep me posted on how they finish up the season."

He imagined knowing her as the season progressed. He imagined a future. The prospect both confounded and comforted her.

Not knowing what to do with them, she pushed thoughts of the future aside and focused on the announcers' lively banter, tried to grasp their fast assessments of the game. And as she sat there with Ryan, eating soup and watching baseball, feeling the warmth and delight that was so welcome and yet so foreign and delicious, she tried to work out what path she could possibly navigate that might allow her to have Ryan in her life. If that was to be even a remote possibility, if what they shared were to evolve, she had work ahead. Maybe, when the time was right, she could reveal what she'd struggled for so many years to conceal. Maybe he'd understand.

Ryan touched her hand, making her jump.

"Come to a game."

He twined his fingers in hers and stroked the back of her hand with his thumb. She was becoming way too fond of what he could do with his thumb.

"I mean, how long's it been since you've been to a game?" He squeezed her hand. "You could bring Sam and Molly."

She pulled her hand away and turned to the TV.

"I really can't." It wasn't as though she could tell him that there'd be people at the stadium who would recognize her, people who knew her and who knew her family. She didn't want to pile on another lie, so she didn't make up an excuse. And was grateful when he didn't press her for one.

And was even more grateful that her questions about his experiences playing baseball lit him up and brought an ease to the evening. How much longer she could've borne the earlier tension, she wasn't sure.

During a pitching change he muted the TV and walked

over to her bookshelf. Like a homing pigeon, he pulled out the most valuable book among the many precious volumes.

"My mom collects old books," he said as he opened the tooled-leather cover of a first edition of *Oliver Twist*.

Her dad had sent the book, along with four other volumes that really should have gone to a museum. He had a perverse love of having things in his personal space that others would have to wait in line just to look at behind roped-off exhibits or thick panes of glass. Just last month he'd suggested sending her a Renoir that had hung in her grandfather's study. Even though it was her favorite painting, she'd put a quick stop to her father's scheming. No one in Albion Bay had security systems; just trying to put one in her cabin would be a joke.

Ryan let out a slow whistle.

"This is one heck of a valuable book." He looked back at her, eyebrow raised.

Her brain whizzed into high gear.

"It's been passed down in my family for ages," she said. "Sort of an old family legacy."

Who knew a ballplayer from Texas would know anything about the value of old books? No, of course *anyone* might have such knowledge. Her prejudices needed some deep adjusting.

As did her housekeeping.

"I'm trying to get my mom to come out to see my ranch. My dad probably won't come. He's got a bug up him about me buying property here. I'm working on him, though." He looked over at her and held up the book. "If she comes, I'd like to show this to her. She's got all sorts of catalogs with pictures of books like this, but it'd make her day to hold the real deal."

"Sure," she said, not knowing what else to say. Knowing the man, she'd like to meet his mother. But that would be taking things way too far. Maybe he'd forget about the book.

"She binds books, it's her thing. It's what she loves."

So much for forgetting about the book.

He put the Dickens carefully back into place. "My mom's the one who wouldn't let me give up on playing, even when my dad threw fits and argued that I'd be better off doing my homework. She always said that if a person doesn't do what they love, they're wasting their life."

"I'd have to agree with her," Cara said. He couldn't know the knot of anxiety his words were firing in her.

He pulled another book from the shelf. "Is this the guy you were telling me about?" He tapped the cover. "The guy who writes about how your brain can trick you into focusing on the bad and letting the good slide off?"

She nodded, glad he'd moved to another topic.

"I tried it last week—and hit a triple. But he's right—it's ridiculously easy to let good experiences slip into a phantom realm and go unnoticed."

He narrowed his eyes.

"What is it?"

"Nothing." He shifted his weight and rolled his shoulder. "Just a random thought."

Her curiosity was piqued, but she had no right to pry. She wanted to know so much more about him, and the strength of her wanting dismayed her. But asking questions wasn't fair, given the circumstances. And fairness was a value she wouldn't give up.

After he left, she scrubbed at the pot she'd burned and thought about what he'd said about the joy of doing what you love well. He loved baseball, that much was clear. But what had surprised her was how his entire countenance had changed when he'd mentioned phantom realms, as if something haunted him. The man was full of surprises.

Before he'd left, he'd pressed her for a date. Turning

138

him down was the hardest thing she'd done in years, even though she knew it was the right thing to do. But she hadn't so much turned him down as put him off. The turning down would come, just as the sun would rise. She dreaded having to do it.

But as she climbed the stairs and replayed the buzz his goodnight kiss had sent through her, confusion settled in like a dense winter fog. Keeping her steps on the path she'd so carefully drawn for her life was starting to turn into one damned painful journey.

CHAPTER THIRTEEN

"HOW OFTEN DO YOU GET OUT HERE?" RYAN ASKED Alex as they rounded the last of the curves on the coastal highway and headed down the hill into Albion Bay. They'd won their day game against Arizona, had kept a solid five-run lead into the ninth.

"During the season? Maybe six or seven times. The vineyard takes up most of my free time. But Jackie's out here every couple weeks, working at the lab."

Alex had planned to retire the year after he'd won the Triple Crown, but Ryan didn't have to ask why he hadn't. No one really wanted to leave the game unless pain or poor performance forced an early exit.

Ryan nosed his Jeep into the middle school parking lot and helped Alex with the bags of equipment they'd brought for the team.

Sam Rivers ran up to them, already short of breath.

"I can help," he said as he reached to take a bag from Ryan.

"Sam, this is Alex."

"I know." Sam extended his hand under the bag, and Alex bent to shake it. "You're taller than you look on TV."

Alex laughed. "Trick cameras," he said. "Fools the competition."

"Huddle up," Dave Jenkins called from the bench.

"Sam, get over here." Dave nodded a greeting to Alex and Ryan and proceeded to bark out the starting lineup.

Alex nodded toward the taco stand. "Is that her?"

Ryan nodded.

"Taco time," Alex said. "I'm starved."

Cain wasn't there, but Cara was, and she was studiously filleting a slab of fish.

"She wields a mean knife," Alex said as they approached.

"I'll store that fact away," Ryan said.

"She wields more than a mean knife," Molly Rivers said as she hauled a bag of ice to the cooler. "You should see her drive a bus. I couldn't for the life of me."

"Molly, meet my buddy Alex. Molly is Sam's mom. And this is Cara West."

Cara looked up from the cutting board and waved a vinyl-gloved hand. "You'll thank me for not shaking your hand." She smiled. "Hello, Ryan."

Two words. *Hello, Ryan.* That's all it took to settle him. He was more hooked than the fish she was filleting had been.

Molly turned to Alex. "Where's that wife of yours? She walked off with our ice chest last week."

"Hawaii, this week. Alaska the next."

"Guess I'll have to go to Hawaii to get our ice chest back—hardship duty. You two want tacos?"

"Ryan here tells me the proceeds go to a good cause," Alex said.

"Yup, equipment for the boys and gas for the bus." Molly winked at Cara. "Cara has a heavy foot."

"You won't be wanting that ice chest back," Alex said. "Don't loan Jackie anything you don't want smelling like day-old seal-tissue samples."

Molly wrinkled her nose. "I'll keep that in mind." She

threw tortillas onto the grill to warm and then turned and nudged Cara. "Hey, I forgot to tell you that the community center got a five-thousand-dollar grant for the irrigation system. Straight out of the blue. The garden committee wanted to thank the donor, but the company that called to announce the grant told Perk the donor insisted on remaining anonymous." Molly threw a slab of fish onto the grill. "Don't you think that's odd? You'd think they'd want to be thanked. And Perk doesn't even remember the town submitting a request."

Ryan saw Cara's knife slip on the slab of fish she was preparing. He stepped around the table and took the knife from her.

"Let me do that. Put my ranch skills to work."

"I didn't know they had fish on ranches," Cara said.

Though her comment was meant to be humorous, he knew her well enough to know that something had shaken her. If he hadn't heard it in her voice, he'd seen it in the way she'd stiffened when Molly broke the news about the grant. It didn't make sense, but right then all he cared about was helping her with the task at hand. That and securing another date with her.

"I won't tell you what we cut up on ranches," Ryan said as he angled the knife on the fish. "Not in mixed company."

Alex groaned. "That's why I stick with grapes. I leave the bloody work to Jackie."

Sam came running. "Mom—did you hear? Ryan's *staying*." He turned to Ryan. "You are, aren't you? We heard you got a gazillion dollars for six years to play for the Giants. Is it true?"

Ryan had hoped to break the news about his contract to Cara in a far more subtle manner. But Sam's innocent, beaming smile made it impossible to be irritated. He again bit down his impulse to ruff Sam's hair. The kid just got under his skin, but in a good way. If he had a boy, he'd like to have one with Sam's enthusiasm. But without the asthma. That scared the hell out of him.

"Guilty," Ryan said. "Staying right here."

"Does that mean you can get us tickets to a game?" Sam asked.

"*Sam.* That's not polite."

Sam colored at his mom's chastising tone.

"If he won't, I will," Alex jumped in. "How about Wednesday? I'm throwing a party after the game to celebrate Ryan's contract. It's a day game, so it won't put you all home too late."

Ryan felt color rise in his face. So much for subtly inviting Cara to the party.

"I'd like you to come," Ryan said to Cara. He cut two slices of fish and handed them to her to put on the grill.

"Let me think about it," she said without looking up. "I need to look at my calendar."

"Come on, Cara," Molly chided. "What could possibly trump Ryan's party in the city?"

"Right." Cara shot a quick glance at him. "I guess I could come."

Angels could've blown three trumpets and they wouldn't have matched the joy blasting through Ryan.

But after he and Alex had finished helping the boys with their game, when he looked around for Cara, she was gone.

Ryan shook the dust from his boots and closed the back-pasture gate. He picked up his coffee mug and glugged down the lukewarm remains. It'd take more than coffee to clear his head this morning. The party had gone late into the night. And Cara hadn't shown.

Ten more fence posts and some wire work and he'd be ready for the first of the rescue donkeys. They were trailering them in from Nevada in a couple of weeks.

He blew on his hands to warm them before sliding them back into his work gloves. Already the nights and early mornings were chilly. He was glad he'd insisted that his contractor install a heater in the barn. When his dad found out he was paying to heat rescue donkeys, he'd never hear the end of it. But the animals were half-starved; they'd need help over the winter until they gained enough weight to insulate them against the damp and cold.

He'd called his parents that morning and invited them out for Thanksgiving. His dad had passed the phone to his mom without committing. Ryan was pretty sure he could get them there. He'd send tickets and a car to take them to the airport, offer to pick them up himself.

The wire cutters slipped, barely missing his finger. He'd better call it a morning—his mind wasn't on his work. It hadn't been in the game yesterday and though he'd enjoyed the party, his heart hadn't been in it either. Every time he shut his eyes he saw Cara. Already he'd nearly driven himself mad replaying their evening together. He wished he'd had the control to have loved her slowly, gently. But, no, he'd ravaged her like some depraved beast. That she'd met his every move and even upped the ante a few times hadn't made him feel better about it. But even so, the evening hadn't gone as he'd planned. As he'd hoped. But he was pretty sure she'd be interested in a follow-up. He might not be a genius at reading women, but he knew she was more than interested.

The sun slanted gold rays through the oaks behind his house. He glanced at his watch. Nine in the morning. Even if he zipped over to Cara's, he could still make it to the stadium with time to spare. That she hadn't invited him didn't matter. He had a bone to pick with her. You just didn't go around accepting invitations and then not showing. Not even in Texas—hell, *especially* not in Texas. And women didn't blow a guy's mind and then drop him cold. At least not without a fight.

CHAPTER FOURTEEN

C ARA RUBBED AT HER BACK AS SHE BENT OVER THE row of carrots she'd spent the best part of an hour weeding. She'd made it only halfway down the row. The weeds were growing faster than the volunteers at the community center could pull them. But it was a gorgeous Indian summer day, so she had few complaints. The breeze wafted the scent of the ocean up from the cliffs, and the sun was warm on her back. She was grateful for its warmth, for the blaze of light that helped her clear the grogginess from her head.

She hadn't slept well.

Sneaking out of the middle school game to avoid Ryan and then avoiding Molly's phone calls had made her tense. Canceling her meeting in the city with Alston hadn't helped. His return message telling her she had to fly to New York for a family meeting dialed up every anxious cell in her busy brain.

A nettle stung her through a hole in her gloves, and she rubbed the back of her hand against her jeans to calm the stinging.

"You didn't answer my calls."

She jumped at the sound of Ryan's voice.

She tilted her head up, but the sun was directly behind him, so she couldn't see his face.

"I was busy." It was true. She'd spent the evening cooking up excuses to avoid the meeting in New York and hadn't come up with one that would fly.

"You missed the game."

"Molly and Sam said it was fantastic. I think Sam hopes you'll adopt him."

"I'm not in the market for adopting," he said. "That is, anything other than donkeys."

Of course he wasn't. She didn't even know why she'd said it.

"You didn't come to my party."

Now *that* she had a perfectly legitimate excuse for missing. She'd seen the photos from the party on the Internet early that morning, before she'd come out to do her volunteer work in the garden. The paparazzi had been all over his party. All over him. And they would've been all over her—*Disappearing Heiress Resurfaces*—a great scoop for any one of the tabloids. Too bad she couldn't tell him her excellent alibi.

Feeling awkward kneeling in front of him, she stood. And wished she hadn't. She saw the anger in his eyes, but what she saw under it nearly did her in. She hadn't meant to hurt his feelings. She knew that experience too well herself. But she had let everything go on too long—and any further interaction would either make it harder for him to forgive her if she did decide to accept the reins of the foundation and take on all that came with it, including revealing her identity. If she took that path, she wanted to be able to make her case to him, to remind him that she'd put the brakes on until she could be honest with him. Part of her wanted to believe that would make a difference. And if she chose not to change her life and to turn her back on what she felt for him, any trail of hope that she didn't squelch would just lead to more hurt.

"Ryan, look..."

Look *what?* As she sought words, she knew she wasn't very well prepared. How did one prepare for possible disaster? Her heart did a little flip in protest of what she was about to do. She stepped back and nearly tripped over the carrots she'd so carefully weeded. "I'm not really what you're looking for—"

"I can make that call."

Anger and hurt made for a powerful offense.

She rubbed at her still stinging hand, knowing the delay wouldn't help. "Well, I *am* making that call." Her voice wavered, but her resolve did not. "Now."

At first she thought he was going to reach out and grab her. And maybe part of her wished that he would. But instead he fisted his hands to his hips and held her in the most gut-ripping gaze she'd ever experienced. Then without a word, he shook his head and turned and walked away.

As she watched him get into his Jeep, her heart broke, just a very little bit. Just enough to send pain arcing through her.

Just enough to send her to her knees.

The sounds of New York's Fifth Avenue still lived in Cara's blood. Ambivalence settled in her as she walked along the busy street. She passed familiar landmarks, places she'd spent much of the early years of her life—the private school she'd attended near the park, the stable where she'd learned to ride, the bagel shop, the Madison Avenue boutiques her mother had dragged her to.

For many, living in New York was a good life, the life they sought to make for themselves. Some twist of genes or fate kept her from being one of them.

She rubbed at her neck. She'd tried to sleep on the plane, but the memory of the look on Ryan's face sliced through even her most well-practiced meditation routines. So much for enlightenment.

Cara turned the corner at Sixtieth Street. The familiar red awning of the Metropolitan Club stretched out, welcoming the privileged few who had the pedigree, influence and wealth to pass under it. The club's wrought-iron and gilded gates flanked gleaming marble columns that stood, stately as ever, like old actors always ready to play their parts in an ongoing drama.

Maybe there wouldn't be too much drama today.

Right.

Since it was her family gathering, how likely was that? And though she'd angled for another meeting place, her father had sloughed off her suggestion. Maybe she was paranoid, but the Metropolitan Club *was* favored by athletes. She'd checked the Giants schedule; they were in town, playing the Mets. But of course she was being ridiculous. Ryan wasn't a member; the Club hadn't accepted a new member in four years. Besides, it wasn't the sort of place Ryan would favor. Too stuffy and far from the downtown hotels.

The doorman recognized her and tilted his cap.

"Haven't seen you around much, Miss Barrington."

"I've been away, Jasper. How's your boy?"

The smile he beamed warmed her. He was proud of his son.

"He's at USC, got a baseball scholarship. Not really a boy anymore."

Jasper held the door for her and for the woman behind her.

"Caroline?"

Cara turned. The woman's voice was familiar, but Cara

149

couldn't place her face.

"Olivia Astor," the woman said, holding out her hand glittering with diamonds. "Ashley's mother."

Ashley and Cara had been best friends at Brearley until they'd graduated and gone off to different universities. Mrs. Astor must've had a facelift; Cara barely recognized her.

"How is Ashley?" Cara asked as she shook Mrs. Astor's hand.

"She's in Paris. You two should get together when she comes home for Christmas. She'll be thrilled to hear I ran into you." She glanced at her watch. "I must hurry and eat, or I'll be late for my hair appointment. See you at Christmas?"

Cara just nodded. Parties like Mrs. Astor's stuffy holiday celebration were just one of the many events she'd been happy to leave behind.

Cara's mother and father were already seated at their usual table when she walked into the dining room. The breeze from the open windows stirred the crystals of the chandeliers and sent waves of glittering light dancing in the opulently decorated room. Every color was muted, as if someone had taken a dab of sepia to a brush and coated everything in it. Even the sounds were muted, as if secrets were being told and no one was meant to hear them.

"You're so thin," her mother said when Cara settled into the chair the waiter held for her.

"And *you* look lovely as ever," Cara said as she leaned forward and brushed a kiss to her mother's cheek. "Hi, Dad. No golf game today?"

"I'll play tomorrow. Alston insisted that we all get together." He took a sip from his martini and sent the curl of lemon peel dancing in the glass.

Her mother patted her hand. "What's this Alston tells me about you not wanting to take over at the foundation?"

"Rebecca."

Cara bristled. She hated it when her dad took on his arrogant, bossy tone. Especially when he used it on her mother.

"We weren't going to pressure her, remember?" He took a bigger sip of his martini. "I think you've made a good decision. Dray's doing a great job. No need for you to wrestle with all that."

Her mother toyed with her salad fork. Cara could tell that the position her father had taken regarding her grandfather's foundation didn't sit well with her mother. Not much about her father sat well with her mother these days. Ever since her mother had gone back to school and earned her counseling degree, there'd been tension in the family. He didn't like that she worked, much less that she was a psychologist. In his mind there was nothing classy about the profession.

"We should discuss Cara's plans," her mother said.

"If Cara wants to stay holed up in a godforsaken backwater town, it's her business."

For once her dad was right. But he rarely took a hands-off position toward her or her brother. Maybe Alston was right. Maybe Dray Bender did have something on her dad. Something serious. And maybe her mother had no clue.

"I told Alston and I'm telling you both now—I'll think about what I want to do about the foundation, okay?" Cara sipped from her water glass. New York might be a crowded, noisy, busy city, but it had great water. It came straight down from the Adirondacks and it was delicious. Well water from Albion Bay never tasted good.

"What's Bender's focus for the foundation?" She watched her dad take in her question.

"Pharmaceuticals," he answered in a short tone. "Saving lives. That sort of thing."

"You mean funding research?"

"Something like that."

Cara knew then that her father had no idea what Dray Bender was funding. And evidently didn't want to know. Alston's suspicion was taking hold in her. She'd discovered that what happened to her grandfather's legacy was important to her. She'd read through the last ten years of grants from a list that Alston had provided. Grandpa had prided himself on making grants that made a difference, that actually changed lives. And she'd seen first-hand the impact that pivotal funding could make in a community that needed it. But she wasn't going to get anywhere questioning her father.

Cara nodded to the empty seat beside her. "Where's Quinn?"

"China," her father answered flatly.

"He's investigating a project in a southern mountain province," her mother said. Cara heard the touch of pride in her voice. "Children from the mountain villages live too far from the schools in the valleys. I think Quinn said it was a three-hour journey over treacherous roads, roads that aren't even passable in the winters. The project provides housing and food for the mountain children, so they can live in the villages and get an education. Quinn wanted to personally see where the money was being used." She shot a look at Cara's father. "Personally. Up close."

Cara's father raised his empty glass and instantly a waiter brought another chilled martini.

"I didn't raise children to have them running off to all ends of the earth," her father said.

"Last I checked, California was still a state in the union." Cara bit back her retort about China. Her father's class prejudices were topped only by his deeply rooted racism.

"By the way, your father and I *are* coming out for Thanksgiving. No arguments, Cara. You may not understand it, but I want to see your place." She tapped Cara's hand again. "It's a mother's duty to make sure her children are well situated."

"I don't have a guest room," Cara said, grasping at any excuse to keep her parents away from her world.

"They do have hotels in your town, don't they?" her mother said with a wink. When Cara shook her head, she added, "Well, we can stay at the Mark Hopkins in the city. There's an impressionist exhibit at the Legion that I'm dying to see."

"All I need is the two of you traipsing around Albion Bay. It'd take less than an hour for you to wreck what I've spent three years carving out for myself."

"That's *ridiculous* darling. We know how to be subtle. Your father prides himself on his diplomacy. We'll be discreet."

A waiter brought bread and olive oil to the table. Cara didn't reach for it as she usually did. The idea of having her parents roaming around her world made her stomach contract just at the thought.

Her father lit up. "I'm sending that little painting out next week," he said with a smile. He smiled so rarely, Cara wanted to nod in agreement. But she didn't. And when he saw her open her mouth, he said, "No, I won't hear any argument. It's yours and you should have it. It's small; surely you'll find a good place for it."

Little painting.

It was a Renoir. Unsigned, but a Renoir all the same. It was unusual and would've been a key piece in the exhibit her mother was talking about. But she had to pick her battles, and this was one she wouldn't win. And he was right; the landscape had been a favorite since she was old enough to

153

say so. She'd just have to tuck it away upstairs.

"Langley Terrence asked about you." Her father slanted her a look over the rim of his martini. "He's throwing a party this week to christen his new yacht, and he specifically asked me to invite *you*. Now there's a good man."

Langley Terrence had nearly spent through his fortune before he'd left Harvard. Cara knew too well why he was interested in her. Escaping the pursuit of those sorts of men was one reason she'd fled New York. She was beginning to question her father's discernment in any matter, particularly his ability to size up people and their motivations.

"I'm leaving at seven thirty tonight," Cara said.

"I was hoping you'd stay at least through the weekend," her mother said.

"I have a bus run early Monday morning."

"Ridiculous." Her father scowled. "You don't need a job."

"Russell, stop. Cara has her reasons, even if you don't understand them." She turned to Cara. "But I do hope you'll take an interest in the foundation. You could do so much good."

"Now it's you who's meddling, Rebecca," her dad said.

Clearly he didn't want Cara anywhere near the foundation. Yet his put-offs were inciting not only her curiosity, but a deeper, heartfelt concern for her grandfather's vision. A vision her father clearly did not share.

Cara suddenly realized that this *emergency* meeting was Alston's way of making her face those facts. For a mild-mannered guy, Alston was a surprising master strategist. She should've felt irritated with him, but she wasn't. She smiled to herself, making a note to surprise him with an unusual gift for his insights.

"I think you'd make an excellent president," her

mother said. "It makes a difference to have something meaningful to do every day." She looked over to Cara's father, whose scowl had deepened. "Your father doesn't understand, but I do."

"Driving the bus means something to me." Cara picked at her food and then gave up and set her fork aside.

"We can talk it over later," her mother said in a firm tone as the waiter cleared their plates. Her mother was all family counselor in that moment, and Cara was surprised to see her dad settle back in his chair and drop the subject. Maybe there was hope for them.

The waiter brought dessert menus. Her dad listened as the man rattled off the specials and then ordered the crème brûlée. "But don't bring any coffee." He turned to Cara. "The coffee here is undrinkable. Apparently the good people who run this place want to keep it that way."

"I think I'll skip desert," Cara said. "I might hit traffic on the expressway."

As she stood to exit the dining room, she thought she saw Alex Tavonesi walk in with Ryan and another man. Her pulse rocketed to a racing beat, and she ducked back into her seat, hoping neither of them had seen her.

Of course the Tavonesis would be members; most prominent families on the West Coast had memberships in New York clubs as well.

"Is something wrong, darling?" The look of concern on her mother's face was genuine.

"No, I'm just dizzy. I must've stood too quickly."

"You don't eat enough, Cara. It's not good for you. You hardly touched your meal."

Who could eat with the two of them trying to move her around like a pawn on a chessboard?

"I'm fine, Mother. Really."

Cara glanced across the room. The waiter had seated

Ryan and Alex with their backs to her, just past a bank of potted palms. Explaining what she was doing in the most expensive, exclusive club in New York was a scene she had to avoid. When Ryan picked up his menu, she kissed her mother on the cheek, nodded to her father and fled. At the entrance to the dining room, she darted a quick glance back over her shoulder. Through the screen of the palms she saw Ryan stand up and stride toward the dining room entrance.

She practically ran to the street entrance of the club, grateful that Jasper always kept a cab waiting for members in a hurry. As the cab pulled away, she looked back and saw Ryan exit the club and look up and down the street. Her heart didn't slow its pace until the cab reached the midtown tunnel.

CHAPTER FIFTEEN

T HE RISING SUN SENT SHAFTS OF LIGHT THROUGH HIS house as Ryan stumbled toward his kitchen. If the damned espresso machine didn't cooperate, he'd have no time to linger over breakfast at the diner as he liked to do. And he'd have to make cowboy coffee in a pan like he used to do back in Texas.

He glanced out the window and saw two trucks down at the barns.

The first of the rescue donkeys would arrive in ten days. He'd asked if the donkey rescue center could hold off until the end of baseball season, but the guy just said if he didn't make space for seven more animals that next week, they'd be snuffed. Animals and ranchers didn't give a damn about his baseball schedule.

He loaded coffee into the fancy filter and levered it onto the machine, just like Cara had shown him the day she'd visited. The day her kisses had screwed with his brain. Actually screwed with more than his brain. He'd been having dreams again. On the team plane back from New York last night he'd dreamed she'd lured him into a New York City penthouse and had done all sorts of edgy, ball-rocking things to him. He'd met her moves and raised the ante, exploring her body and making her wait until she was speechless with throbbing desire. In his dream he'd loved her as she should be loved: slowly, thoroughly and completely. When the flight attendant woke him to fasten his seat belt for landing in San Francisco, he hoped she hadn't seen the very real signs of his arousal. Her sultry smile told him that maybe she had.

Since the day Cara had basically shoved him out of her life, he'd run every moment he'd had with her over in his mind multiple times. She hadn't said he wasn't what she wanted, not outright. But her push-away could've been a face-saving way of telling him he wasn't the sort of man who lit her fire.

But he didn't believe it.

He'd felt the energy pulsing between them when they'd had sex. He'd felt the power of their kisses. He might like the rational, but he knew the forces that drove rationality were mysterious and powerful. Forces that maybe he couldn't explain, but that he trusted. And he trusted her, her responses. She wasn't a woman who could fake her response to anything.

He'd just have to find a way to win her.

He'd start with something simple. He knew from looking around her place that she liked pretty things. He'd buy her something to brighten up her place. At least it would be an excuse to see her again.

The light on the espresso machine glowed a dull red. It took only three minutes to heat, but it felt like an age.

The pain in his shoulder had returned, and he'd fought through a sleepless night. He wasn't superstitious, but after two bummer games against the Mets, he was having a hard time fighting off superstitious impulses. His defense in both games had been good. He'd snagged balls that would've been home runs, made plays that had even the Mets fans roaring with respect.

But he hadn't hit worth a damn. He tried drilling up his mental game, practiced calling up the good, but every time he did, there was Cara floating like some sort of Disney hologram in front of him.

And his mind was playing other tricks on him as well. He'd been sure he'd seen her in New York, but knew even as he'd chased after the woman leaving the Metropolitan Club that he was being ridiculous. What would Cara be doing at a high-end place like that?

The espresso machine sputtered. He grabbed a towel and stood back, prepared to smack it down if necessary. To his great relief, the machine spewed thick, dark coffee into his cup. He grabbed it and headed for his barn.

Adam Mitchell's beat-up truck was parked next to that of his contractor from the city. He had nothing against Adam, other than the fact that he was sniffing around Cara. And this week he needed the guy's fine skill and efficient work.

Ryan kicked at a stone in his path. He might not have any right to wish that other men didn't take an interest in Cara, but he wished it anyway.

He actually liked Adam. He just wished the guy would take an interest in Molly or any other woman in town. Anyone but Cara.

Ryan's eyes adjusted to the dim light in the barn. The floor paving for the drainage was in, and it spruced the old place up more than he'd expected. His old barn was getting to look like something out of a movie. His dad would probably rib him about that too.

"Looking good," he said to his contractor.

"Better than that," Marvin said with pride. "The slope below the pavers means you won't have any trouble hosing this place in the wet season. You can spray down these stalls in about ten minutes." He pointed down to the last of the stalls. "My crew can come back from that city job in a couple of weeks, and we can have all this wrapped up by mid-October."

Ryan eyed Marvin. "I can't wait that long. The first animals are coming in ten days."

Marvin crossed his arms. He didn't know Ryan, didn't know he'd grown up on a tough-assed ranch. Crossed arms weren't a deterrent.

"Just finish wiring in the heaters and get the fans in before you leave today," Ryan said in a level voice. "Adam can finish up the stalls and the feed room. Your crew can come back and deal with any finishing work later."

It was always best to give a guy a way out.

Marvin nodded. "We'll get the heaters wired, don't you worry. But there's no way I can be back here in less than a week."

Ryan fisted his hands in his pockets. Marvin had told him he had to pull the crew off by the end of September and get to a job in the city. It was Ryan's change orders that had put the work behind schedule.

"I'll send my electrician back tomorrow to wire in the fans," Marvin conceded.

Ryan nodded. "That'll do." He turned toward the back of the barn. Adam had a hell of job ahead of him.

He poked his head into the last stall. Adam looked up from screwing a hinge to the gate.

"Thanks for coming in on short notice," Ryan said.

Adam stood and shook his hand.

"It's a great project," Adam said. "It'll be finished in time." He tilted his head toward the door. "Your contractor hasn't seen what Albion Bay men can do."

If Ryan had known about Adam, he would have had him on the crew in the first place. Ryan liked providing work for locals. He'd asked around and discovered that Adam had a reputation for great work. He also had a reputation for being a ladies' man. Ryan wished that last part was none of his business.

Ryan left the men working and cranked up the Bugatti. It'd been a week since he'd had her out for a spin. Even during the busiest weeks he liked to get in at least an hour of solid country driving, blow out the carbon, keep the car running smoothly. He had five hours before he had to be in the city, five blissful hours to ease the tweak out of his shoulder and take in the countryside.

In his rearview mirror he saw the school bus go by the end of his drive as he backed out of the barn. Though there was no reason for it to stop or even slow down, he was disappointed when it did neither.

Besides, he liked a challenge. And he'd been handed a clear one when Ms. Cara West had kicked him out so baldly.

He cruised onto Highway One. As he shifted into second gear, the ping of pain below his shoulder blade felt like a hot rubber band snapping. The week of pain-free days now seemed like a far-off oasis he'd never reach again. The plane trip last night hadn't helped. Driving probably didn't either, but he longed to click off some miles and settle his feuding thoughts.

He shot around the bend and saw the school bus jutting at a strange angle about a tenth of a mile from the driveway to the middle school. A line of kids were running down the shoulder of the road toward the school, shooting backward glances to where Cara sat beside the bus, clutching someone in her arms.

Gravel flew as he skidded to a halt behind the bus. He jumped out and ran toward her. As he neared, he saw that she was holding Sam Rivers.

"I told one of the kids to call 9-1-1 as soon as they reached the school," she shouted. "There's no cell reception here."

Whatever was wrong with Sam, it didn't look like waiting half an hour for the Point Reyes EMTs would do the boy any good.

"Let me take him," Ryan said. He lifted Sam from Cara's arms before she could protest.

"C'mon, let's get him in the car. You hold him, I'll drive. You can give me directions to the hospital and explain on the way."

She grabbed the blue backpack at her feet and followed him to the car.

"Seat belt," he ordered.

"Right." She snapped the seat belt over her, and he laid Sam in her lap. He'd gone limp and his lips were a little blue, but he was breathing, although shallowly.

"He's seizuring," Cara said.

"He's not," Ryan said in a forced calm tone. He hadn't expected the panic he heard in her voice. "He's having an asthma attack. My grandmother has them."

Ryan slid behind the wheel and had them on the road in seconds. "Look in his backpack and get his inhaler."

She leaned over Sam and grabbed the pack.

"Just lunch. And a bottle of water."

"Punk."

Sam moaned as if to protest, but didn't move in Cara's arms. Cara shifted him so his legs could stretch alongside hers to the floor of the car.

"He's breathing, right?" Ryan didn't take his eyes off the road.

"Barely."

"He'll be okay." Ryan said. "Trust me."

Cara nodded.

Though he wasn't sure Sam would make it, he needed Cara to stay calm.

"Call the hospital," Ryan said when they reached the stretch where he knew there was cell reception. "Tell them we're coming."

Cara fished for her phone. "I left my purse on the bus."

"Use mine."

Ryan hoped Sam didn't register the anxiety in her voice as she spoke with the emergency room.

"Molly already called in," Cara reported. "She can't be far behind us."

Ryan pushed the Bugatti and the roads to their limit. He heard Cara suck in her breath as he took a sinewy curve at high speed.

"Cara, relax. I know the limits of this car. And I know my own." He glanced quickly at Sam. "And you just hang in there, buddy—got that?"

Sam nodded weakly.

Ryan snapped his eyes back to the road. And gave silent thanks that driving in extreme conditions was a skill he'd mastered early on.

It was all Cara could do to stay calm for the last few hundred yards to the hospital. Ryan ran two red lights and left drivers swearing in his wake as he pulled into the rotunda fronting the hospital emergency room.

As she opened the car door, a nurse and two men in surgical scrubs pushing a gurney came rushing out.

"I'm Dr. Goldfeld, the pediatric triage resident," said a short man with glasses. He and the nurse pulled Sam from her arms. He turned to the nurse. "Respiratory distress, red alert activation."

"I'm the triage nurse," the nurse said to Cara as they loaded Sam onto a gurney. "Mrs. Rivers called ahead. She'll be here soon."

Cara's heart sank as the doctor snapped an oxygen mask over Sam's face.

"How'd it come on?" the nurse asked as they wheeled

Sam through the double glass doors.

"I don't know," Cara said. "He was fine when he stepped onto the bus."

"Could've been anything," Dr. Goldfeld said in a voice that told Cara he was worried but didn't want anyone to panic. "We'll get him shaped up." He eyed the Bugatti. "Good thing you two have a fast car."

"Good thing he knows how to drive it," Cara said, feeling awkward. The doctor thought they were a couple. And in that moment, they were. A couple that had just rushed her best friend's son to the ER, that had maybe saved his life.

She looked over to Ryan. He took her hand.

"Let's get you some water, maybe some coffee?" He squeezed her fingers. "I'm not making it, so you're safe."

"I want to stay with Sam."

"Sorry," the nurse said, blocking her way. "The doctor's taking him directly into triage. You can see him when he's through giving him a workup. He may need to insert an endotracheal tube—he won't want you around for that."

Cara opened her mouth to protest.

"He'll be fine," the nurse said with a touch of irritation. "Just let us do our job, okay?"

"Looks like you're stuck with me," Ryan said, leading her away with the firm pressure of his hand.

While Ryan went to the counter in the café for coffee, Cara called the school, telling them she wouldn't be able to do the afternoon bus run. Then she pressed her palms to her eyes and willed away the headache threatening to form behind them.

"Caffeine," Ryan said as he plunked down a paper cup of dark steaming coffee. "Probably the most underrated substance on the planet—next to water." He grinned, but it dissolved when he looked into her eyes.

"Hey." He put his hand on her shoulder. "He'll be okay. We had a guy on the Red Sox with a case of asthma worse than Sam's. Last I checked, he's in the running for a Cy Young."

She had no idea what a Cy Young was, but appreciated his attempt to calm her nerves. She took a sip of the hot, black brew, felt it melt into her and warm her. But as Ryan sat in the seat across the small table, it wasn't just the coffee warming her. His confidence—no, his excellence—delved into the worry that gripped her and teased it apart, giving her space to breathe.

"It's a pitching achievement," he added.

She blinked, then nodded. It was uncanny how he seemed to know what she was thinking, and even odder that he knew how to say all the right things to take her mind off her worries.

"Cy Young played in the late eighteen hundreds and early nineteen hundreds. During his twenty-one-year career, he pitched for five different teams. Some of his pitching records have stood for a century. Young compiled five hundred and eleven wins, the most in Major League history."

"If you're trying to distract me, it's working."

He wiggled his brows. "I have my ways," he said in a comic voice that made her laugh. "But honestly, I don't know how they do it. Pitchers, I mean. My shoulder would make it through about two innings and then *I'd* be through. For life." He sipped his coffee. "Pitchers have reputations as prima donnas, but now that I've seen up close the heat and accuracy the guys in the majors have, I recognize that most deserve the accolades and special attention."

He leaned back in his chair and laughed. "If you repeat that to the press, I'll be marked for life."

She wasn't getting anywhere near the press.

"Have your donkeys arrived?"

"In ten days. I hired your guy Adam Mitchell to finish up the critical work. The rest will have to wait."

When she became aware that he was searching her face for a reaction, it dawned on her that he was jealous of Adam. The thought warmed her even though it shouldn't. He had no reason to be jealous. No man could crowd Ryan out of her thoughts or dreams.

Ryan stretched his legs out along the side of the table. She tried to ignore the fire that simply watching him move kindled in her belly.

"The strangest thing happened last weekend." He was still watching her face closely. "I joined Alex Tavonesi at his club, some stuffy place in Manhattan. I thought I saw you there."

Her coffee stuck in her throat. She hoped he didn't see the effort she had to make just to swallow it down.

"I have one of those familiar faces."

She felt the seconds crawl by, slowly, as though time had been slowed down, like the seconds were being metered out by one of those old-fashioned grandfather clocks with heavy, weighted pendulums. Only the racing of her heart told her they hadn't really slowed.

He reached across the table and uncurled her fingers from her cup.

"You have a beautiful face, Cara West." He lifted her fingers to his lips. The noises of the café dissolved into the background. All she could hear was the pounding of her pulse in her ears. "A face I could look at for a very, very long time."

He lowered her hand and his to the table and kept his covering hers. She felt the cool surface of the table under her palm and the almost blazing sensation of energy where his hand rested on her skin.

"You kept your cool really well," he added when she didn't respond.

Her heart stuttered. She had no ready answer to explain what she'd been doing in an exclusive club in Manhattan.

"Not many people could give good directions while holding a gasping child."

Relief flooded her. She'd thought he'd been referring to spotting her in New York.

"Thank you."

She slid her hand out from under his and picked up her coffee, took a sip and was grateful that she hadn't had to tell a blatant lie. Each partial truth now felt like a weight being piled on top of her head, added to a stack of previous weights and slowly sinking her below the surface of what once had been a blissful, peaceful, serene body of water that she'd called her life. The surging waters of the past day's events were lapping just under her nose, and soon she'd have to hold her breath or she'd drown in the mess she'd made of everything.

But one thing she couldn't deny was that she wanted Ryan Rea. Wanted him in a way she'd never have imagined. Wanted him in places in her heart and soul and body that had never before spoken up with their insistent desires.

But she'd sent him away—would he even be interested in trying again?

Maybe it was the rush of adrenaline, the aftermath of her horrible concern that they wouldn't make the ER in time, but whatever the cause, no finer torture could've been invented to torment Cara into breaking her silence than Ryan Rea. He tempted her to breach the boundaries she'd erected, to give over to the power that screamed for her to leap into his arms and confess all her secrets.

If Molly hadn't come rushing into the hospital café, she just might have leaped.

CHAPTER SIXTEEN

THREE HOURS LATER CARA HELPED MOLLY AND SAM into Molly's old Toyota. Ryan had had to leave for his game, but he'd waited until the last minute to get the thumbs-up from the emergency room doctor before he would go. Seeing Ryan joking around with Sam, trying to cheer him up before he'd left, shot a web of happiness around Cara's heart. No, more than that. A feeling of... Jeez, she might as well say it. A feeling of love.

And Ryan had wisely told Cara to drive Molly home. Molly, though she tried to appear unflappable, was in no shape to drive.

"I thought we'd get to ride in the Bugatti," Sam fussed as Molly buckled him into the back seat.

"You *did* ride in that car," Molly said.

Cara heard the strain in her voice.

"But I don't remember it very well."

Sam sounded more than tired, he sounded defeated. Cara suspected the mode of transportation had little to do with his glum mood. When the doctor had asked why Sam hadn't had his inhaler, he'd answered that he hadn't needed it for two weeks—he'd thought he was "over it," he'd told the doctor. The doctor had squeezed his arm and told him it might be a few years before that happened.

On the way out, the doctor had whispered to Molly

that Sam might have attacks for the rest of his life and that she and Sam had better plan accordingly.

"Maybe Mr. Rea will take you out another day," Molly said as she shut the door and slipped into the front seat beside Cara.

In the rearview mirror, Cara saw Sam give a wavering smile and curl up against the window.

Cara headed west, out of town and over the hill that separated Albion Bay from the rest of the world.

Molly glanced into the back seat. "He's asleep," she said in a low voice. "Thank God you and Ryan got him there in time."

"Ryan did. He drove like a demon. I never thought I'd appreciate a man or a car so much."

The praise escaped her before she had a chance to edit it. Her appreciation didn't escape Molly.

"He's sweet on you, Cara. Everybody sees it."

"I'm not ready for a man in my life."

Molly clucked. "Whoever broke your heart is going to have me to answer to if he ever shows his face in Albion Bay."

The good feeling that settled around Cara's heart as she heard Molly's almost sisterly support warred with the bad feeling underneath. It wasn't a guy that forced her to be so cautious—it was her own careful, determined choices that made it impossible for her to have a relationship with Ryan. Letting him in that close, at least right now, just wasn't an option.

"What about you, Molly?"

"You're kidding, right?"

Cara shook her head and kept her eyes on the road.

"Chemistry, honey," Molly said in a tone normally reserved for three-year-olds. "It's called chemistry. You two could blow a powder keg. You can't fake that."

169

Chemistry.

A little word for the sometimes fatal power of attraction. If her mother and father hadn't had such a strong chemistry between them, they'd have split long ago. Without the bond of such strong chemistry, her mother might have freed herself from the never-ending, play-by-play descriptions of golf games and endless social obligations. Only recently had it occurred to Cara that maybe those interactions that appeared so irritating to an observer were like a secret language between them, a code that only they could decipher and find meaningful.

"Besides," Molly added, "Ryan's too much of a city boy for me."

"He grew up on a ranch," Cara pointed out. "In Texas. *East* Texas."

"You know what I'm talking about."

She did, but she was surprised Molly had taken such precise measure of Ryan so quickly. And that her own response had been so easy to read.

"Sam adores him."

"Cara West, you are digging a deeper hole with every word you say. Now I *know* you like him."

"*Every*body likes him."

"I'd say I've got you backed in that hole you just dug, like a gopher hiding from a terrier." Molly tapped her fingers along the dash and shot Cara an *I told you so* look.

Cara was in no shape to defend herself, and anything she said would just dig the hole deeper.

"We need the town planning committee to vote through an interim step for a clinic, at least for a doctor," Cara said, shifting the subject. "You have clout in the community." And her son had nearly died for lack of adequate emergency access. "Maybe they would listen to you."

Molly sighed. "There aren't any funds for that." She took in a long breath and let it out slowly. "I didn't want to be the one to tell you, but I think you had best hear it from me before we get back to town. The county cut the funds for the school bus service. It was announced at the parent-teacher meeting this morning."

Cara pressed her back against the seat and willed the leaden feeling dropping in her chest to stop. She'd seen the cuts coming—anyone who read the newspapers would have. She'd even made plans in her head to organize a car-pool system. But she hadn't expected the cuts to come so soon.

Molly patted Cara's arm. "Don't worry. We'll all help you until you figure out what to do. I heard there are some jobs in Point Reyes. I mean, I know it's a commute, but it's only bad during heavy rains."

Molly's heartfelt concern washed over Cara like a blessing. But Molly couldn't know that it wasn't the loss of the job that disturbed her; it was the loss of her role in the community. For two years things had rolled along smoothly. And now nothing was going as she thought it would. Dealing with decisions about the foundation, having Ryan shoot through her boundaries and steal into her heart, maybe even her soul, and now losing her job—how could her carefully plotted life unravel in a few short weeks?

"It's okay," Cara said, even though it wasn't.

"It's *not* okay. Cutting your job with no notice is awful. And nothing about cutting schools or school services is okay. Don't those fools realize it's the *future* they're messing with?" Molly lowered her voice. "We'll be a nation of illiterates if this sort of nonsense keeps up."

Cara knew it was stress talking as much as the aftermath of shock. She just nodded and let Molly talk on.

Molly looked back at Sam. "I know it's just because he's mine, but he looks like an angel when he's sleeping.

When he's sleeping I can imagine that he'll have a perfect, healthy life."

"He will, Molly. I just know it. He's got you. You see him for who he is. That's worth a lot."

"I guess so. But I shouldn't let him play sports, especially baseball. All the spurts of running after standing around, all the adrenaline. If his dad were still alive, he'd talk some sense into him."

"He loves baseball."

"Yeah. More than anything."

Cara made the turn into Albion Bay. Both she and Molly had tough choices ahead.

The cold, crisp scent of approaching autumn met Cara as she stepped onto the bus the next morning. The sun burning through light fog promised a warmer day ahead. She pulled into the gas station and hooked the nozzle into the gas tank. Then she sorted through her backpack, but couldn't find her favorite wool scarf. The collar of her jacket would just have to do until the sun did its job.

She'd called the school principal and announced that she intended to drive the bus without wages, but was told that she could continue the bus run only until the end of the week. After Friday, they'd no longer be insured. The announcement had shocked Cara. She'd been so sure her offer to volunteer would solve the problem. But just like that, the end of her job was in sight.

Cara had worried about how the other kids would treat Sam after his asthma attack, but when she swung the lever and opened the bus door, he hopped on like nothing had happened. She needn't have worried; Sam was a hero. He'd ridden in the Bugatti and gotten out of a whole day of school, both major coups in the eyes of the other kids.

Before she let the kids off, she stood at the front of the bus and waved them to attention. She told them the bus run was ending on Friday. The bus sizzled with their protests. When she explained that the parents were putting together a car pool, the older kids groaned.

That they'd rather have Cara driving them than their parents made her smile, even though she shouldn't have. She finished the bus run and headed back to town for the town council meeting.

Three more days.

Three more days and she'd have to sort out more than just losing the routine of driving the bus. She'd lose her day-to-day connection with the kids. Driving them had anchored her in the community. Driving the bus meant more to her than anyone would ever know.

Cara slipped into the back of the town council chambers. Molly sat next to Cara as the meeting droned on. When the subject of the clinic plans came up, Cara ignored the butterflies in her stomach and walked up to the small podium.

"I know that everyone wants to hold out until there's enough funding for a proper clinic." The PA system buzzed, and she backed away from the mike a few inches.

She looked out over the faces of the people she'd come to love. Perk was already shaking his head; he knew where she stood and didn't agree. Belva sat with her arms crossed, her lips pressed into a firm line. Cara swallowed down the lump of emotion in her throat. The race to the hospital with Ryan and Sam had changed everything. It wasn't just her life she held in her hands anymore. Alston would just have to work with her and find a way to funnel funds to the town.

"If we can secure funds for a couple of on-call doctors while we look for funding for a full clinic"—she tried to ignore Perk shaking his head—"it could save lives."

Belva stood, surprising her. "Cara's right. We could hold some fundraisers and pull together enough to get a doc in here for a few days a week. McFarley's old dentist office could be fitted up. I have a few things I can sell. They're just old antiques collecting dust. And some of you would do well to clean out your attics."

"I'll pitch in forty thousand."

Everyone turned to see who had spoken. Cara knew Ryan's voice, knew it too well. She hadn't seen him slip into the meeting.

Perk stood, hands on his hips. "That's generous of you, Mr. Rea. Very generous. But it's a mistake to tackle this piecemeal—the road to Hell is paved with piecemeal projects. We need a real clinic out here, a twenty-four-seven operation. If this past week has shown us anything, it's shown us that."

"Get off your high horse, Mr. Mayor," Belva said in a tone that only a lifelong friend could use with Perk, one that had a few of those in the audience chuckling. She looked to the back of the room. "Mr. Rea—Ryan—we accept." She waved her hands at the crowd. "And the rest of you, dig in those pockets. Deep."

Perk reddened and waved his hands. "Belva, this is town business, you can't—"

"Perk Norman, don't you go telling us what we can and can't do. I say we vote on it."

Cara walked back to her seat, stunned. Ryan's generosity had solved one problem, but he couldn't know the tumult he'd set into motion in her. *She* hadn't stepped up. She could have, but she hadn't. She wasn't ready to face the consequences.

Perk was the one holdout in the vote approving the plan to hire an on-call doc and fit up the old dentist's office.

After the vote, Cara slipped out of the council chambers and headed back to her cabin. She couldn't face Ryan right then. Or anyone else. Maybe not even herself.

~~~~

Cara turned in to her driveway and saw the crated package leaning against the front door to her cabin.

Her foot caught on a piece of rotted decking when she leaned down to pick up the crate. Adam had asked if it would be okay to work on Ryan's place for a week or so, and after hearing about what the donkeys had been through in their short lives, any contribution to Ryan's effort to provide them a good home was a small price to pay. Her decks could wait.

She looked around to see if anyone was about and then hauled the crate in and propped it just inside her door. She was beginning to feel like a bad actor in a low-budget spy film. Her life didn't even feel like it was hers anymore. She felt like a ball set in perpetual motion, banging around inside a steel box, hitting the side and bouncing to the opposite side, leaving no impression and just bouncing, moving, with no direction other than that caused by the impact with the wall. If she believed in evil spells, she would have thought she'd tumbled into one.

She uncrated the painting her father had sent by overnight express. He hadn't even insured it. A three-million-dollar Renoir, dropped off on her front porch like a package from L.L. Bean.

She stared at the perfect landscape. Renoir had captured the light of the south of France so that the painting seemed to glow. The birds along the horizon looked alive, as if they could take wing and fly through her cabin.

Her father was a thickheaded blunderbuss, but he was

right—she loved the little painting. Always had. It called to the part of her that had set out to find her place in Albion Bay, the part of her that wanted to live close to the land, to the sea, connected to the lives of the people around her.

She read the note that her father had taped to the back of the frame.

We all need beacons in our lives. I know this painting is one of yours.

She took the painting and the note upstairs to her bedroom. She put the note on the bookshelf next to her bed, nestling it alongside the owl feather she'd found her first day in Albion Bay. The paper slipped down and she propped it up, reading her father's slanting script once again. For the first time it occurred to her that her father might be just as lost in the life he'd cobbled together as she was in hers. To her surprise, she felt a camaraderie with him, a kinship she'd never expected.

She hung the painting on a wall opposite her bed, right next to her faded poster of wildflowers of the California coast. Though mismatched in their value to the outside world, both held equal value to her. She stepped back and adjusted the plastic frame of the poster and couldn't help smiling. The two pieces of art seemed happy together. When Renoir had stood in the fields of southern France, painting in the afternoon light, he couldn't have known that centuries later his small painting would command such a dear price. She hoped he'd be happy to know it was cherished simply for its beauty rather than for profit or status.

On the way to her kitchen, she pressed the button on her answering machine. Alston's phone message was vague, but his tone gave her hope. Surely there was some way she could stall until Alston found a clever way to help her. Ryan's gift to the town was generous, but as much as she didn't want to admit it, Perk was right—hiring an on-call doc was a stopgap. The town meeting had put a knife-edge on her resolve to find a way to funnel money to the clinic project and yet stay securely anonymous in the background. There had to be a way. And there had to be some way to get rid of Dray Bender other than for her to take on the presidency of the Barrington Foundation.

Her stomach grumbled. She grabbed the stack of papers she'd picked up from the post office and headed into her kitchen. She could read through them as she ate lunch. In the kitchen she focused on the soup pot, staring into it. At the bottom were the slightest remains of charring from the night she'd made love with Ryan. Clutching the pot, she sank into the chair by the table.

For three years she'd convinced herself that community was enough. For three years she'd kept herself aloof from entanglements with men. Until Ryan.

She ran her fingers along the back of her hand. The previous night she'd slept for the first time in weeks. Exhaustion fueled it, exhaustion and nerves. And she'd dreamed. Dreamed vividly and emotionally.

The sensations from her dream swept through her, as fresh as they'd been when she'd awakened, stunned. She pressed her palms to her eyes. Images rushed back. Ryan had held her, their bodies melded in the ecstasy of passion and... and in a pure sensation that she had no words to describe. He'd pressed her back across a bed that morphed into a lake of billowing clouds and together they'd floated— weightless, touching and tasting. He'd come to her from a world beyond her consciousness, beyond anything she'd ever known, and together they'd twined their hearts and bodies into a primal, wordless dance that left her breathless and disoriented when she'd awakened.

She thought of those children's games where you take the pieces apart and put them back together and the thing you construct in no way resembles the creature you had in your hands just moments before. Like such a creature, her parts were the same, but a new spirit inhabited her, enlivened her.

She swept her hand over her forehead and tried to ignore the knot forming deep in her belly, tried to reconcile the lively feelings with the lurking, gnawing sensation that told her events were moving too quickly for her to process. Ryan had opened territory she hadn't ever expected to experience.

She locked her fingers in her hair and tugged, felt the pull along her scalp and tried to center herself in the familiar sensation. There couldn't be a worse time to start out on any kind of a journey, especially one she hadn't planned for.

Frustrated when the power of the dream wouldn't release its hold on her, she opened her eyes and set the pot on the table, pushing it away with her fingertips. Then she picked up the stack of papers Alston had sent. She read through every grant application that Dray Bender had approved in the six months he'd been at the helm of the Barrington Foundation. After reviewing the reports, she was sure that Alston's suspicions that Bender was getting kickbacks from the projects were true. If she wanted hard evidence, the best way to find it was to track the money. She read through the information Alston's team had gathered about Bender's financial dealings. He'd purchased stock in the pharmaceutical companies he was funneling grants to. Clearly the companies were feeding him information that could be considered insider trading. It wasn't legal, but there were always loopholes. Loopholes Bender apparently had every confidence no one would challenge.

The laws seemed to be written so that plundering by those in power, by those who wanted to bend the rules to their own purposes, couldn't be easily discovered or stopped. A mechanic who made a mistake on his tax return could be charged a steep fine, even face jail time, but a person of means and very few morals could walk off with illegal millions and never even get his wrists slapped.

Her grandfather had based his entire life on the principle that what was good for the everyday citizen was good for the country as a whole. Bender was exactly the sort of guy that he would have taken to the mat.

Why her father didn't see any of this... She shook her head, considering. Maybe he didn't want to know. And maybe she didn't want to know what Bender had on her dad. But resolve jelled in her. There was no way she was going to let a man like Bender misuse her grandfather's legacy. It wasn't right.

What it would take to stop him, she wasn't sure. But with Alston's help, she would. She wouldn't take on the role of president of the foundation, but she'd find a way to oust the current president.

She wrapped her arms across her chest and sought the blissful feeling she'd had—was it just that morning? But she couldn't call it back to her. She eyed the stack of papers on her table. Her brain raced with options and scenarios, none of them ideal and all of them less than welcome. Knowing the destination of the road ahead and finding her way along it were two very different ventures.

CHAPTER SEVENTEEN

RYAN LEVERED THE FIFTY-POUND SPOOL OF FENCING wire and rolled a length of it between the last of the fence posts needing reinforcement. Pain shot through his arm as he twisted the wire cutter, and he cursed.

"That doesn't sound like fun."

He turned and saw Alex Tavonesi walking toward him on the rutted path. He'd forgotten Alex had invited himself over to the ranch that morning. He was forgetting too many details he usually wrangled with ease.

Ryan dropped the roll of wire into the dry grass at his feet.

Alex surveyed the line of fences and whistled. "Anyone ever tell you you're crazy?"

Ryan wiped his sleeve across the sweat beading his forehead. "If I remember correctly, you're the guy who risked a Triple Crown batting title to chase down armed kidnappers on a cliff side."

"Kidnapper," Alex said, still eyeing the fences. "There was only one. And yes, guilty. But there was a life at stake."

From the posture of Alex's stance, Ryan knew the shock of nearly losing Jackie still lived in his friend. Trauma had a long tail and a hard lash. He'd spoken in jest, without thinking. But it didn't do either of them any good to duck the truth. Trauma only got stronger if you tried to bury it.

"Well, there'll be fourteen lives at stake here." Ryan knew Alex's fondness for animals. "So you're just the guy I need."

He took off his gloves and handed them to Alex. "The rescue centers are at overcapacity, so some of the donkeys are coming directly here before they've been rehabbed. I intend to make good on my promise to provide a safe and humane environment for every one of them."

"Then let's get on with it." Alex donned the gloves and then picked up the spool of wire by the wooden dowel running through its center. "One thing a vineyard teaches you is how to run wire."

Alex had wire-cutting and fastening techniques Ryan had never seen used on the ranches in Texas. Evidently cowboys didn't know all there was to know about high-tech fencing. He followed Alex's instructions and admired the deft moves of his teammate.

When he'd been traded to the Giants, he'd never imagined finding guys like Alex and Scotty on the team, guys who weren't only excellent players but who had more than the usual team spirit. Most of the guys were like that, as if they'd been hand-picked for their sense of camaraderie and cooperation as much as for their stats and ability to perform.

They worked through the morning and finished reinforcing the last of the weak fences. The sawing and banging slowed in the barn, and Ryan hoped that meant Adam was coming to the end of the work in there.

"How's the shoulder?" Alex asked.

"I tweaked it a few days ago loading a barely breathing kid into my car." Tweak, ping, zing—that was about all any player admitted to unless he was on the training table. And sometimes not even then would they admit to anything more drastic.

"I thought you were rescuing donkeys."

Ryan told him about the emergency run with Sam and Cara.

"It's the damnedest thing," Ryan said. "When I think about her, the pain goes away." He didn't mention his phantom pain theory. Scotty had already ribbed him hard for that.

"Better keep her in mind, then," Alex said with a chuckle.

Though Ryan felt foolish, he had to ask.

"How'd you know, I mean *know*... with Jackie?" He didn't say the word love, didn't want to. Though he wrestled with the word in his mind, pushing it away, it kept bobbing to the surface of his thoughts whenever he thought about Cara. Alex had found a great woman to share his life, everybody could see that. Ryan trusted Alex's opinion on the subject.

Alex leaned on the fence post and crossed his arms. "It's not something you know. It hauls down on you and you'll wish it hadn't—it's never convenient." He raised a brow as a half-smile lit his face. "Maybe that's the real yardstick—if it's painful and inconvenient and you still can't help yourself or can't stop thinking of her, then she's the one."

"She's pretty much keeping me at arm's length." He could admit to Alex what he tried not to admit to himself.

"Maybe you'll get lucky." Alex grinned.

Maybe he would.

The next morning Ryan took the back road to Cara's place. The early morning sun speared shafts of light through the low-hanging coastal fog, circling the oaks and coyote bushes with a soft, golden hue. He pulled his Jeep into her drive.

He sat for a moment admiring the colorful flowers that

banked up against the front deck of her tiny cabin. Everything about her place seemed to whisper the praises of the simple beauty of country life. Of her.

He pulled the Mason jar filled with daisies from the cup holder. He'd cut them just before he'd left his house so they'd be fresh. He leaned over and lifted the carefully folded knit scarf from the seat beside him and headed up the path.

Words formed in his mind as he stepped onto Cara's front deck. Words he'd rehearsed. Words he hoped would serve as stepping stones into her world.

He knocked at the door.

As he waited, his carefully collected words fled, and he began to frantically search for new ones. Words had never been his strong suit. When Cara opened the door, sleepy-eyed and tousled, wearing only a robe, his mind went blank.

"It's six thirty in the morning," she said with a puzzled smile.

He looked to his watch. Water splashed out of the jar and onto the leg of his jeans. Great, that was a ridiculous move; he knew what time it was. He righted the jar and held it out. The daisies stood like colorful guardians between them.

"These are for you." Embarrassment washed through him, and he quickly held out the scarf. The scarf gave him a legitimate reason to be there. "And this. You left it in my car."

She propped the door with her foot, then took the scarf and wrapped it around her neck. "I thought I'd left it at the hospital," she said, patting the scarf. "Molly made it for me." She looked up at him. "Thank you."

She reached for the Mason jar holding the daisies. Her fingers brushed his, and she took in a breath. What she felt, he wasn't sure, but with that light touch he knew the path he wanted to take, words or no words.

"These are lovely."

"You didn't seem the long-stemmed red-rose type."

She stiffened, and immediately he regretted saying such a stupid thing. Maybe she did like red roses. When she pulled her hand away, he wished for better words.

She opened the door. "Have you had breakfast?"

"Hours ago," he said, wishing now that he hadn't.

"Would you like to come in?" She motioned toward the living room.

"That'd be great."

He stepped into the room and caught the scent of her. Though it was familiar, her scent always caught him off guard. Like it snuck into some place in his brain that was otherwise closed off to him and started firing up synapses.

"TV working?" he said, not knowing what else to say.

"Brilliantly."

She set the daisies on the table beside the TV. She bent to arrange them, giving him a very good look at her beautiful backside hugged by the silky robe. He tried to talk down his arousal, but it was hopeless. Good thing he'd tied his fleece jacket around his waist, or he'd be busted.

"How's Sam? I wanted to call Molly but didn't have her number."

Cara turned to him. A smile played along her lips and revved up his hope. "He's great. He's a hero now, thanks to you."

Ryan raised a brow.

"He's the only kid in town who's ridden in your Bugatti."

"Might be the new version of a pony ride," he said. "Maybe I should charge a fee."

She laughed then, and he felt his shoulders relax.

"Would you like a coffee?"

184

"Is it safe?"

She laughed again. "French Press. No rocket-science machines in this house."

"Cara."

He put his hand on her arm and closed his fingers around it. She lifted her chin, and he saw her lips quiver. Under his fingers, she trembled. It was clearly not his morning for wordsmithing. He pulled her into his arms and lowered his lips to hers.

She opened to his kiss and let him snug her against him. It was the green light he'd dreamed of. He pulled back so he could look into her eyes, so he could touch her face. Then he kissed her again.

Tender good-morning kisses led to passion and then to need. He lifted her in his arms, and she tipped her face to his.

"Upstairs," she whispered. "First room on the right. But I can walk, you know."

"I'm not taking any chances."

He would've run up the stairs, but he'd promised her this time he would go slow. It would take every bit of discipline he could summon, but he would love her slowly, properly, with everything he had.

He was vaguely aware of the muted colors of the room as he laid her across her bed. She fisted her hands in his shirt and tugged him to her, pressing her lips to his. In the searing heat and heady taste of her, his resolve for going slow was ripped from him. She nipped at his bottom lip, and that resolve simply died.

He pressed up and away from her lips and called up his willpower, the willpower that gave him an edge on the field and made him better than good at the game. But when he saw the smoldering look in Cara's eyes, he knew that no practice, no training, had prepared him to harness the desire she fired in him.

He hauled in a breath and willed his body to submit to his command. Then he parted her robe and cupped her breast. The sensation of her smooth warm skin and the beauty of her body tested him. He ran his thumb over her already hard nipple. She arched up with a gasp that he hoped was pure pleasure. He smoothed his hand down her belly, then followed it with his lips. When she tried to sit up and reach for him, he pressed her back to the bed with his forearm. And gave silent thanks that his physical power could constrain her and allow him to continue on the path he'd charted for her pleasure. He held her pinned and traced his mouth along the crease of her thigh. When he parted her folds with his tongue and tasted her silky, salty wetness, she cried out and plunged her hands into his hair. He resisted her effort to draw him away and back up to her mouth.

"I promised you slow, Cara."

He teased her with his tongue and wasn't sure when he heard her muffled sighs, when her hands gripped the sheets and her hips bucked up against his mouth, that he had the control he'd imagined. But he focused on her pleasure, drinking in her cries and keeping her pressed down into the bed. He circled his tongue over her and felt her shudder, drank in her moan and slid a finger into her. Her muscles contracted around his finger as she cried out his name. Never had his name sounded so good. She grabbed his hair again and tugged, hard, making him more intent on staying right where he was and doing exactly what he was doing.

"Ryan—"

He dipped a second finger inside her, and she gasped.

"Ryan, you've"—she dragged in a breath—"you've proven... your point." She tugged at his hair once again, harder this time. "I'll die if I don't feel you inside me and—Oh!"

He loved the feeling of her hands in his hair, the passion her grip telegraphed. He moved his fingers slowly inside her, angling them to the spot that would send her over. He ignored the insistent throbbing in his groin and traced slow, near-teasing circles with his tongue. A shudder of ecstasy took her, and her legs tightened around his shoulders as she arched up. And then she went still.

He stood and kicked off his jeans, pulled his shirt over his head. She leaned up on her elbows, the aftermath of pleasure still pooling in her eyes, the glisten of sweat lighting the curves of her body. Her cheeks were flushed, and she looked thoroughly loved. When her robe slipped from her shoulders, she wriggled free of it. Ryan drew on a condom and watched her watching him as he unrolled it up his erection. And prayed that the insane pulse of want that flooded him was his to harness and control.

She held out her hand and he took it, pinning it above her head. He took her other hand and did the same. Her eyes went wide as he teased her, circling and barely dipping the tip of his erection inside her. She fought to free her hands, but he held firm. She moaned and bucked up against him, sheathing him with her heat, her muscles contracting around him and flooding him with intense sensation. He held her captive as he stroked into her, holding his weight up and away from her so that the only place they were joined was inside her and at their palms. She tossed her head in the side-to-side almost uncontrollable rhythm that revealed her pleasure and matched each of his deep thrusts. She tried again to release her hands, but he met her effort with deeper thrusts. How long he could hold back, he didn't know. All he knew was that in that moment, she was his. His. And he'd do what it took to keep her that way.

He wedged his hips between her thighs and released her hands, running his palms up her hips to cup her bottom and pull her tightly to him. She wrapped her legs around his hips, and he plunged, each thrust taking him nearly beyond his control. He slowed and dipped down to once again taste her lips, and met the ecstatic thrusts of her tongue against his.

Never had he wanted to pleasure a woman as he wanted to pleasure her. Never had he known such beauty as he saw in her. He wanted the moment to last, wanted to hold time back and to forever feel the power coursing between them. But she arched into him, pressing her breasts against his chest, digging her fingers into the muscles of his back and writhing against him so that her nipples danced over his, and he was lost.

He lifted her hips high and drove into her until her cries and his were indistinguishable, until the fire in him exploded and he could hold back no more. He held her gaze as the power took them, shuddered with the force of it and the stripped-to-the-bone pleasure that flooded her eyes.

He lowered to his forearms, holding his full weight off her and willed his breathing to settle. She looked up at him, and he had no words for the emotion he saw in her eyes. He touched his forehead to hers, then kissed her cheek and then her lips.

"I'm thinking that you can't possibly know how beautiful you are," he whispered against her lips.

Her eyes widened and even through the flush of their lovemaking, he saw her blush. He kissed the tip of her nose and slid out of her.

"I thought you didn't." He propped himself up on an elbow and brushed a strand of hair back away from her face. "And you know why?"

She shook her head. Her breathing hadn't settled. She shivered, and he pulled the edge of the duvet to cover her. "Because there aren't words for such beauty."

She laughed. It was a laugh like he'd never heard—a laugh that a person who believed in heaven or angels might hear from a creature inhabiting those realms. Nothing could have made him happier.

She lifted up to her elbows and motioned for him to lie beside her.

"I'd be lying if I told you that the power I feel when we connect doesn't scare me," she said in a soft, still-breathless voice.

"No," he said, stroking her cheek with his thumb. "There's no need to be scared." He lifted his other hand and cradled her face in his palms. "Our bodies are meant to harness this power, to share it. But I'll admit it's a mystery. It's as mysterious as knowing before a pitch is thrown that I'll connect. The resonance between people, no one knows what it's made of."

She put her palm to his chest, above his heart.

"I hadn't meant to love you, Ryan."

Love. The word stopped him. *Light speed.* That seemed to be the pace of what was happening between them. From the way Cara colored and slipped her gaze away from his, the speed had taken her by surprise too. And though she said she loved him, she'd said it as if it were a painful confession rather than something she was happy about. That she'd be unhappy about her feelings for him hadn't crossed his mind.

And he sure didn't want their morning together to end on an unhappy note. That wasn't part of his plan. Not part of his plan at all.

He looked around the room, searching for something to say, something to do, some bridge to stretch between the life-rocking moments and the day-to-day world. He saw a small painting hanging next to a poster of wildflowers. A painting of the countryside.

He stood and walked over to the painting. It was simply done; the stippled colors reminded him of the hills near his childhood home in the spring. "This is beautiful," he said. Words were still stubborn, elusive, not at his beck and call. He peered closer. The painting looked remarkably like the ones he'd seen at the exhibit opening that Alex had dragged him to after a day game the previous week.

Perhaps he imagined it, but Cara darted between him and the painting as if there was something she didn't want him to see.

"How about that coffee I promised?" she said.

Her voice had a cool tone, but he could feel the heat of her body even though she was inches away. He batted away a ridiculous ping of warning and reached for her.

"Um... sure. But first—"

He pulled her to him and cradled her face with his hand, dipped his lips to hers and tasted. Their bodies were still slick with sweat, and he felt her nipples go hard against him as he pressed her closer. She didn't stop him as he tracked his hand down the curve of her belly and slipped it between them, lowering it to touch her slick, wet sex.

An alarm sounded from beside her bed.

She groaned and walked over to silence it.

He glanced at his watch. Though it seemed like hours had passed since he'd carried her upstairs, it was only seven thirty. "Do you have to drive the bus?"

"Parent-teacher day," she said with a near-wicked smile.

He moved toward her.

"No," she said, backing away. "*You* may have had breakfast, but I haven't."

She lifted the robe from her bed, slipped it on and tied the belt. Maybe she knew that the silk hugged her curves and accentuated the swell of her breasts beneath it. Maybe she didn't. Either way it had the same effect on him. He hoped it'd be a quick breakfast.

190

In the small kitchen she moved like a dancer running through a well-rehearsed routine. Her movements lent a grace to the simple activities as she scooped a gray porridge-like cereal into a pan on the stove and made coffee. The aroma of the coffee melded with the scent of their lovemaking.

He'd never think of coffee the same way again.

He was grateful for the simple routine, the activities of her making breakfast. He'd felt awkward after sex in the past, but never had he felt odd tension that gripped his chest as he watched her move about the kitchen. Making love with her had cut through to a place he hadn't even known he'd needed to guard. As he watched her, it occurred to him that she might feel the same vulnerability. Though it wasn't kind to wish it so, he did. He'd hate to be traveling that territory alone. She hadn't spoken of the sex that'd just blown his mind, but she had used the word *love*. Evidently he'd made an impression. But the way she'd said it, it felt almost like past tense. He was still sorting through his thoughts as she poured two mugs and set them, along with her bowl of steaming cereal, on the table.

"Why a ranch, Ryan?" She sipped at her coffee. "I mean, I get the donkey rescue. Love it, really. But how'd you decide to buy the ranch in the first place?"

She spooned a bite of the cereal from her bowl, and he had a hard time not staring at her lips as she ate it off the spoon. She saw him staring and smiled.

"Are you sure you don't want some?"

He shook his head.

"I'm always curious how people figure out how to orient their lives," she said. "I'm still working at that myself."

She'd lost her job, and he hadn't even mentioned it. He felt like a heel. Her livelihood had been pulled from under her and here he was acting like everything was fine, selfishly chasing after his own dreams.

"I was sorry to hear about your job."

She rested the spoon in the bowl and shook her head. "It's okay, I'll get another one. But I liked driving the bus. The kids. The routine."

She nibbled at a half-burned piece of toast. He resisted the urge to lunge across the table and kiss her.

"But really," she went on, "I'd like to know how you decided to come out here, buy the ranch and get involved with the town."

He was grateful for a topic he could talk about easily. Since they'd come downstairs, his mind had been reeling with scenarios he'd spun of a future with her, scenarios it was way too early to explore. At least he knew how to talk about the ranch.

"I came out here to..." Why exactly had he come out to Albion Bay? He knew the steps he'd taken that had landed him in the town, but they didn't add up to the reality.

"Well, the first thing you should know is that baseball's as addictive as a drug for guys like me who've loved it most of their lives. It seems like the hankering's always been in me, driving me, and it only settles down if I'm playing."

He tapped his fingers on the edge of the table, remembering. "For years it was all I cared about. But when I got called up to the majors, I wasn't prepared for the warp-shift. Most guys aren't. All of a sudden, the game has a world spun around it, like arms and legs of a strange creature—the press, the fans, the lifestyle. Nobody's ever ready for the mind-bending ramp-up when it happens. And it happens fast if you're lucky. If you're not, you can wallow down in the minors and watch it all go by."

He stopped. "Sorry. You asked about the ranch, not baseball."

"No. I want to hear what you're moving toward, what you left behind, what comes up—that's all part of it. It is for me."

"What did you leave behind?" He knew so little about the woman who'd just rocked every cell in his body.

"We were talking about you," she said. "I want to hear, Ryan."

And to his astonishment, he wanted to talk, wanted to see how she'd respond to the rest of his world, not just his body.

"You probably guessed that I'm still working out the money thing. I grew up without it. My parents never talked about money, never told me that we were poor, but it didn't take a genius to see how my mom took on odd jobs so I could have a new bat or glove, saved so she could get a second car to drive me to games in the summers."

He stood and paced to the sink, looked out the window at the pots of herbs and vegetables she'd planted. Looking for the threads of the story he'd never told before.

"My dad, he just worked all the time. He'd rope me into jobs on the ranch. I liked those times. When I was doing ranch work beside him, I felt like he saw me. When I played baseball, he didn't. I thought he was afraid that if I gave up my schooling, that I'd be stuck being a ranch hand, that I'd end up just like him. He was furious when I quit college to sign with the Red Sox."

He glanced over at Cara and noticed she'd stopped eating. "Your cereal's getting cold."

She picked up her spoon, but rather than putting it into her bowl, she waved it at him. "How did you end up with the ranch?"

Embarrassment flooded him. He'd been rambling, not making any sense. "I've been told I'm a lousy storyteller, I—"

"Whoever told you that is an idiot," she said with a light laugh.

Her laugh freed something in him. He wanted to tell her his story, yearned to. So what if he couldn't follow a solid storyline?

"When I came out here, I had it in my head to buy my dad a ranch, a place of his own. I found the place up here—well, Alex helped me—and I bought it. I sent my dad the pictures. Told him it was his."

He sat back in the chair.

"He sent me a four-line letter. Four lines. He told me he didn't want a ranch, that he liked his life just as it was. Told me to keep it and see if I could make something of it—that it'd be good for me. That's the closest thing to approval he's ever shown. But I think he was offended. He didn't say so, but I'm pretty sure he was."

Ryan sipped at his coffee and tried not to focus on the cleavage peeking out from under the neck of Cara's robe. Her beauty astonished him. It was like someone had sculpted a goddess and then decided to plunk her down into the countryside and dress her in humble garb. But more than her beauty, he knew now that she was the woman he'd been secretly seeking. A woman who loved the simple things. The important things. A woman who knew her mind, a woman of integrity and independence. If he wanted Cara West, he'd have to do more than just delight her in bed. What he'd have to do, he didn't know, but he was going to figure it out.

She leaned her chin in her hands. "And then what?"

"I walked the ranch for a few days after I got his letter and realized he was right—the ranch would ground me, in a good way. It's an antidote to all the hustle and hype. I should thank him for that." He sipped his coffee. "So here I am. I haven't told him about the donkeys yet. That'll be a leap for him. But I think he'll get it. Eventually."

She spread her hands on the cloth covering the table, stroking it to smooth invisible wrinkles. When she looked up at him, he saw tears pooling in her eyes.

He wasn't sure what he'd said to draw up her sadness. He reached across the table and took her hands in his.

"You're lucky, Ryan. Lucky to have parents who see you, who get you, even if only a little bit. I don't have that, not really." She pulled her hands away and cupped them around her mug. "My mother is starting to come around, but my father is hopeless. It's the world through his eyes or it's not real."

He swept his arms open. "What could they possibly dislike about this place? It's perfect."

"It's not a place that either of my parents understand, it's—"

A banging on her back deck shocked them both to attention.

Before either of them could move, Adam knocked loudly on the kitchen door. Ryan pulled back so that a cabinet blocked him from Adam's view. He did it for her; having the town know that they were an item wouldn't bother him a bit. His Jeep parked in front of her house was a pretty solid giveaway, but it was her choice to reveal their relationship, not his. Old Southern manners ran deep.

"Just a minute," Cara called out. She motioned Ryan into the living room. "I'm sorry. I wasn't expecting Adam back until next week."

Ryan lifted her hand to his mouth. Her little intake of breath as his lips touched her skin made leaving that much harder.

"Will I see you at the community celebration this afternoon?"

The hope in her eyes made his heart do a little dance, but he shook his head. "I have a game."

She pulled her hand away gently. Slowly.

"Of course you do. You made me forget everything," she said with a smile.

"I'll slip out the front." He turned to grab his keys from where he'd left them near the TV.

"Ryan."

He faced her, once again shoving down the urge to carry her back upstairs.

"Thank you," she said. "For more than you know."

"I'll call you after the game," he whispered. "We can pick up where we left off. But this time, I want to hear more about you."

As he climbed into his Jeep, the scenarios of a future with Cara leaped back to life. Spending his days with Cara West sounded like heaven. So did creating a future with a woman who blasted the doors off his world without even trying. A woman he could love, a woman he could trust. A woman he could build a life with.

He wanted Cara more than he'd ever wanted anything or anyone. He turned into the drive of his ranch, grinning and tapping the steering wheel. The choice to live in Albion Bay was looking better every day.

CHAPTER EIGHTEEN

L ATE IN THE AFTERNOON OF THE DAY RYAN HAD made love to her, the day she'd confessed that she'd fallen in love with him, Cara had nearly finished weeding the last row of onions in the community garden when Molly walked up brandishing a glass of lemonade.

She'd been letting her thoughts roam as she worked, replaying every moment of the morning, wondering what she was going to do about her feelings for Ryan.

He hadn't returned her sentiments, had seemed surprised she'd admitted them, though he hadn't seemed shocked or frightened by her admission. Maybe it had simply been too soon for him. But she had to keep so much hidden, so much unsaid, that the emotion had demanded to be spoken.

"All work and no play makes a girl stoop-backed," Molly said with her characteristic throaty laugh. "I made this. My own lemons. See what you think."

Cara sipped the cool liquid. The sweet burst of citrus and mint slid into her. "It's delicious."

"I don't understand it, but it's really true that the things we grow ourselves taste better than anything bought from a store. Except chocolate. 'Course, I've never tried to grow chocolate."

"It grows in pods. In the tropics. You're safe from trying."

"Sam's teachers gave him five-star reports today."

Cara heard the pride in Molly's voice. She sometimes wondered what it was like to have a son who looked so much like his father, wondered if it made it harder for Molly to let go. David had been dead for four years, and she hadn't even dated.

"I heard *you* had quite a morning," Molly said with a sly glint.

Cara was still getting used to how fast news traveled in a small town. They hardly needed a newspaper; anything of the slightest interest made the gossip rounds before sunset.

"My decks being finished?" Cara said, turning back to weeding the onions.

"One Ryan Rea on early-morning rounds. C'mon, spill."

"I like him, Molly."

"Like is an overused word, but in this case it's downright pathetic."

"He has a good heart."

"*Cara.* This is me you're talking to. He has a hell of a lot more than a good heart."

"The good heart is enough."

Molly's face changed from a smile to what looked like might turn into a flood of tears. Cara pressed up from her crouch and wrapped her arms around her.

"Yeah," Molly said between sobs. "A good heart."

Cara just held her. Her own grief for her grandfather wove into Molly's for David. What was it about grief that made it easier to bear when you had someone to share it?

Molly pressed away and wiped the back of her hand across her face.

"We'll be late for the party," she said, pulling herself up and squaring her shoulders. "Those onions can wait."

They traipsed through the rows of carrots and the taller

rows of deep green kale and reached the street. The people of Albion Bay loved any excuse for a party or a homespun parade. Today's celebration was in honor of Mrs. Janis Petersen, the bee lady, who had turned ninety the weekend before.

Cara trailed Molly into the community center meeting room. Someone had run crepe paper along the ceiling in festive rows, and a cake the shape of a beehive stood on a table in the center of the room. She and Molly strolled over to congratulate Mrs. Petersen.

The old lady stood and waved everybody quiet. Then she took Cara by the arm.

"This young lady has only been here for three years," Mrs. Petersen said in her crackly voice. "That's eighty-seven years fewer than me." The crowd laughed. "But she's a gem, she is, and well"—she turned to Cara and handed her a crumpled envelope thick with its contents—"this is for you, honey. We all chipped in. It isn't much, but it should tide you over until you find a new job."

Blood rushed to Cara's cheeks, and her legs felt rubbery.

"I told them that at my age," Mrs. Petersen continued, "a person doesn't need any more gizmos. You're a *much* better way to spend birthday money."

Cara's cheeks flamed. She was both horrified and touched, but mostly horrified. What a web she had woven. She accepted the envelope and turned to the crowd. Most of them she knew, many of them fairly well. They thought they knew her well. Deception had never been her intention, but the heartfelt response of the community made it clear she had to craft a new path. She took a breath, unsure what to say. Ruining Mrs. Petersen's party with a blundering confession was not the way forward. She looked down at the floor and tried to gather her thoughts.

"For God's sake, Janis, don't embarrass the girl," Perk shouted from the back of the room.

Cara had never been so grateful for an intervention in her life.

Belva started a chorus of *Happy Birthday,* and the celebration rolled on with cake cutting and the usual town conversation. Cara took the plate someone placed in her hand and made for a table in the back of the room. Several ladies Cara didn't know sat at a nearby table, their backs to her. Within a few sentences they were deep in a conversation about Ryan.

"He's like those people you see on TV," one of the elderly ladies said. "He doesn't have real problems like normal folk."

"But he's such an honest, straightforward guy," the woman sitting next to her said. "You've got to love that about him. He could throw his status around, but he doesn't."

Cara's face flamed. She dipped her napkin in the glass of cold water she'd poured and patted it to her cheeks.

"He's just the kind of guy who would always tell you straight up where you stand," the second woman elaborated. "I don't have patience for lies, never did. What you see is what you get with that boy."

"What I see is not what I get," the first woman said. The other ladies at the table tittered.

Cara slipped out of her chair and edged to the door, grateful that all eyes were on Perk as he presented Mrs. Petersen with a mock key to the town.

She had to get out of there. She needed to think, something she'd been doing far too little of lately. And she had to make some adjustments.

When she returned home she saw the light flashing on her answering machine. She laid the envelope on the table beside it. She didn't want to count the money. She wished she didn't have the money. Every twenty-dollar bill represented a greater percentage of a townsperson's income than she could bear to think about. The money in the white envelope was tangible evidence of a plan gone wrong. Very, very wrong.

She pressed the button on the answering machine.

"Cara? It's Ryan. You're probably still at the party. I just wanted to tell you what it meant to me, being with you today." There was a hum of noise in the background and men shouting. "Hey, I'll call back later."

She flicked the answering machine to answer on the first ring. She had a lot to sort out before she talked to Ryan. Before she talked to anyone.

Later that night Cara bundled into the sweater Molly had given her and walked down to the beach north of the harbor docks. The moon cast a path of wavering light on the bay. The waves lapped at the beach in a slow, steady rhythm, a stark contrast to her darting thoughts.

A breeze blew a cold wind across the bay, and she wrapped her arms around herself, seeking warmth. She wasn't ready for winter. And she sure wasn't ready for what lay ahead.

She'd have to return the money.

And she'd have to own up to her deception.

But she had some time; she had a little time. Maybe she could orchestrate a rollout that would temper the blow of revealing her identity. Yet whatever plan she cooked up wouldn't work for everybody. Once word got out, a few searches online would reveal far more than she wished to. Worse, she had the feeling that those people she was closest to would likely take her deception the hardest. Molly and

Cain and Belva, not to mention Perk. And she couldn't bear to think about Ryan.

And she still hadn't decided what to do about the foundation. She wanted Bender out, but she didn't want in.

Back in her cabin, the chill had settled in and she gathered kindling to start a fire. When the phone rang, she jumped. She let it go to the machine.

"Cara?" That Ryan always said her name with a question mark, as if someone else might be answering, made her smile. So many things about him made her smile.

"I'm headed home. We won. Maybe you're our new good luck charm. How about a hike on Monday? It'd have to be early. We fly out around two. Call me."

She knew from the way her heart ached as she listened to his voice that she'd let everything go too far.

If she got her head on and figured out a plan, maybe then she could see Ryan again.

But not before.

Making love with Ryan, declaring her love for him, had just dug her in deeper, and if she kept seeing him, there'd just be all that much more to shovel her way out of. But she'd concluded that it wasn't in any way fair to dump her big revelation on him so close to the end of the season, not when the team was battling for the playoffs and he was so close to earning a Gold Glove. Ballplayers took their luck charms seriously. And though it sunk her to admit it, she was pretty sure he thought she was his. He'd just admitted to as much on the phone.

She slumped into the chair at her desk, knowing what she had to do. Just like texting, email was a coward's way out. But seeing him face-to-face, talking with him, would make controlling her voice, her face, impossible to do. He read faces well, too well. Even a phone message would give her away.

She tapped at her keys and wrote and then revised and then deleted what she'd written. Even a coward's way out wasn't easy. In the end she just told him that she couldn't see him just then, that she had some things she had to take care of and would be freed up in a few weeks.

If she left the door open even a crack, she'd be back in his arms in an instant. And though every bit of her wanted that, she knew it was the worst thing she could do if she wanted a chance for any future with him.

She sat back and read the message a fourth time; there just wasn't any way to improve it. She hit Send and slumped down in her chair.

Cara spent the better part of the next day tending to the garden behind her cabin. It had gone from romantically ill-kempt to downright overgrown. By two in the afternoon she'd made little progress. Her empty stomach finally drove her inside to raid the fridge. The irony that all she had was a Ziploc bag of frozen squash soup wasn't lost on her.

After her meal she washed the soup bowl and wiped down the table. Ryan's mug sat where he'd left it. She sniffed at it, but all she smelled was the dark aroma of the dried dregs of coffee. She considered washing it, but couldn't bring herself to wash away the last tangible bits of something he'd touched. The fragile mental state of a Brontë heroine came to mind, and she put her hands to her head. Maybe the road to madness started this simply, one bad decision following another until the snowball effect took over.

Or maybe she just needed a nap.

She pulled the bedroom curtains closed and lay across her bed. But images of being in it with Ryan rushed through her, stirring feelings that struck at her again and again.

Perhaps it was a good thing she'd promised Molly that she'd go with her to the community dance that night. Maybe it would take her mind off her dilemma just long enough for her to think. Realizing that *that* thought made no sense, she rolled over onto her side and curled up in a fetal position.

At least Ryan wouldn't be at the dance. He had a game in LA. She'd sneaked a look at the TV before she'd gone out into her garden.

After getting absolutely no rest, she pushed herself out of bed and dressed in a zombie-like state, pulling on her jeans and sweater with methodical motions.

When she went down to her living room to grab her keys, she stared at the TV. Knowing it was a bad idea, she switched it on anyway.

One of the Dodgers' hitters stood ready at the plate. He stepped into the next pitch, and she heard the distinctive sound as the bat hit the ball, the sound that said *distance*. The ball arched up, and the cameras tracked it to center field. Ryan leaped up and snatched the ball just before it went over the center field wall. He smiled triumphantly and hauled his arm back to fire the ball toward the infield.

The station showed a replay. A thrill rippled in her as she watched him run, leap, grab and then haul back his arm and throw. How could he possibly appear larger, more powerfully muscled, than she remembered? But she remembered the smile he shot out, perhaps to a teammate, perhaps to the crowd. She'd seen that joyous smile up close. Up very, very close.

The announcers spoke in excited voices about the likelihood of Ryan earning the Gold Glove if he kept up his stellar performance.

Their announcement scorched a path of resolve deep into her. Now was definitely no time to tell him that she wasn't the woman he thought she was. She had standards;

ruining another's person's life because of her bad decisions and poor timing wasn't an option.

Already she wished she hadn't sent the email. Surely she could've found ways to simply avoid him. She could've left town, left a sweet note, gone into the city, disappeared until the season was over and she'd made her decision about the foundation and...

She didn't *want* to make any moves. She didn't want to give up the life she loved. Her motives for sending the email had been selfish. And foolish. As if her calling for a hiatus until she could come clean was going to change his feelings when she revealed her deception? As if waiting a couple weeks was going to change how he reacted? What would she say? *Oh, by the way, I wanted to wait until the season was over to tell you I'm living a lie so I wouldn't disrupt your game.*

And then again, maybe her motives weren't entirely selfish—she'd feared she wouldn't be able to hold up, that she'd end up telling him everything, spilling out her heart. She'd been close to doing just that in the moments after they'd last made love. Too close. But the rationalization failed to offer her any comfort.

She watched a few more plays until her heart couldn't take any more.

She was turning out to be one hell of a wimp.

But one thing she was sure of, she wasn't going to wreck Ryan's season, no matter what it took.

More people than usual were crowded into Grady's feed barn by the time Cara arrived at the dance. Word must have spread that the barn dances were a lively and inexpensive way to have fun on an autumn evening; unfamiliar men and women crowded around the refreshment tables and clustered on the dance floor.

"Want to dance?" Cain offered his arm and a smile. "I mean since your boyfriend is busy, the least I can do is keep an eye on you."

"He's not my boyfriend," she said, sounding like a teenager denying the obvious.

"The lady doth protest too much," he said with a laugh.

Cain had earned an honors degree at Cal in literature. Evidently he knew his Shakespeare. And evidently he had her number. Or maybe everybody in town knew by now that she and Ryan were lovers.

She let him lead her into the dancing crowd. When the musicians broke into a slow dance, he took her in his arms and swooped her through the laughing couples. He was a handsome man, and she knew from his reputation in town that he was kind. Just as she knew from her reaction to his touch that it was nothing like the fire of desire she felt when Ryan touched her. She might try deceiving those in Albion Bay, but she couldn't deny that what she felt with Ryan was the real deal. That it was more than she'd ever imagined she'd feel for any man.

"You're a million miles away," Cain said as he led her off the dance floor and to the refreshment table.

A big hand-lettered sign proclaimed that all proceeds from the sale of the baked goods would go to the clinic fund. Cara bit back a sour laugh; there was nowhere she could go to escape the reality of the conflicting demands pressing in on her.

"Just thinking," she said.

"This is a dance, Cara. It's supposed to be an antidote to thinking."

"Where's Laurel?"

"She decided she wanted a landlubber."

"I'm sorry."

"Nah, we were never a good fit. Good of her to figure it out."

Molly walked out from behind a table spread with every kind of baked goody imaginable.

"We've made two hundred dollars already, and it's only seven thirty," she said.

Cara saw the way Cain looked at Molly. Maybe Molly was dense. Maybe there was a reason she didn't notice Cain's interest. And maybe Cara wasn't the only one with secrets. But one thing she did know was that these two friends of hers had sparks arcing between them, sparks that neither of them were letting ignite.

"Cain's looking for a dance partner," Cara said.

"I have to stay at the table," Molly said, her face coloring.

"I need a break; I'll take your shift," Cara said. "I'm good with money."

Why the hell had she added that? To her relief, Cain just offered his arm and Molly took it. Cara watched them as they moved into the crowd of whirling dancers. Maybe she'd done one good deed that day.

"I'll take one of those chocolate chip cookies," Perk said, rubbing his hands in anticipation as he approached the table.

Cara used the tongs and placed the largest cookie on a napkin.

"Two fifty," she said as she handed it to him.

"Robbery," Perk said, his eyes crinkling behind his thick-lensed glasses. "But even so, at this rate it'll take twenty years and four million cookies to raise enough money for the blasted clinic." He took a bite. "I told Belva that this piecemeal approach would stall any real effort. Half the town was baking cookies this afternoon. I couldn't even find my assistant. Turns out she was down at Belva's." He took another bite. "Mixing up cookie dough."

"I'll have what he's having," a tall man with piercing eyes said as he held out five dollars. "You can keep the change."

Cara knew a lord-of-the-universe type when she saw one. Out having fun in the country. The barn dance was a quaint novelty to him. He reached across the table and tapped Cara on the arm.

"That is, if I can have the next dance?"

"She has a boyfriend," Perk said in his deep mayor's voice.

Cara opened her mouth to correct him just as the man flashed a grin at Perk.

"Well, that's too bad. Guess I'll just have to dance with you."

"Cost you more than five dollars to get me out there," Perk stammered. "And I don't play for the other side."

Cara smiled. She knew the man had been teasing, but Perk was clearly flustered.

The man just nodded and walked off.

"Cheeky bastard," Perk said as he huffed over to where Belva sat with a group of locals.

Cara sold all the cookies and tucked the bills into the steel box at the end of the table. And she made a decision as she snapped down the lid. Either Alston found a way to give the clinic the money they needed for the complete project, or she'd find a way to do it herself. She could convince her parents to sign off on their share so she could sell the house in Southampton, the house her grandfather had left to her. So what if it'd been in her family for three generations? It might not fetch four million, but surely it would sell for two. It was a start. She nibbled at a crumb that remained on the cookie tray. A good start.

"You are the absolute *worst* sort of matchmaker," Molly

said as she came around the table. She looked at the empty trays. "But you're darn good at selling cookies." She flipped open the lid of the box and quickly fanned through the bills.

"It's all there," Cara said, attempting a joke.

Molly looked up. She wasn't smiling.

"I'm moving, Cara. To Novato. It's the only responsible thing to do. I lost David. I can't lose Sam."

Fear clouded Molly's eyes. Fear could force even the wisest person into very bad decisions. And didn't Cara know about that.

"The interim clinic will be up and running in two weeks, Molly. Two weeks."

"I've thought it through. Novato has a world-class hospital and good schools." She brushed cookie crumbs off the tablecloth. "I wanted to tell you first. In person. You've helped me so much."

"But this is your home." Cara wrapped her arm around Molly's shoulder. "Maybe give the on-call doc a chance. Fear can muddle your thinking."

"The whole project could stall. The county might not approve the permit—I know Belva said two weeks, but it could be months. I can't risk it. If I thought we'd really get a real clinic..." She tapped the steel box. "We both know cookie sales aren't going to cut it. Even with Ryan's gift, it's just not enough." She glanced at her watch. "I have to go. Tracy's watching Sam for me, and I promised I'd be home early."

Cara watched her go. Then she stacked the tin trays and folded the tablecloth. Couples would be leaving the dance in a few hours, arm in arm, going back to their homes and to their kids. But Cara would be going home alone.

It was the life she'd chosen, and she'd be going to the home she'd built for herself, the home that used to comfort her. But her hideaway was no longer the place of contentment it had been until recently. Loneliness had joined her there, disturbing her satisfaction and ease.

That loneliness now sank into her like a thick fog, winding its way through her and shrouding what little light remained in her heart.

CHAPTER NINETEEN

CARA WOKE ON MONDAY WITHOUT THE COMFORT OF her usual routine. Normally she'd shower, make coffee and head off to drive the bus. But not today. Though there'd been talk of petitioning the county for additional funds, that process would take time. The parents at the middle school had arranged an efficient system of car pools using a couple of the vans and their personal cars. Cara's car hadn't been needed. The staff had hinted that they wanted her to be free to look for a new job. She'd driven for the last time on Friday and said a wobbly goodbye to the kids. She'd see them around town, but it wouldn't be the same.

She stared out her bedroom window. Unplugged from her routine, she wasn't sure what to do. She checked her emails. Ryan wrote to say that surely she could find time to get together before three weeks were up. She stared at the screen, tapped out a very sensible list of reasons why she couldn't, then deleted her reply. No answer would send the better message even if it ran against everything she felt in her heart.

To clear her head she considered driving to the National Seashore at Point Reyes and walking the beach there or maybe hiking Mount Wittenberg. Instead she fussed in her kitchen, organizing and cleaning out drawers and moving objects around that didn't need attention or moving.

Then she poured a third cup of coffee and sat at her kitchen table, put her head in her hands and wept.

A few miserable minutes later, her front door banged, and she heard footsteps crossing her living room. She wiped at her eyes. There was absolutely no one she was up for seeing right then. *Maybe* she could handle Molly. But from the heavy sound of the footsteps, she was sure it wasn't Molly.

"Nice security," her brother, Quinn, said, grinning as he burst into the kitchen.

She leaped up and threw her arms around his neck. He closed her in a bear hug and to her dismay, she began sobbing against his shoulder.

"I was only gone two months," Quinn said. He eased her away and held her by the shoulders. "Want to tell me what's up?"

She pulled away from him and in between hiccupping gulps of air, she told him what had happened since she'd moved to Albion Bay. About the foundation, about Molly and Sam, and about the clinic.

He crossed his arms, narrowed his eyes and gave her his best gunslinger stare. It used to make her laugh. She wasn't up for laughing at the moment.

"What aren't you telling me?"

She paced to the window. There were no secrets between twins.

"I've been thinking a lot about Laci, about her reasons for killing herself." She stared out at her side garden and searched for words to put to her feelings. "I'd nearly put it behind me until Alston called with the news about the foundation." She ran her palm along the frame of the window, followed the newly painted wood with her fingertips. "Laci got swallowed up, engulfed by forces she couldn't handle."

212

Quinn crossed to her and turned her to face him. "You're not Laci, Cara. You're nothing like her. She was, well, fragile, I guess you'd say. Even before that loser left her."

"We didn't help her."

"You tried. We all tried. When she died, I felt guilty too. Guilty for our efforts not being enough. But you have to let all that go, Cara. Laci had to want help. She had to *choose* it. It's not your fault that she went searching for it in men and in a needle, things that couldn't fix what needed fixing." He shook his head and pinned her in the loving gaze she'd missed. "In the end, no matter how much family or community offered help, Laci had to want to save herself. You couldn't change that."

"Why didn't you say this before?"

"You were too raw at first—losing Laci after trying so hard to help her had your body and emotions stressed out. And then we found out that Grandpa was sick. Remember? And then didn't you break up with Roger around the same time?"

"But he was nothing to me. Not really."

"But it was just one more stress on top of everything else." He rubbed at his stubbled jaw. "And I could have been more understanding. I could've hung around and not run off to China that year." He slid his hands from her shoulders and grasped her hands, squeezed them. "And I did try to tell you that what happened to Laci wasn't going to happen to you. But I should have been there to support you."

She wriggled her hands free and closed her arms around him. His words entered her mind, each like a careful stitch helping to pull together the ragged edges of the wound she'd worked hard to seam up. As she rested her head against his chest, she exhaled the sigh she'd held for three years too many.

"You're here now," she said as he smoothed her hair with his hand.

She pulled back.

"Actually, why *are* you here right now?"

"My current version of support," he said in a suddenly cool tone. "And it may not be something you're going to like."

"Spill. *Now.* I don't like being part of your plots."

He glanced around the room and then settled a very determined-looking gaze on her. "Maybe we should have a cup of tea first?"

"*Not* happening. Besides, I've had three cups of coffee." She crossed her arms and took a step back. "I know that look, Quinn Barrington. I am *not* going off to China or wherever with you—I have *responsibilities* around here." Although now that she didn't have the bus driving, what did she really have?

"You'll wish it were as simple as refusing a junket. I'm here to kick your butt. To get you to get back in the game." He planted his hands on his waist. "You need to boot that SOB Bender out—put yourself in the president's chair and do your thing."

"Quinn—"

"I'm not kidding. You *love* to give, you love making sure every last dollar gets to those who need it or who can put it to use. You've always been that way, which is why Grandpa drew up his will the way he did." She opened her mouth to protest, but he held up a hand. "Don't try to deny it. Alston's kept me in the loop. I know what you've managed to do with the limited resources of your own foundation."

He rubbed at the back of his neck, a gesture *she* made when she was about to make her case for something, one of the many gestures they shared.

"Cara, you know I prefer to go to the sites, dig in for a few months, see what the needs really are. And I admit it—I get distracted by the causes themselves. I don't want to muck around with the finances and the contracts and all that. I want to roll my sleeves up or pull my boots on or spend two months with the people we help, building something with my hands. But I suck at the grant-making part of it, the weighing the benefits, the decision making. You love it; I don't. You'll make a great foundation president."

"Quinn—you *don't* get it. It's not just taking the reins of the foundation that's the issue—if I do that, I'll lose what I love about my life here, lose everything that's helped me keep it together and not melt down into a disaster like Laci." She caught herself rubbing at the back of her neck and pulled her hand down to her waist. She had to make him see. She needed someone to understand what was really at stake.

"Out here people see me just for who I am. I used to hate not knowing why people smiled at me. Why they agreed with me. Why... why they wanted to spend time with me. Not being able to trust people—to trust that the connection is genuine—it's no way to live."

"I can't change our family and neither can you," he said in a flat tone she rarely heard from him. "And you can't change that you have a *responsibility*. It might be one you didn't sign up for, but Grandpa's money, he made it fair, by providing something of value, and *someone* is going to disperse that money back into the world. It should be you, Cara, you and a team you put together. Not some hairball ass that Dad owes a favor, and not the government. Grandpa intended that the funds go to causes that can make lives better, and make the world a better place." He gestured to her small kitchen. "If you hide out here, you're making a choice about where the money goes, but you're letting a jerk direct it. You're giving him power he doesn't deserve."

"Laci felt worthless," she said, not following his train of thought.

Quinn whirled toward her.

"Cara, Laci's problem was different, we've been over that. You have to let all this stuff about her go." He tilted his head, as if her words were just registering. "And you can't possibly think that if people know you for who you are that they won't like you—that you're not worthy of people's affection."

She looked away. Hearing Quinn state her fear so baldly made it seem both immense and ridiculous at the same time.

"Cara—you're kidding me, right?

She shook her head.

He wrapped his hands around her neck and pressed his forehead to hers.

"You knucklehead, of course you're worthy. I love you, don't I? And Mom and Dad, for all their quirks, they love you. And then there was Grandpa. He was a pretty good judge of character. *He* liked you. Hell, even that mean old dog of his liked you. And she used to bite my ankles any chance she got."

Cara laughed as hot tears spilled down her face.

"And haven't you found friends here, in this town?" He wiped at her tears with his sleeve. "Don't they like you for being the delightful pain in the ass that you are?"

She slugged him, and he pulled away laughing.

"So... ?"

So... He was right, the jerk. "Yeah, I've got some good friends."

"And I repeat, *so*... ?"

So what did it mean? It meant that she was worthy of

being a friend, worthy for just being herself. She'd proved it, but holding on to the snarled tangle of her old fears, she just hadn't been able to let the realization register.

"Anybody whose affections change because of this isn't someone you should be friends with in the first place." He picked up a knife from her table and tossed it from hand to hand. "Lesson one in dealing with being a Barrington." He pointed the knife at her. "And you'll just have to suck up the hangers-on and trust that I can help you with that bit. It's not as hard as you think."

Why had it taken her so long to see what Quinn had nailed in less than half an hour? She grinned—how she hated when he was right and she was wrong. But this was one time she was happy he was right.

But then it struck her. She might be ready to face stepping into a leadership role in the world of philanthropy, especially if she could do it on her own terms, and she might be ready to face the reactions of her friends and the people in the town, but in no way did she feel ready to face Ryan. Now that she'd discovered what love felt like, she wasn't ready to lose it.

She turned away as a shudder ran through her.

Quinn spun her to face him.

"Want to tell me what other demons we need to slay today?"

He slashed his arms through the air using the knife as a pretend sword, and she couldn't help but smile.

She sat down at her table and told him about Ryan.

He shot her a grin. "Little Sis lands an All-Star, huh? Think he can get me tickets to the game tomorrow?"

He liked calling her Little Sis, even though he was only seventeen minutes older than she was.

"Quinn, it's not funny. I finally meet a guy I care about, and he thinks I'm everything I'm not." She closed her eyes.

"He wants everything I'm not."

"Hardly. He just doesn't know that you make twenty times more than he does. Might scratch his ego."

"It's not his ego I'm worried about. He has integrity. He hates lies. *I* hate lies. It's a disaster."

"You can talk to him and explain. But wait till the season's over. I want the Giants to win the pennant, and he's their best bat. Don't want to screw with that," he said with a laugh that told her he was only half-joking.

"You'll be glad to know I've already guarded against screwing up his season. I'm dodging him. And everybody else." She glanced out her kitchen window. "Which car did you bring?"

At this point worrying about cars in front of her house was ridiculous, but she couldn't help it.

"It's a rental. A Ford. Your secret's safe." He held out his hand. "Let's go into your living room. I have something I want you to see. Something worth flying three thousand miles to show you."

He sat down at her desk and fitted a thumb drive into the side of her laptop. A document spread across the screen with several columns of numbers, narrow paragraphs below each.

"Alston's suspicions about Dray Bender were right on." He reached and tugged her to his side. "Look at this."

She scanned the columns and numbers, read Quinn's careful notes alongside each.

"He's skimming funds," she said, not hiding her dismay.

"Boat loads. But he's shrewd. He's cleverly disguised his trail; we won't be able to prosecute him. Alston says we can't prove anything." He clicked the document shut.

"I still can't believe Dad hired him."

"He hired him by phone," Quinn said. "From

Australia. Our illustrious father didn't want to interrupt his golf tournament; an ostrich had just eaten his balls."

She laughed, but she wasn't so easily put off track.

"It's easier for you, Quinn, easier for you to step up. You fit the lifestyle. You love it."

Quinn pressed his lips into a line and crossed his arms.

"Don't tell me you don't," she said. "It's me, remember? I shared a womb with you."

He wrinkled his nose. "Damn close quarters." He looked around the living room. "Sort of like this place."

She punched his arm.

"Okay, I like your place. Especially the roads leading to it. Perfect for a new Veyron Legend."

"Not happening. This town already has one Bugatti. We hardly need another."

"I might like this Ryan guy."

"That's the problem—you *would* like him. I think I love him."

Quinn whistled. "If he breaks your heart, I'll flatten his tires."

"I'm touched. But my deception is a gap even an All-Star won't be able to leap." She leaned her hip against the edge of her desk. "I told him I couldn't see him for a while."

"Foul play, Cara. You're making his decisions for him. I might remind you, being male, that I know something of the male mind. We hate having decisions being made for us. *Hate* it."

"It seemed the right thing to do at the time. What happened to you not wanting me to mess up his season?"

"I said that before I knew how serious you two are." He jumped up from the chair. "Look, I can help you sort out your All-Star later. Right now we need to hop into my very slow, very boring rental car and go see Alston. Whether you step up as president of the foundation or not, we need a plan, one with teeth that can oust Dray Bender. Grandpa wouldn't like any of this."

"He should've had another plan," Cara said. She didn't like the defensiveness in her voice.

"Maybe this plan was his best shot. Maybe you were."

"You sound like Alston."

"Been practicing," Quinn said. "Cara, you can help thirty people or you can help thirty thousand—or three hundred thousand. You could fund this clinic you're so worked up about. Hey, you could even help me with Moonbird."

"*Moon* bird?"

"It's the name of a very special Rufus red knot, a bird that flies every year from the Canadian Arctic to Tierra del Fuego."

Quinn's eyes lit with the fire she'd always envied. He lived his passion, jumped into projects with his whole heart.

"This particular guy is a survivor—he's about eighteen years old, and all told, he's flown a distance greater than the one between the earth and moon."

"You've always loved your birds."

"He's a poster child—poster bird—for the whole species. The populations are in trouble. The lords of industry have discovered that the birds' critical meal for their midflight refueling—the eggs of the horseshoe crab in the Delaware Bay—are also a source for lysate, a chemical used by the medical industry to test for contaminants in injectable drugs or implants. Lysate is a two-million-dollar-a-year industry."

"Horseshoe-crab eggs?"

He nodded.

"Bender's probably funding the pharmaceutical firms you're trying to stop."

Quinn pressed his lips together, but didn't laugh.

He paced the room. She knew his stride, knew how he ran a hand over his face when he was thinking. She'd missed him. Since she'd moved to Albion Bay and he'd begun the work with migratory birds and the project in China, they'd rarely seen each other.

"We're hoping to get the Rufus listed as a threatened species. And maybe train egg collectors to harvest eggs in ways that won't kill off the crabs." He shook his head. "You don't want to know how they do it now."

"No fair playing the abused-creatures card," she said, only half-joking. "You know I have no defenses against that argument."

He stopped midroom and planted his feet wide. Jammed his hands to his hips. "The work will take more money than I have at hand, more than my foundation can grant." He grinned. "See, it begins already, the path to your door. Even I have an ulterior motive."

He sat on the arm of her sofa.

"You can do this, Cara. I know you. We can work out the details and the timing. Maybe keep it under wraps for a while until—"

"Quinn, you don't get this town. And you don't know Ryan. I can't explain what I feel for him. It just feels right, like he's my future. I'm afraid to lose that. And stepping up, acknowledging who I am, acknowledging my connections... Well, I'm afraid that will destroy what Ryan and I have... destroy everything."

She heard herself say the word *afraid* and remembered the advice she'd given Molly: fear never solved anything. She pressed her palms against her eyes, felt the pressure, savored the calming darkness.

She could run, but she couldn't run forever. And she was tired of hiding.

Quinn was right. It was time to face her fears. Time to

step up. Time to stop using Laci as an excuse and instead stand in the shoes of the person she'd become. And it was time to take her own advice and practice turning up the positive. High time. She'd been touting the benefits of the practice, but now she needed to dig in and use it.

She pulled her hands from her eyes and held a hand out to him. "I get it," she said. "I'll do it—I'll take the position."

He took her hand. "I knew you would."

"No gloating."

"Can't promise that." He grinned.

As his fingers curved around hers and he pulled her from the sofa, she felt a strange lightness, a lifting, as if the forward motion of her decision was already at work in the world and in her. But the slow churn in her stomach warned her of the shadowed path ahead.

"But I still need some time."

"Alton's a master," Quinn said. "I imagine he can pull off a stall or two."

She grabbed her purse from beside the TV.

"Nice TV," Quinn said. "Not like you."

"It was a gift from Ryan."

"He must love you if he bought you a forty-eight-inch flat screen."

"You have been living in cities for *way* too long. Love is not determined by the size of screen diagonals."

A grin curved across his face. "Sis, someday you'll realize that most guys still believe size matters."

She ribbed him as they got into his rental car and then quizzed him about his recent trip to China. But with each mile they covered as Quinn drove toward San Francisco, Cara ran her decisions over and over in her mind.

Maybe there'd been another way to carve out her life, one not based on deceit, one that wouldn't have required such machinations. But what she'd done had seemed her

222

best shot. And though she was a realist, the trace of optimist in her fought to hold on to the hope that she wouldn't have to give up loving Ryan. The realist knew better, of course. She'd be lucky to come out of the web she'd spun with any friends at all.

And wouldn't *that* be ironic, running off her true friends through her own actions, through the inescapable confession of her reasons for seeking out real friends and community in the first place.

Ryan bounded into the hotel bar and spotted Alex right off. Now that he was out from under the paternity suit, Boston took its place once again as Ryan's favorite road trip. He loved the bookstores and the sophisticated fans. A guy could actually go out for a drink and not be interrupted by well-meaning fans. They'd wait in the wings until he paid his bill, then politely hold out whatever they wanted signed. Very civilized, Boston.

"I'll have what he's having," Ryan said to the bartender. Copley's Bar was a favorite with its wood-paneled walls, old gaslights and cushy leather barstools that had probably been used for a century. It was no wonder his mother loved visiting her girlhood home. Everything had an air of mystery, of history, and the city was damned gorgeous. Except in the winter. He'd never want to live buried under ice and snow; he hadn't gotten that gene from his blue-blood mother.

The bartender plunked down a tumbler with a couple fingers of amber liquid. Ryan lifted the glass and sniffed. "Angelfire?"

"You bet," Alex said as he sipped from his glass. "Best whiskey around."

223

"Good for plotting and scheming?" Ryan sipped at his drink, felt the fire burn down his throat. "Because we've got some work ahead."

"Whatever you say, this fundraiser you're planning must have you jazzed. You hit the hide off every ball tonight. The cycle, man—Boston is still reeling." He raised his glass in a low-key toast.

"I sweated that last hit—wasn't sure it would get over the fence." He'd never hit for the cycle before; there was nothing like a single, a double, a triple and then a two-run homer to set off a good buzz. "Eight games to go. We win three and we've clinched our spot in the playoffs."

"Don't count those chickens yet," Alex said with a finger wag.

"I'd rather count up the advance pledges we've got for the Albion Bay clinic."

"I'm in. Scotty and Chloe are too. We'll have to work on the rest of the guys. Most of them have never heard of Albion Bay."

"The Pacific-Union Club is all set. Walsh pulled some strings for me."

"You have it bad, my boy," Alex said over the rim of his glass.

"You're one to talk. Scotty told me you're going to the Pribilof Islands for marine mammal research at Christmas. You do realize those islands are *between* Alaska and Northern Siberia? It'll be thirty degrees—*below* zero. Not counting wind chill."

"Wind chill's nothing compared to telling Jackie I wouldn't go with her," Alex said with a somber look. "I'll be the one in the Nanook suit, bearing flasks of brandy."

"What we do for love," Ryan said, shaking his head.

"We're talking love now, are we?" Alex drew his brows together. "Glad to know these efforts are for the big prize."

"It's for the clinic," Ryan countered, not yet willing to lay himself bare.

A smile lit Alex's eyes as he raised his glass. "Well, then, here's to the clinic."

CHAPTER TWENTY

CARA SIPPED AT HER COFFEE AND READ THROUGH THE foot-high sheaf of papers that Alston had given her after she and Quinn had met with him in the city.

Alston had been pleased that she'd decided to take the reins at the foundation and had agreed to put protocols in place that would help maintain her anonymity, at least for a while. Both Quinn and Alston were doubtful about her ability to delay, but Alston had gone along with her plan. She'd have to fly back to New York at the end of the month and meet with the board; there was no way around that. And she'd have to deal with Bender sooner than she'd hoped. It hadn't helped that her dad had given Bender her cell number. Bender had wasted no time in calling and leaving two artificially calm and yet subtly threatening messages. She'd asked Alston to do all he could to keep him away from her, at least for a while. It was going to be a pleasure to eventually oust the guy.

If all went well, she'd bought herself three precious weeks.

She shoved the stack of papers aside and sorted through her emails, reading for a third time Jackie Brandon's request that Cara meet her later that afternoon at a café a few miles from Albion Bay.

She had no idea why Jackie wanted to meet with her so

badly. She looked Jackie and Alex up on the Internet. When she saw the stories about Jackie—*Lady* Jacqueline Brandon—and how she'd shunned her aristocratic past to set up shop as a veterinarian—with marine mammals, no less—a creeping unease swept her and she wished she'd stalled or at least put off meeting with Jackie for a couple of weeks.

Jackie's face had seemed familiar on the day they'd helped with the sea lion, but Cara still couldn't call up where she'd seen her before.

Scores of scenarios shot through her mind as she drove the winding road to the café. Perhaps Jackie had heard she lost her job driving the bus. She shuddered at having to discuss job leads. Maybe she wanted to ask Cara to volunteer at her lab, or maybe she needed an assistant in her office up there.

But as Cara pulled into the gravel parking lot next to the café, the sense of unease squeezed deeper into her chest.

A grove of redwoods nearly hid the rustic building housing the Lagunitas Café. It served the locals as general store, coffee shop and meeting place. Jackie sat at one of the outdoor tables, shaded from the sun by an umbrella that looked to be as old as the faded wood siding.

"It's a lovely day," Jackie said in her perfect English accent as Cara sat at the only other chair at the rickety table.

Weather was a safe topic.

But as Jackie leaned back and appeared to be taking Cara's measure, Cara was pretty sure she hadn't brought her out here to talk about the weather.

"Perfect," Cara said in a light tone.

"I'm not one to draw out suspense," Jackie said as she leaned forward and rested her elbows on the table. "I met you at Wimbledon. Six years ago. Your brother and your parents were with you. I remembered you because you took such an interest in my work in the Okavango Delta."

Cara sat silent, stunned.

227

"And because your brother was tracking the Moonbird," Jackie continued. "Not many people even know it exists." She gestured to her own face. "I had short hair and a hat; it doesn't surprise me you had trouble placing me. But I remember you well. You suggested that I write to your grandfather to fund my work."

Jackie appeared calm, as if revealing world-shattering secrets was an everyday occurrence.

"I want to thank you for that suggestion," Jackie added. "His funding allowed me to finish up the species survey."

The memory flashed. "You had seats next to ours." Though her heart raced in her chest, Cara felt like a load was lifted from her shoulders. She looked Jackie in the eyes. "Busted."

"Not exactly." A smile teased at the corners of Jackie's lips. "I'm good at keeping secrets." She pointed to the hand-lettered sign listing a variety of espresso drinks. "Want a cappuccino? We may be miles from nowhere, but they make a killer cappuccino."

Cara nodded. While Jackie went in to get their coffees, her mind raced almost as fast as her pulse.

Jackie placed the coffee in front of Cara, the smiley face the barista had swirled into the milky foam staring up at her.

"Thank you," Cara said. "For the coffee." She looked up at Jackie, who held her face in the gentlest of expressions. "And for not outing me. I'm about to do that myself."

"I don't envy you that. I know something about running from the restrictions of a world you'd like to leave behind."

"I saw the reports online," Cara said, feeling that she should own up to her snooping.

The press had hounded Jackie after Alex had rescued her from a crazed kidnapper intent on murder. He'd risked his career and his life to save her, but all the press had wanted to report was the discovery that Jackie was an aristocrat hiding her roots. A wealthy blue-blood hiding out as a vet in a bungalow in California made for sensational headlines.

Cara lifted the cup to her lips, but it was too hot to sip. "Life has its ways of forcing one's hand."

"Doesn't it just," Jackie said.

Cara told Jackie in the plainest terms about her dilemma. About her grandfather leaving her the foundation, about her reasons for seeking a quiet life in Albion Bay. About the problem of the clinic. And about Laci.

"I'm afraid I'll be pulled back into the world I grew up in, afraid I'll be engulfed and never come out. Afraid I'll lose everything I've worked for."

A thoughtful expression played across Jackie's face. "I know that feeling. And I'm sorry to hear about your friend. It's tough when you want to help and can't."

Cara lifted her chin. She could've looked the world over and not have found anyone like the strong and experienced woman sitting before her. Jackie was a person she could trust.

Cara told her about Ryan and about her decision to cut off her relationship with him until she could pull herself together and tell him the truth. She hauled in a breath and added, "What I'd like to know, what I *need* to know, is how Alex took it—you not telling him about your family."

Jackie waved her hand as if batting away an unpleasant memory, but then surprised Cara with an impish smile.

"One thing about a life-threatening trauma, it puts other factors in perspective. In the end, Alex wasn't happy that I hadn't trusted him enough to just tell him the facts."

Cara stirred the foam in her cup and watched the happy face dissolve into a frown of bubbled milk.

"I wasn't ready to tell anyone. I'm still not. Maybe I should have trusted Ryan, but things between us got rolling and then it seemed too late to say anything."

"You love him," Jackie said.

"I hadn't intended to."

Jackie laughed.

"You're like me, thinking that love is something you can control with your mind. It doesn't work that way." She tapped a finger to her head. "Love alters activity in your brain," she said in what Cara imagined was the voice she used to lecture colleagues or volunteers. "And it triggers parallel changes in the other person's body and brain. Love doesn't belong to just one person; it resides in the resonance between you. If it's love, it'll survive all this."

"But—"

"It's *science*, my dear." Jackie shoved her sunglasses to the top of her head and nailed Cara with an unwavering gaze. "You ignore such a strong power at your own peril. I've discovered that love is a stronger power than fear; I owe that lesson to my relationship with Alex. But if you don't use the power love offers, other forces will shape your brain and your life for you."

Cara clasped her hands under her chin, aware of the prayer-like gesture. At that moment, Jackie and her words—her wisdom—were a tether to the life she dreamed of. A floating sensation washed through her, and she held herself still, as if any movement might banish the hope coming to life inside her.

Jackie tapped one finger on the table. "I nearly lost everything by trying to ignore love. It bites back if you ignore it." She lowered her sunglasses against the glare of the sun. "All those other details? You'll sort them out."

"I want to work them out *before* I tell Ryan, before I tell anybody, but especially before I tell him." She pushed her cup away, to the center of the table. Her hands were shaking, and she clasped them in her lap. "And I don't want to do anything that might upset him right now, not while he's playing so well and the team is in the running for the pennant."

Jackie shook her head. "If I've learned anything being married to Alex, it's that you can't rule your life by the game."

"Even if I were prepared to tell Ryan, it's not like I can just go up to him and say, *Hey, you know the simple woman you're so into? Well, I'm really one of the richest women in the world; I just didn't want anyone to know.* Like that will fix everything and he'll go out and hit home runs?"

Jackie pressed her lips together. Cara wished she could see her eyes.

"I understand your reasoning. It's considerate of you and perhaps not off the mark." She removed her sunglasses and set them on the table. When she looked up, there was no humor in her eyes. "There is something you should know. It's not like I'm telling a secret since anyone with an Internet connection could turn this up. Alex told me that Ryan was horribly deceived by a woman claiming that he'd fathered her child. The truth came out recently that she'd schemed the whole thing, but Alex thinks the experience, the deception, left its mark."

The coffee soured in Cara's stomach. She put her hands on the table to steady herself.

"I thought you might not know," Jackie said. "And I can see that you didn't," she added as she read the shock in Cara's face.

Cara swallowed and tried to counter the heaviness weighing down her limbs, sinking her into the chair. "That explains the sense I've had of being auditioned. It's subtle, but I feel it with him, as if he's testing my motives. You'll laugh now, but I think he was worried that I'd like him for his money."

Jackie didn't laugh. And Jackie's response made Cara realize they had more in common than she'd surmised.

"I'm afraid I'll lose him, which is crazy since I don't even have him—since we don't even know twenty things about each other. But I love him. That's the thing that scares me the most."

It was the first time she'd said it without reservation. Each word was like ballast, tilting the ship of her life and sending waves crashing over the sides.

Jackie put her elbows on the table and leaned toward Cara. "Fear can make you overlook opportunities. And when we let fear win, we dream smaller dreams."

Cara flattened her palms against the table and straightened her spine. "I do have a plan. But what you just told me, well... my plan may not be enough."

She told Jackie about the strategy she'd set up with Alston. And hoped that Jackie was right, that love was a stronger power than fear.

As she drove back to Albion Bay, her hope wavered. But she knew what she had to do. Step by step, Alston had said. She had a couple of weeks to go step by step. By then the baseball season would be over. By then she'd have sorted out the best way to break the news to her friends in Albion Bay.

Yet no matter how carefully she rehearsed her lines in her head, she dreaded breaking the news to Ryan. No plan she came up with for that confession featured anything close to a happy ending.

CHAPTER TWENTY-ONE

MOLLY WAVED FROM CARA'S FRONT DECK AS CARA pulled into her drive.

"Amazing, amazing news!" Molly said as she ran out to greet Cara. "Ryan has arranged for a fundraiser in the city for the clinic." She spilled the news before Cara could even turn off the car. "His teammates are coming. They have money, Cara, loads of it. It's Wednesday, after the day game. It's at a swanky club; Belva told me it was the Pacific-Union." She opened Cara's door for her. "Belva's in such a state, I think she's going to bust an artery. I told her to wait till we have a clinic."

"That's wonderful," Cara said, unable to laugh.

There was no way she was going into the city and *especially* not to the Pacific-Union Club. Her dad was a member. He liked to throw his weight around when he came out west, and it was the most exclusive club in San Francisco. There'd be people she knew there. She had weeks of work before she'd be ready for something like that.

"It's the break we've been waiting for, Cara. Imagine getting to make our case to people with real money. I have a great feeling about it."

"Does this mean you're staying in Albion Bay?"

"Yes. I thought about what you said. And this fundraising effort gives me hope. Plus Sam doesn't want to

233

change schools. He wants to stay and play with his team. He pulled out all the stops. Told me—me!—that the stress of moving would be worse for his health than any risk of an attack. The little weasel."

Cara did manage to laugh at Sam's antics.

Molly walked Cara to her front door.

"You'll need a dress," she said. "I'm going to make one for you. I think red. You'll look stunning in red."

"That's sweet of you, Molly, but I can't go. I have to—"

"You *have* to go! Ryan put this together. I can think he cares about this town, about my son, and I'm sure he does, but we all know he's doing it for you."

"I don't think that's true," Cara said. At least she hoped it wasn't.

"Don't be ridiculous; the guy's smitten. And I *am* making you a dress. I'll come over tomorrow and fit it on you."

Cara raised her hand to say an emphatic no, but Molly fisted her hands to her hips.

"I won't let you refuse. You're too darn modest. This is the biggest thing to happen to help this town since Grady built the feed barn. We have to look our best. And by the way, Cain's my date. Four years is long enough to mourn, and it's not doing Sam or me any good. Anyway, Cain asked to go with me and I accepted. But he'll have to buy a suit."

She turned on her heel and headed to her car.

Before she stepped in, she held up two fingers in a victory sign. "See you at two tomorrow—two o'clock sharp."

Ryan sat in his office at the ranch and made the last of the calls that topped his to-do list. Everything was set for the clinic fundraiser at the Pacific-Union Club that night. Then he called his dad and convinced him to come out for Thanksgiving. He didn't tell him about the donkeys, but he rehearsed the lines he'd say when he saw his dad face-to-face. It was time to own up to the truth about where he was headed with his life. But his lines for Cara, they didn't come as easily.

But the dreams did.

He walked along the west fences, checked and double-checked them. And decided to add a higher section of wire to the most vulnerable section that bordered the creek. But it wasn't donkeys that filled his mind as he worked. The dream he'd had late in the night was as real as the steel wire he molded with his hands.

He shut his eyes and remembered.

At first he'd been caught in the cloying darkness of his recurring nightmare. His arms were bound, his shoulder pinched and aching, and he was stuck in layers of a filmy yet cloying web twisting around him and crushing his chest. Elaine Mooney's image rose before him, her head thrown back in a soundless laugh. Terese stood over him, drawing the web tighter until he gasped, unable to breathe. He fell, tumbling, and no force of his will or his struggle slowed his sickening descent. A faint light appeared, burning brighter as he fell toward it.

He crashed against a hard surface and felt the bruise forming on his back. Pushing against the web binding his arms, he struggled to free himself, but each motion only shrank the cords tighter around his body. He gasped as the web contracted around him, wrapping him in an icy, otherworldly chill. Death called to him seductively with a siren song promising release from the pain racking his body, enticing him to give in. He knew this nightmare too well, had thought he'd left it behind. But never before had there been any light. Pain laced through him as he turned his head toward the glow in the periphery of his vision. The light flared brighter and moved toward him like a slow-moving tumbleweed. He forced himself to focus on the river of light trailing behind the approaching specter. He fought to take a breath and not give in to the darkness. But he couldn't hold on and his world went black.

Fingers touched his throat. Warm, almost searing. He wanted to cry out, but his body heeded no command of his mind. Slowly the fingers eased the web from his throat. He gasped in a breath and opened his eyes.

Cara crouched over him, her fingers working at the web, loosening it. Light glowed around her and trailed her body as she bent closer to him, leaving a phosphorescent image against the pure darkness surrounding them. He saw alarm in her eyes as she focused on unwinding the cable-like strands of the web, her hands dissolving them as if they were no more than spun sugar. He couldn't take his eyes off her face. Wordlessly she freed the web from his shoulders and the pain eased. She worked her hands down his chest, pulling at the strands that bound him. His heart stuttered, and he tried to speak. She put her finger to his lips, her eyes sending a silent warning. She traced her palm down his bare chest, and he realized he was naked.

Sensation returned, and he felt grass pressing into the skin of his back, smelled the sweetness of the air. She drew both her palms to his shoulders, and heat and wholeness pulsed under her touch. A smile lit her eyes. He reached for her and the light fell away from her like a cast-off cape, revealing the beauty of her body. He pulled her close, his lips blazing as they met hers. The warm, honeyed taste of her dissolved the chill that had threatened to snuff him. His pulse raced as he slid his body against hers. When she tipped her head and deepened her kiss, astonishing power passed

236

between their lips, coursed into and through him, the kind of power that beat at the heart of every living thing. A power that called forth life and hope and not death or despair. The all-consuming power of love.

A horn sounded in the distance, growing louder and insistent. With each blaring blast, more of Cara dissolved from his arms. He clutched at her image, willing the spell-breaking noise to stop, desperate to hold on to the sensual, heart-binding, life-giving bliss.

But the noise grew louder, and she disappeared.

He'd jolted up in his bed. In the blur of waking he'd grabbed his blaring alarm clock and thrown it against the wall. Then he'd sat, stunned, at the edge of his bed, running his hands over his chest and shoulders. And lower, to his throbbing hard-on. Though his body screamed for release, after such a dream his heart wasn't in a quick hand job.

He wanted Cara and he would have her. However long and whatever it took. Her last email didn't daunt him. In fact, it fired him up for the challenge of winning her.

He didn't need a dream to tell him she was the one. How he'd managed to find a woman with such integrity, such kindness and a body that sizzled passion through him the way hers did, he didn't know. Maybe there was a God. Just in case, he said a silent prayer.

He repeated the prayer as the memory of the dream once again ran through his thoughts. And then he turned his mind and body to the task before him.

The sun was high before he finished running the wire in the westernmost section of fences. He'd have to reinforce two sections and put in two taller, stronger posts. He checked his watch. That work would have to wait until another day.

Before he left for the stadium he pulled the zippered garment bag that held his favorite suit from the back of his closet. The last time he'd worn it had been to his grandfather's funeral. At least this time it would see a happier occasion.

CHAPTER TWENTY-TWO

A LEX AND SCOTTY HOPPED OUT OF RYAN'S JEEP, STILL laughing about the razzing they'd taken from the guys in the clubhouse. Though their joking had been good-natured, several of them had wisecracked about the big price tag to help Ryan land a lady. Knowing they didn't mean anything, Ryan took it in stride. Most of the team were attending the fundraiser, and Ryan hoped those who didn't might soften up and send a check.

Ryan took the stub the valet handed him and followed his buddies up the stairs of the Pacific-Union Club. The brownstone was one of only two buildings in the area that had survived the San Francisco earthquake and resulting fire in 1906. The club was exclusive, members only, exactly the sort of venue to entice guests who'd otherwise never have a chance to cross the club's threshold.

One of the Giants owners was a member and with Hal Walsh's help, Ryan had talked him into sponsoring the party to raise funds for the Albion Bay clinic. The guy was so happy that Ryan had signed the six-year contract with the team, he threw in expenses for the food and drink as well. His enthusiasm made Ryan think that his agent could have negotiated a higher salary, but fifty million was more than enough. If only he'd had it up front, he could've funded the clinic himself.

They'd arrived a few minutes early. Waiters in variations of tuxedos and other staff in red and gold uniforms hustled efficiently through the marbled foyer, setting out food on long, high tables.

Ryan had worried when the game had been tied in the eighth that it would turn into one of those legendary fiascoes that went nineteen innings. But Alex took care of that in the bottom of the ninth. When the Giants won four to three, Ryan had never been so happy to have a game end.

"Look at that ceiling," Scotty said as they nosed around the various rooms. "It must've taken an army to carve that thing."

Although the arched ceiling was impressive, Ryan wasn't interested in the architecture. His mind was on the speech he'd rehearsed. His job was to make clear the need for the clinic.

His mind was also on Cara. He wasn't sure she'd come. He'd emailed and left two phone messages, but she hadn't replied. He'd gone over every damn moment they'd spent together, but he'd been unable to add any of them up into a reason for her silence.

He'd rehearsed a few lines for her too. If she attended the fundraiser, he hoped the event and the conversation he'd imagined having with her more times than he could count would melt through whatever qualms she might've dreamed up about him.

But he had a hell of a lot more confidence in the words he'd strung together about Albion Bay and the clinic. His feelings for Cara didn't lend themselves to rehearsed lines and imaginary conversations. Hell, his feelings for her didn't lend themselves to anything that made sense.

"Champagne?" One of the tuxedoed waiters held out a tray of glasses.

Ryan took one and handed it to Scotty. Took another and started to down it.

"Whoa, a toast," Scotty said, tilting his glass to Ryan's. "To the Ryan Rea Clinic."

"No way it's being named after me. I have an aversion to anything being named after me." He clinked Scotty's glass. "But here's to success tonight."

Scotty motioned Alex over to join them.

Alex pulled an envelope from the breast pocket of his suit jacket.

"We wanted you to have these," Alex said. "To get you started."

Ryan opened the envelope. The check on top was from Alex's foundation. Ryan squinted in the light. It really did say eight hundred thousand dollars. He looked at the second check. Three hundred thousand dollars written on the foundation account Scotty had set up with his wife, Chloe.

"People always like to come in after the first gifts," Alex said. "And now you've got those first gifts, so they don't have any excuses."

"This is more than a gift," Ryan said. He still wasn't used to money. Maybe never would be.

"Hey, let's get this thing funded," Alex said. "Who knows, my intrepid wife might be the first customer, given the risks she takes. Consider it insurance."

Sam Rivers came bounding through the hall. He looked tiny and fragile in the cavernous space.

"Great hit!" he said as he ran up to Alex. "Mom let me watch the game in the sports bar down the street. She thought we might hit traffic and be late, so we came to the city early." He turned his face up to Ryan. "I practiced my story."

Sam was Ryan's ace for the night. He'd asked Sam's mom if it would be okay for Sam to recount his experience of the day Ryan and Cara had to rush him to the emergency room in Novato. He'd also used the opportunity to ask if

241

Cara was planning on coming. Molly had assured him she was *and* told him Cara had a surprise for him. He tried to wrangle the surprise from her, but she'd told him to wait and see.

Ryan snagged an iced tea from a passing waiter and handed it to Sam. "You're our DH."

"I'd rather be a pinch hitter," Sam said, suddenly serious. "Designated hitters only get to hit in opposing leagues. I want to hit a lot."

The men laughed. Sam colored, but then grinned and laughed along.

"Where's your mom?" Ryan wanted to ask about Cara, but took the oblique route.

"She's in the ladies' room. With Miss West."

"Perhaps they should call it the West Clinic," Scotty teased. "She seems to be the instigating factor."

Ryan glared at him.

"Just saying," Scotty said with a shrug and a wink. "C'mon, let's get this boy something to eat."

Scotty and Alex walked off with Sam, leaving Ryan standing in the center of the marble rotunda. It reminded him of pictures he'd seen of the Roman Forum, of the sort of place where treachery and intrigue unfolded over the ages.

He saw a flash of red pass between two of the columns. Then he saw Molly. But she was wearing a blue dress. Then the flash of red came around the column nearest him, and his throat swelled with the surging of his pulse. Molly looked pretty, but Cara looked like a goddess. A goddess who'd cast a spell on him. All his carefully rehearsed words fled his brain.

Cara stopped when she saw him. Then she linked her arm through Molly's and sauntered toward him. He couldn't read her expression, but Molly was beaming.

"Told you he'd like it," Molly said. "I told her you'd like red."

More than like. The soft fabric of the dress hugged Cara in every way possible. She had on makeup that made her eyes sultry, almost smoky. Her lips were a deeper shade of red than the dress, and he couldn't help staring at them. He'd give anything to forget about the party and plunder those lips. Heat shot to his groin at the thought of kissing her.

"Hello, Ryan."

He hadn't heard Cara's voice for days. It rolled over him like a warm tropical wave and had him wanting to have her in just such a wave with him, naked, laughing and—

"Yes, hello, Ryan." Molly said, her voice pulling him out of his fantasy.

Cara watched his face. With her standing close, he could see from her gaze that he wasn't struck off her dance card. In fact, unless he was losing his ability to read faces, he was pretty sure she was as glad to see him as he was to see her.

"You came," he finally managed to get out.

"Molly is a persuasive agent," Cara said, squeezing Molly's arm.

He fought the urge to drag Cara off to one of the alcoves and kiss her senseless. Maybe he'd do it later. Why a club that normally didn't even allow women inside had alcoves obscured by palms made no sense. The sheltered, intimate spaces were perfect for what he had in mind.

"Mom!" Sam ran up and tugged his mother's arm. "They have a picture of Babe Ruth! You have to come see!"

"See you two later?" Molly asked, as if he and Cara might be able to disappear. At that moment, Ryan wished they could.

Cara pulled the shawl that rested on her arms up to

cover her bare shoulders. "Molly made this too. Dyed to match."

"It's lovely," Ryan said. "You're lovely. Look, whatever I said or did to make you back off, I—"

"You didn't do anything."

She shivered, and he took off his jacket.

"Here," he said, offering it.

"Molly would kill me," she said. "This dress is her pièce de résistance."

Molly had that right. If he'd had in mind resisting Cara, he couldn't have, not with her looking like the hottest woman on the planet. He shrugged back into his jacket. Then he pulled the envelope Alex had given him from his pocket.

"One million one hundred thousand dollars," he said, tapping it with his fingers. "Alex, Scotty and Chloe wanted to give us a good start." He hadn't meant to put such emphasis on the word *us*. It had dropped from his lips like a phantom force.

She looked down at the floor. When she looked up, there were tears pooling in her eyes. He had expected her to be happy, but tears? Maybe it wasn't enough. Maybe he shouldn't have said *us*. Maybe it spooked her.

"Hey," he said, "we'll get there. A couple of the guys are thinking about getting places up near Albion Bay. They're going to pitch in."

She shook her head. "It's wonderful, what you're doing. Truly wonderful."

But she didn't look like she thought it was so wonderful. Maybe it was just the stress of having to dress up and come into the city; maybe she was overwhelmed by the opulent club and felt out of place. Yet she didn't look out of place; she probably looked finer than any woman who'd been in the joint. But looking the part and feeling at home, well, didn't he know the difference.

"Let's go find Scotty and Alex," he said. "Chloe's coming up in an hour. She'll miss Sam's speech, but not the party." He wanted to say, *Let's duck into one of the back rooms and let me get that dress off you*, but that would have to wait.

"Sam's giving a speech?"

"I pulled out all the stops," he said with a grin. "Who can resist an earnest twelve-year-old?"

She smiled then. And he knew he was in love. Like a throw that landed just right, snug in the pocket, it all came together and he just knew. He reached for her hand, twined his fingers in hers. And took a breath when he felt her hand relax in his.

"If I'd known you were going to be dressed to take everyone's breath away, I might've had you give the speech instead," he said.

He leaned down and kissed her cheek. To his surprise, she curved into him, and he held her, felt the motion of her breathing against his chest. She was a strange one—he never knew what to expect. But he'd take this. Just as he started to trail his fingertips down the curve of her back, she drew away and looked toward the door.

"Your guests are arriving," she said. "Looks like I'll have to share you."

"There's always the after-party."

She pressed her lips together and shook her head. He regretted saying such a bull-headed thing. The fire that drove him to her left any finesse he once could've mustered in a pile of ashes.

He greeted his teammates and the people from Albion Bay. Belva had on some sort of spangled blouse that caught the light as she moved. Cain and Perk wore suits, Perk looking much happier in his than Cain did. Most of the guys from the team headed for the bar.

Twenty minutes later he hadn't spotted Cara once in the crowd milling through the club. But when Sam stepped up with him to the microphone, he saw her standing in the back of the room.

Ryan announced the funds they had in hand and pledged half a million of his own.

"But before we go on," he said with a wave at Sam, "this young man has a story for you."

Sam pulled himself up, beaming.

Then he proceeded to give a blow-by-blow and very embellished account of Ryan's car and the drive to the hospital.

The crowd laughed.

"Um, Sam?" Ryan said as he leaned down to Sam's eye level. "Tell them about your asthma."

"Oh, that. Well, if Ryan hadn't had such a fast car and been able to drive like Jimmie Johnson, I might be dead now."

He turned to look at Ryan. "That what you meant?"

"Sort of," Ryan said over the roar of laughter from the crowd.

Ryan called Belva up to the stage.

"If you folks can match the funds we have in hand, we'll be eighty percent there. I don't want to do some sort of public step-up routine. I know that's what people say works, but it's not my style. If you're inclined to help, Mrs. Rosario will—"

"Call me Belva, please," Belva said, crossing her arms and smiling out at the crowd.

"If you're inclined to help, *Belva* will be accepting your checks and pledges. She'll send out an email and let you all know how we did." He paused and scanned the faces he was coming to know. "It means a lot that you all came out for this."

246

And before he said something mushy that he'd regret, he stepped away from the mike and down off the dais.

People clustered around Sam and others headed off to the bars scattered throughout the club. He went up to the nearest bar and ordered a beer. Next he was going to find Cara and kiss her, no matter how much she'd try to wriggle out of it. He knew there was fire between them. He just needed to stoke it a bit and remind *her*.

"That was a good show up there," an unfamiliar voice said.

He turned to face a man his height, maybe an inch shorter, with a face that said he'd spent years in the sun.

"Ryan Rea."

The man took his hand. "Henry Beaumont." Henry took the martini the bartender handed him and motioned Ryan to the side of the room.

"You know, if you really want to wrap up this project, you should hit her up."

He pointed to Cara, who stood with Molly near one of the potted palms.

Ryan laughed. "You're kidding, right? She drives the school bus. Or did before the county cut the funding."

"Now you're the one who's kidding. That's Caroline Barrington. Her twin brother plays on my polo team when he's in the Hamptons. Her family's worth billions."

Ryan took a swig of his beer and swallowed down his urge to tell the guy he was nuts. If Beaumont really traveled in high-money circles, maybe he was considering a donation. Ryan couldn't afford to insult a donor.

He laughed a second time. "Perhaps she just has one of those familiar faces."

Even as Ryan said it, Cara looked up at him and smiled, gesturing as she spoke to a group of ladies from Albion Bay. But when her gaze shifted and she saw the man he was talking to, her face froze midsentence and she turned and raced out of the room.

"Excuse me," Ryan said.

Her reaction drove the stranger's words through his mind. More than that, it drove images through his head, images of inconsistencies he'd seen but ignored. The valuable painting and book, the way she handled the coffee machine, her utter lack of reaction to the Bugatti, her studied ease and well-practiced mannerisms. Seeing her in New York...

Damn, he *had* seen her in New York. And none of it made any sense.

She was fast, he'd give her that. But as he raced down the marble hall, he was faster.

He reached her and wrapped his fingers around her wrist, turning her to face him.

"Whoa, not so fast. Mind telling me why you're in such a hurry?"

She didn't look at him, just pulled her hand from his grip. "I saw you talking with Henry."

"You know him?"

"Not well. My... my brother does."

"Is it true?" He bit back the anger threatening to flood him.

"Is what true?"

"That you have billions?"

She tipped her head back. "Ryan, I—"

"Just tell me if it's true."

"Not quite." She put her hand to her throat and held it there. "Not till next week."

He felt like someone had pumped air into his veins.

"Then you *are* Caroline Barrington?"

"Some part of me is."

She lowered her hand and started to reach toward him, but whatever she saw in his face made her pull back and clasp her hands in front of her.

She stood unmoving. Silent.

He tried to convince himself that she was the same person she'd been just minutes before.

But she wasn't.

The force of her deception crashed into him.

He couldn't breathe.

He turned and dropped his forearms on the cold marble wall. If it hadn't been solid, he might've punched it.

Still might.

Anger and images of the day he'd stood in court—publicly defending himself and his honor against the deceit of a lying woman—washed over him, buffeting him. Slamming into him. And now he discovered that another woman had lied to him. And not just any woman. *Cara* had lied to him. Deliberately. Systematically. *Cara*. He pounded the marble under his hands. She'd pretended to be something, someone, she wasn't.

Images and emotions came flying at him—the summons to appear in court, the day he'd read over the DNA test results, the day he'd admitted to himself that he'd been taken in by the woman scheming to mold his life to hers. And then there were the images of Terese. Of Terese lying to him, knowing in her bones—all the damned while *knowing*—that he'd have slain dragons for her.

Cara might not have been scheming to bend him to her plans, but she'd deceived him. And worse, he'd fallen in love with a woman who wasn't what she appeared to be. A woman who'd deceived not only him but an entire town.

She'd pretended to need a job, for God's sake. She'd pretended everything. Hell, he didn't even know who she really was. A name. A family. But the person?

Emotions flooded him so fast that he knew he couldn't trust his reactions.

"Ryan, I—"

"I need some air," he said without looking back at her. "Alone."

He went out the first door he saw and found himself facing the massive spires of Grace Cathedral. Her family probably built it. Or could have. He raced across the street and hailed the valet.

Lies.

They ripped out your heart and left an abyss in their wake, a fathomless abyss that couldn't be crossed.

CHAPTER TWENTY-THREE

CARA STARED OUT THE WINDOW OF HER HOTEL ROOM. From thirty stories above, San Francisco looked like a glittering octopus. It was a fanciful thought, something to take her mind off her betrayal of Ryan. But the city didn't hold her attention for long. It couldn't. What she needed to escape was inside her, and nothing on the outside could heal that inner pain.

After the scene with Ryan, she couldn't face going home to her cabin or returning to Albion Bay. Just as she'd imagined, everything had gone horribly wrong. The look on Ryan's face told her more than she needed to know. Though she hadn't directly lied to anyone, she had lied by omission and she knew it. Omission was just as much a lie as telling a direct untruth. It didn't matter what her motives were, what her dreams had been, what scared her. There was no way to paint her actions in any other light but a negative one.

She'd walked the streets for hours before checking in to the hotel, and though it was now well past midnight, there was no way she could sleep. She replayed the scene with Ryan over and over in her mind. He hadn't given her a chance to explain. She hadn't expected that he would. And she didn't blame him. How exactly was she going to explain the motivation for her deceit? Or tell him she was waiting for the right moment to reveal that she'd kept her true identity from him—that at her core and in her heart she really was the simple woman he'd fallen for? That her money didn't make any difference?

But the money did make a difference. It was the reason she'd run from her roots and started her quiet life in Albion Bay, away from all the hype and constraints and expectations.

He'd reacted with such burning anger; likely everyone else would as well. On the outside they might not be unkind, but she'd never live again at the heart of the town, as one of their own.

She'd lost Ryan and when the news broke, she'd soon lose everything else she'd spent three years building, moment by moment, action by action.

At least she'd felt for a brief time what it was like to belong to a community. Maybe that was enough. Maybe she could start over somewhere else.

Of course she could. People did it all the time.

She closed her eyes.

She didn't want to start over. She wanted Albion Bay and Molly and Sam and Belva.

She wanted Ryan.

She opened the lock on the mini bar and fingered a bottle of wine. Then she put it back and snapped the lock shut. What she had to sort out would take more than a miniature bottle of wine.

No part of her wanted to return to New York and go through the motions of being Caroline Barrington again. That was the coward's way out.

She had to burn a new path no matter how much it scared her. And now that she'd met Ryan, now that she'd felt what it was like to love a man—a man who lit a fire in her that time could never extinguish—a flame of courage burned in her. She could only hope that its power was strong enough to fight back her fears.

Exhausted by adrenaline and drama, she drew the curtains, shutting out the lights of the city, and then fell across the bed.

~⌒~

In the morning Cara picked at the breakfast she'd ordered from room service. It hadn't helped her state of mind that she'd slept fitfully and when she *had* slept, images of Ryan had snaked through her dreams. Worse, an anguished Laci had risen in the darkness, reaching pale arms toward Cara and crying out. But Cara couldn't reach her, and she'd slipped back into the blackness. In the strange fog between dreaming and waking, Cara knew that Quinn was right: she wasn't Laci. They'd tried to help her friend fight her demons, and they'd failed. But they'd failed because Laci couldn't, wouldn't, face what it would have taken to pull her life together. Though her grief for Laci might never dissolve, Cara felt the tight knot of guilt release in her belly.

And she made the decisions she'd fought with in the dark night.

She shoved her breakfast aside, pulled her cellphone from her purse and called Alston. He listened as she told him to draw up the papers for her to sign, that she intended to start running the foundation immediately. He asked if she wanted him to draft a letter to fire Dray Bender, but she told him she wanted to do it herself. She owed her grandfather that, at least.

And she might as well get some pleasure out of her new position. She was looking forward to telling Bender what she thought of him and his shady practices and his kickbacks.

Her cellphone rang as she went to slip it back into her purse.

"Cara, thank goodness you answered." Jackie sounded alarmed.

"Is something wrong?"

"When you didn't return home last night, Ryan called here. I had to talk both him and Alex out of calling the police."

She glanced at her phone and saw that there were messages.

"You heard what happened at the club?" she asked Jackie.

"In colorful detail; I can understand why you didn't answer any calls. I knew you were holed up somewhere, that you were okay, but the guys were hard to convince." She heard Jackie take in a breath. "I would've done the same."

"I stayed in the city last night. I needed to think. But I'm headed back now."

"You sure you're okay? Do you want me to come with you?"

"And leave the marine mammals of the world without their champion for an entire day?"

"I could do some work up at the lab."

She told Jackie about her decisions and her conversation with Alston.

"I have to do this on my own, Jackie. All of it. And I have to talk with Ryan. He may slam the door in my face, but I have to try."

"The madder he is, the more you mean to him."

"You don't know Ryan."

"It's true, I don't."

There was a commotion in the background. Cara heard Jackie tell someone to put an animal under anesthesia and that she'd be right there.

"Anesthesia sounds good to me right now," Cara said, trying for a humorous tone. "I'll stop by. Maybe you could numb my heart."

"The trouble with anesthesia is that when you wake up, nothing will have changed. Look, drive safely, okay? I have plans for you."

Jackie hung up without explaining. Cara stared at the phone. What plans could Jackie have for her?

Cara called for her car and headed back to Albion Bay. She didn't care if it was seven in the morning—Ryan had awakened her earlier than that, was it only a week ago?

She would say her piece. And then it was up to him.

Hope was a devious devil. It drove her ever forward while at the same time the ground was washing out from under her feet.

Ryan's Jeep was in his drive. She stepped out of her car, smoothing her moist palms against the silk of her party dress. It was hopelessly out of place against the backdrop of the ranch. And perhaps so was she.

But she would make Ryan say it to her face.

CHAPTER TWENTY-FOUR

RYAN GAVE UP ON THE ESPRESSO MACHINE AFTER THE third try and made coffee in a pan on the stove. He grabbed at a mug and heartily wished that after he'd returned from the Pacific-Union event the night before that he hadn't dived into the bottle of scotch that now sat empty on his kitchen counter. His head was thick and his thoughts thicker.

The knock at his door sounded like a giant hammering on an anvil. He really shouldn't drink scotch. He shot a look to the clock in the hall. Seven forty-five. Adam had finished the last of the stalls in the barn the day before, so Ryan wasn't expecting him. Maybe he'd left some tools.

He threw the door open.

Adrenaline flooded him when he saw Cara. Cara safe. Cara unharmed.

Even his best anger management tools hadn't prevented him from putting his fist through his bathroom wall at three in the morning when he'd driven to her place for the third time and she still hadn't returned home. Not that he'd wanted to see her. He just wanted to know she made it home safely.

He only hoped he could rope in his driving wish to throttle her.

"May I come in?"

He hated that voice. It was the proper voice of highfalutin' city people, of TV news anchors, the measured voice of cold reason.

But as he looked into her eyes, he thought maybe not. Maybe he was mistaken. She didn't look like a woman driven by reason. If she were, she surely wouldn't be standing on his front porch. Not in the face of what he had loaded up to say. Not wearing a party dress that looked like she'd slept in it.

Against his better judgment, he nodded and stood aside to let her in.

"Thank you," she said.

He heard the waver in her voice and saw the tremble in her lips. But his heart shut, hard, like steel walls around a compound. A wavering voice and trembling lips weren't going to do her any damn good.

"I had hoped to tell you about all this properly, in due time."

There it was, that formal, *snotty*, tone. It stoked the fire in him, and he barely contained his roar.

"Properly? All this?" He waved his arms. "Like there's a *proper* way to tell a person that everything about you is a lie? Like there are specific words that make deception okay?"

He *was* roaring now and couldn't stop.

"The bake sales, Cara? The community raising money to tide you over? Do you even *know* how hard it was for some of those people to give? Some of them are on social security and welfare—how will you explain to them that you took their money when all along you had billions of dollars?"

He crossed his arms. It was the only way to keep from punching another wall. "I earned my money. I know what it takes—what it took—for them to give."

"No one *earns* ten million dollars a year. Or a billion. It's a responsibility, Ryan. At least I don't spend my money on fancy cars and houses and God knows what else."

The pounding in his head intensified. He tightened his grip on his elbows. Maybe he would smash a wall.

"You're going to lecture *me* about responsibility? About how I spend my money? That's *ripe*. Really ripe."

"And *you*—what about you? What about the walls you've built around yourself? Not even Mother Teresa could gain entrance to the inner kingdom of Ryan Rea. How long will you let events of the past color what's happening now, color how you see people?" She drew herself up. "I'll have you know that I *never* lied to you."

Her voice didn't waver now. And from her comments, evidently she knew about the paternity suit. She'd known and still she'd kept up her deception. She was in full-on defense mode—he could see it from the way she squared her shoulders. Good. If she wanted a battle, she'd have it. He planted his legs wide and fisted his hands on his hips.

"Deception is the silent partner of lying," he said hotly.

The veins in his neck throbbed, and her eyes went wide as she backed away.

"I can see that you can't forgive me," she said in a quieter voice. "But don't say anything to anyone." She took another step back. "Please. I want to tell the people here in my own way."

"And in the meantime you continue to hoodwink them like you have me? Are you a pathological liar? Or do you just get your kicks from fooling those who trust you?" He felt heat rush through him. Instead of cooling down, his anger was ramping up. "And how do you figure out the *right* way to tell people that you've been hiding who you really are? That you took their money, that you could've funded a clinic on your own? That you could've funded *ten* clinics? I suppose you have some fine-tuned plan for that?"

She shrank back against the wall. Great. All his studied

practices for turning up the good did absolutely nothing when he needed them.

"I couldn't have funded the clinic," she said in a low voice. "In fact I can't fund it until next month, maybe even longer. I don't expect you to understand that. But please, Ryan," she said with a look that made him feel like the bully he was being, "just give me this—let me break the news in my own way."

She turned to the door. And then she turned back. "I wasn't lying when I told you I loved you."

She tossed her hair and walked to her car. And drove off without looking back.

A wrecking ball could have hit him and he wouldn't have felt it, he was that stunned. She loved him? *Sure*. The woman was damned good at deception. And she was still practicing it.

No, not practicing; she'd already perfected her technique.

He closed his eyes.

He rubbed at his head, then found himself rubbing at his chest, at a spot over his heart. Both his head and his heart ached. But Alex was wrong: pain and inconvenience did not add up to love.

He slammed into the kitchen and downed two Tylenol with a mug of cold, bitter coffee. Then he stared at nothing.

And he let his brain exercise some control over his emotions.

He could've probed deeper about the painting and the book—his instincts had told him they were out of place in the home of a woman who had little money.

And he should've pressed her about New York. She hadn't said she wasn't there; she'd just put him off with that crack about a familiar face. He'd overlooked the way she evaded personal questions with her smooth manners and easy way of turning conversations. He'd fallen for her misdirection because he wanted to believe it; he wanted her answers to fit his illusion.

He could've asked her more about her life, but no, he'd just spilled his guts about his own life, rambling on about his dreams and blathering about his fight to get his head around money.

And she'd let him.

She'd listened to him.

She'd listened...

Even through the throbbing in his head he began to recognize the role he'd played in this charade. He'd been stuck in his *own* damn deception.

He'd been one hell of a fool.

CHAPTER TWENTY-FIVE

THE NEXT MORNING RYAN SLIPPED INTO A SEAT IN THE last row of the crowded town hall meeting room. Evidently everyone in Albion Bay had seen the flyers plastered around town announcing the special meeting.

A few hours before, he'd ordered the same breakfast at the diner that he always did, but he'd pushed it around his plate, unable to eat. The fight raging in him snuffed his hunger and made it hard for him to think. He had a game later; he should've stayed home and worked out, stretched, and then driven to the stadium. As it was, he could stay for only half an hour; he had to make batting practice on time.

But no amount of working out or stretching was going to dissolve the heaviness that hung in him. He'd spent the hours he should've been sleeping tracking back through every conversation he'd had with Cara and then, when he was sure he wouldn't sleep, he'd spent hours reading about her on the Internet. And while it was true that she hadn't directly lied to him, the result was the same: she'd managed to trigger every distrusting cell that still lived in him and trigger them good. And though he didn't want to admit it, the woman she was—Caroline Barrington, wealthy socialite—kicked up a wall of wariness he'd never felt as strongly before. He'd never been outflanked by a woman, and Cara could outflank just about anyone on the planet if she wanted to.

Excitement buzzed in the room as Belva and Perk stepped up to the podium. Ryan gave a silent prayer of thanks that he'd had the foresight to have Belva take the pledges at the fundraiser. There was no way he could stand up in front of the good people of Albion Bay and say anything at that moment. What should've been a celebration to announce the funds they'd raised for the clinic had morphed into a macabre charade. At least for him it had.

He looked around the room and didn't see Cara. A public meeting probably wasn't her idea of a good forum for breaking her news. She probably had an army of PR people helping her figure out how to spin her confession. PR people could spin anything—they'd made aborigines believe they needed deodorant, hadn't they?

But as he sat there, the thoughts he'd wrestled with all night and through the morning kept surfacing—relentless, nagging and undeniable. They gnawed through his cynicism and forced him to face the role he'd played all along in Cara's drama.

"This thing working?" Belva said as she tapped at the microphone. A sharp squeal of feedback from the PA system shot through the room. "Guess so," she said with a shrug. She drew herself up and held out an index card, squinted at it and then laid it on the podium. "I don't need notes." She tilted her head toward the mayor. "Perk here thinks I do, but I don't." She tapped the card with her finger. "The zeros on this card are a bit overwhelming, but I can tell all of you that thanks to Mr. Rea's efforts and those of every one of you who pitched in, we have two and a half million of our four-million-dollar goal for the clinic build-out."

Ryan's heart sank as the crowd cheered. He'd thought his teammates and some of the front office brass would've been more generous, would've given enough to move the needle closer to the goal. But they didn't live out here, and a remote country clinic wasn't at the top of their lists. And two and a half million *was* a good start.

Cara came in through the side door that led to the kitchen. The purplish circles under her eyes told him she hadn't slept any better than he had. To his surprise, she didn't take a seat but instead walked up to Belva and whispered to her.

"Cara would like to speak to us," Belva said as she stepped aside and stood by Perk.

Even from where he sat in the back of the room, he could see Cara's hands trembling. She placed them on the podium.

"Nothing has ever meant so much to me as the relationships I developed since moving to Albion Bay," she said.

It was a good thing there was a microphone, because her voice was barely above a whisper.

Ryan saw the puzzled looks on the faces of the people seated near him. Cara speaking about the relationships she'd developed with people in the town wasn't the segue they'd been expecting.

"This town is a true community," Cara went on, her voice becoming steadier. "You help each other, care about each other, reach for the future together while at the same time helping each other heal the wounds of the past." She stopped and looked out at the crowd, but the sweep of her gaze didn't reach him. "I'm not sure that you realize how rare that is in today's world."

People were listening intently now, but Ryan felt tension building in the room. Belva had crossed her arms and though a half smile curved her lips, her body language betrayed her bewilderment at Cara's speech.

Cara pulled an envelope from her pocket and handed it with shaking hands to Belva.

"I rehearsed scores of ways to say this to you"—she turned and looked back out at the crowd—"to all of you. But the simple truth is what you deserve."

A murmur waved through the room.

"Unfortunately, sometimes... Well, maybe always, there's nothing very simple about simple truths." She turned back to Belva and pointed to the envelope.

"I'm returning the money that you all so generously raised for me and—"

"Oh, honey, for goodness' sake, you don't have to do that," Belva said, stepping closer to Cara.

Cara held out her hand to keep Belva at arm's length.

"But I do"—she pointed to the envelope again—"I do have to. In that envelope is not only the money I'm returning, but also a pledge for two million dollars for the clinic. From me."

A few people clapped before a stunned silence fell over the room as what Cara said sank in.

For a simple woman, she had a flair for drama. But Ryan reminded himself that she wasn't a simple woman. What she was, he was still trying to get a grip on. All night he'd imagined the life she must've come from. Embarrassment had wound through his feeling of betrayal as he'd remembered his foolish fear that she'd love him only for his money. He'd tried to dam up the burning feeling of shame, but it oozed through his defenses and squeezed hard, taunting him.

"I... I wanted to come out here and have a fresh start."

She said it as though she'd been in prison and didn't want people to know of her criminal past. Ryan crossed his arms and pushed back into his chair.

"I wanted to be accepted for who I am and what I could contribute."

She wrung her hands in front of her and shut her eyes. Then she opened them and gestured to Belva.

264

"I will be forever grateful to have been a part of your lives here."

She said it as if she was already gone, as if her life in Albion Bay was over.

People shifted in their seats, uncomfortable with the tone of her speech.

But he knew what was left for her to admit.

Though he sizzled with the anger he hadn't tamed, some part of him wanted to leap up and go to her. He could only imagine the anxiety flooding her as she took a breath to go on.

"Next week, I will take my place as president of the Barrington Foundation, an institution whose sole purpose is to find individuals and groups and organizations who need money and then provide that money. It was my grandfather's wish that I take over his position at the foundation after his death, take over his duties and follow up on his legacy. And though I fought stepping into his shoes, I know that since I share his vision and his values, I should be the one... I need to be the one..." She shook her head. "No, I *want* to be the one to carry on where he left off." Her fingers tightened on the podium. "I want to continue the good work—the great work—he gave his life to."

Her voice cracked, and Ryan thought she would cry. But instead she angled away from the mike to clear her throat before again looking over the group.

"I can't turn my back on my responsibilities, and I can't turn my back on him. I thought I could, I thought I had reason to, but I can't. And because of his vision, because of his hard work and the careful and conscientious shepherding of his resources, I can provide the rest of the funding for the clinic."

A few people clapped again, jarring into the silence of the room.

"I wanted to tell you before the news is announced in the national press next week."

She put her hand to her throat; Ryan now recognized it was a gesture of fear.

"Maybe it was a coward's way out, but I chose to hide my family's wealth, my wealth, from all of you. I was afraid that you wouldn't accept me. Or that you'd treat me like I was used to being treated back East."

When the women in front of Ryan shifted, he did the same. He needed to see her face as she spoke. He needed to use all his senses, because he wasn't sure his mind was getting the right message.

"My purpose for coming to Albion Bay three years ago was twofold. I needed to get away, away from poseurs and hangers-on, from the fake and the phony. But more than that, I needed to get away from those who only got close to me because of my money."

She licked her lips and looked quickly, sightlessly, around the room.

"I had few friends, not many real ones. Not the kind who like you no matter how silly you are or who call you on your crap. No one called me on anything—they played up to me.

"But they didn't know me. They didn't... they didn't care what was important to me. I was just a piggy bank to them. Men and women wanted to be with me, be seen with me, Caroline Barrington, but not Cara. They wanted the dividends that the association with me and my family name brought them.

"And no, I'm not boasting; my name carries value. I know that quite well."

She pushed herself upright. "But no one gave a damn about me, the woman who likes to harvest vegetables and tell silly jokes and drive a-a rickety b-bus."

Held in place by her words and by the feelings those words were lancing through him, Ryan knew he'd be late, but he couldn't move. He looped his hands around his neck so he wouldn't check his watch.

"I know that sounds selfish, poor little rich girl with no friends. But it was hell. Hell to live without trust."

She tipped her chin down and then lifted it suddenly. Her eyes were glassy. Even from the back of the room Ryan could see the tears backed up in them. She waved her hand out toward the crowd.

"*You* know friendship. And you know love, real love. I see it every day in your faces and in your words and in your actions. I wanted to live with that same kind of friendship and love.

"And so my second reason for coming here was to reach out for that friendship. I wanted to have friends. I wanted to be a friend. I wanted... God, I just wanted to be Cara. To be a part of everyday life here, with all of you."

The spell of stunned silence broke as people began whispering. Ryan heard shock in their voices. But worse, he heard small-mindedness and a sense of betrayal lacing through some of their words, the same small-mindedness and sense of betrayal that had made him act like a jerk.

They'd thought she was one of them. They hadn't had a long, restless night to think things over. They hadn't had an opportunity to look Cara up on the Internet and find out that she was one of the richest women in the world, to think about what could drive a person to do such a difficult and desperate thing as to hide her identity, to run from wealth.

He'd had time to think it over. And it hadn't made a damn bit of difference.

And just acknowledging that made him want to laugh at his whacked-out responses. He apparently wanted the town to forgive her while he nursed his grudge and felt righteously offended.

But as he stared at her, and saw—hell, *felt*—her dammed-up tears, the angry thoughts and negative emotions he'd wrestled with started to dissolve in the face of her sincerity.

"I've taken up too much of your time," she said over the continuing murmurs. She looked out over the room, and her eyes met his. What she saw, he couldn't guess, but even at a distance he saw the tears begin to spill down her face before she turned away.

"I understand that many of you may be angry with me." She wiped at the tears with her sleeve. "And of course you should be. I expected, demanded, trust from you, but I didn't extend it. I just assumed..." She angled toward someone in the front row. "Molly... Molly, I'm so sorry."

Molly stood, but she didn't move near Cara or step away. She stood with both arms wrapped around her body, watching and listening. From behind her, Ryan couldn't tell what she was thinking.

"And even if none of you forgive me, I want all of you to know that being here, working beside you and living in the heart of this town, has shown me love in action. For that, and for your acceptance of me, a stranger, I thank you. I won't forget your lessons and your welcome."

Without fanfare, she turned and walked out the door she'd come in.

Ryan dashed out to the parking lot and saw her pull away. He knew better than to follow her, but he sure didn't want to stick around to hear more of the townspeople's reactions to her revelations. His own blistering, conflicted reaction was enough to deal with. And he didn't want to answer the inevitable questions: Had he known? Had he suspected? What did he think? He'd probably punch somebody.

As he crossed the Golden Gate Bridge and drove toward the stadium, it struck him that other than her words to Molly, she hadn't said she was sorry, hadn't apologized. She'd just given the reasons for her choices and left. He had to admire her for that.

~

To Ryan's surprise, he played well against the Dodgers. Focusing on the game kept his mind from racing out of control.

The team had one of those nights that felt orchestrated. Matt Darrington made a barehanded grab at short that would've taken Ryan's fingers off. That the guy pivoted and fired it home had Ryan cheering in the outfield. When Scotty got a base hit in the sixth, it had everybody jazzed. He couldn't help but laugh at the bemused look on the Dodgers' first baseman's face as Scotty landed on the bag. No one expected pitchers to hit well; not many could hit at all. Maybe he'd get Scotty in the cage over the winter so his hits wouldn't be such a rare occurrence. All night guys made plays that stretched them to the limit and thrilled the crowd. It was like there was something in the air, but only he and his teammates could harness it. The Dodgers had to suck up the loss and scratch their heads.

After the game, he cornered Alex in the clubhouse.

"I need to talk to you," he said.

Alex pressed his lips together. "I already heard about the town meeting. One of Jackie's volunteers filled her in."

"Cara didn't trust me."

"*Should* she have trusted you?" Alex pulled his jersey over his head and balled it in his hands. "Money makes for some major complications."

"Right. I'm still getting used to that part."

Since he'd signed the big contract with the Giants, Ryan had had to shut down his social media accounts.

269

Women were offering him embarrassing things. Women who had no idea who he was, what he cared about, what plans he had for his life. And not only women. People he didn't know were asking for money for this and that, sharing their laundry lists of needs. Now that he'd had a taste of the craziness big money could bring, he'd begun to understand Cara's unenviable position. She and her team would have to be wise and knowledgeable to avoid getting ripped off. Hell, they'd need to have armor just to keep the unscrupulous at a distance.

Alex crossed his arms. "If you'd known about her situation, would you have pursued her?" He gave Ryan the hawk-like stare he was famous for, the stare that put fear into the hearts of even the most hardened veteran pitchers. "If you'd known she was richer than the Queen of England, would you have danced with her, dated her, allowed yourself to fall for her?"

"Cara never felt like a choice. It was like some power rearranged me and nothing made sense but each step to win her."

Alex raised a brow and nodded. "I get that. Sounds familiar. *Real* familiar." He rocked back on his heels and narrowed his eyes. "It's called love, Ryan. But don't shoot the messenger."

Hearing a tough-ass slugger like Alex say the word *love* shocked reality into him. He cleared his throat, wishing he could clear his mind.

"Got some making up to do?"

"I think I burned all my bridges," Ryan admitted.

"I don't picture you as a quitter." Alex turned to his locker and proceeded to finish stripping. "And sometimes anger is the only thing that burns through our thick-headed ability to fool ourselves," he added. "Especially when it comes to women."

270

Ryan drove by Cara's place after the game. There were no lights on, and her car wasn't there. He idled at the end of her drive and then decided morning would be a better time to talk with her. Long ago he'd made a vow not to have difficult conversations after dark; they never turned out well for anyone. But as he sat staring out the window of his Jeep, his thoughts spun out of control. Maybe she'd been in an accident. Maybe someone had heard the news and had kidnapped her and was holding her for ransom. Maybe she was in the arms of some rich guy who shared all the elements of her world.

He slammed his palms against the steering wheel and pulled back onto the highway.

Maybe he was a nut job and needed to get some sleep.

CHAPTER TWENTY-SIX

THE SOUND OF A HEAVY TRUCK PULLING INTO HIS drive woke Ryan. His housekeeper had turned his clock so he couldn't see the LED numbers in the dark. He banged his knee on his dresser as he fumbled for his jeans, then he grabbed at the clock. Five thirty. Who the hell was making a delivery at that hour? It couldn't be the feed store; they'd delivered the week before. He jammed his legs into his jeans and yanked a shirt over his head.

"Mr. Rea?"

Ryan nodded at the wiry man standing on his front deck.

The man tilted his head in the direction of the truck. "Got some mighty tired donkeys for you."

Ryan squinted at the truck. "You're a week early."

"Didn't know that." The man scraped off his cap. Ryan saw the exhaustion puckering the skin around his eyes. "The rescue center was supposed to tell you I was on my way."

Though Ryan would've liked to have had the week to take care of a few final details, there was no use busting the guy's chops. And though he'd planned to head to Cara's first thing that morning, he'd have to help the guy settle the animals in first.

"Then let's get on with it. Want some coffee?"

"Only if you have a to-go cup." The man nodded again

toward the truck. "I think we'd better get those animals into the barn." He paused and appeared to be assessing Ryan. "You see, little Liza—she's my favorite—well, she's about to foal. Any minute."

Ryan wasn't sure he'd heard right.

"Now?"

The man nodded, reminding Ryan of a poorly constructed bobblehead. A bobblehead who'd just told him one of his newly adopted donkeys was about to give birth.

"The barn's open," Ryan said. "It's the one on the right. I'll be right there."

He slid into his boots and grabbed his gloves from the table beside the door. He picked up the pan of coffee he'd left on the stove the day before. It looked worse than cowboy coffee and it was cold, but it'd have to do. He poured two mugs and raced to the barn.

They glugged the cold coffee and set their mugs onto the gravel drive. Then he helped the man—Gus Thompson—guide the donkeys to the stalls. He'd spread hay in the feed troughs the day before, and the donkeys began consuming it with gusto.

"I'll need your help to coax Liza from her spot. Once a jenny picks a birthing spot, it's hard to get her to move."

The little donkey left the truck easily enough, but Ryan saw that her steps were labored. They led her to the closest empty stall. Ryan spread straw in a corner of the stall, studied it, and then spread some more. He latched the gate, just to make sure she didn't bolt. Not that she looked like bolting.

"She won't give a fuss," Gus said. "She's a good girl."

Liza let out a sharp, high-pitched bray.

"That sound usually means they're lonely or there's a predator nearby." The man studied the donkey. "Or she's due any minute."

The little donkey paced circles along the back wall.

"She don't look right to me," Gus said. "You have a vet in this town? I'm decent at wrangling but know next to nothing about all this."

Ryan reached for his cellphone. In his haste he'd left it on the table beside his bed.

"I'll call from the house. But just in case, I'll bring towels and some sheets."

"You know something about foaling?"

His surprise rankled, but was understandable.

"I grew up on a ranch, so I know a little. But probably not enough."

Ryan raced to the house and called Laird. He cursed when Laird's answering machine picked up. He was probably out tending to some medical emergency in town. Ryan left a message urging him to get over to the ranch as soon as he could.

Then he raced down the hall to the linen closet and grabbed an armful of towels and sheets.

"Mighty nice towels, Mr. Rea," the man said when Ryan opened the gate to the stall. "Mighty nice place all around."

"My name's Ryan."

Liza let out another bray, this one weaker and sounding more pathetic.

"Is the vet coming?"

"No answer."

Gus patted Liza's neck. "Something's not right— donkeys are stoic animals. They almost never show pain."

Liza lay down and stayed down. She rolled from side to side, braying. Ryan wished he could do something to help her pain. Avoiding her kicking legs, he knelt and lifted her tail. And his heart sank in his chest.

Instead of the bluish-white membrane of the amnion, a

ballooned, red membrane extended from her.

"The membrane didn't break," he said to Gus, trying not to sound panicked.

"The what?"

"She's red-bagging—it's premature placental separation. The membrane separates from the uterus, depriving the foal of the oxygen supply. Because the foal is still inside, within the membrane, it can't breathe. It could suffocate."

Ryan didn't bother taking the time to roll his sleeves. He used the strength of his hands to rip through the bag, plunged through the gush of blood and heat, groped past the hooves and latched on to the head of the foal.

"C'mon, baby, hang in there." Ryan's heart slammed against his ribs as he wrapped his hands around the back of the foal's skull. At least the baby was positioned right, with its head between its front hooves, poised like a swimmer about to dive into the world.

He used his legs for traction against the floor of the stall and pulled the foal free of Liza's quivering body. He ripped at the shroud-like membrane still covering the foal and tore it open. He peeled back the membrane with his fingers and wiped the unmoving foal's nostrils clear of mucus. The nostrils flared, and the foal took a few breaths. Only then did he realize he'd been holding his own. He let it out as the foal closed its lips around his hand and sucked.

"Holy Mary," Gus said in an awed tone.

"We've got a live wire." Ryan eased his hand away from the foal's lips.

He knew better than to cut the navel cord. Liza would break the cord when she got up, or it would snap as the foal struggled to her feet. But he stayed close, knowing that these precious first moments were the time to imprint on the foal. If Liza let him, the foal would accept him and the closeness those first minutes developed would make it much easier on him, any caretakers and, in the long run, the little donkey.

The little foal turned to him and nuzzled, wiping a trail of slime and wetness along his jeans. A trail of slime and wetness that made him a very happy guy. He'd been accepted.

Liza rose to her feet, breaking the umbilical cord. Gus reached a towel toward the foal, and Liza nipped at him.

"I'm your friend," Gus sputtered as he recoiled against the wall.

The new mother ignored him and began licking her foal dry.

"That licking action is very important," Ryan said to a near-spellbound Gus. "Especially if this is Liza's first foal, which I suspect it is. The licking stimulates her mothering instinct, gets her milk flowing, and perhaps most important of all, prevents the foal from getting chilled."

He stood and flipped the switch to the overhead heater. And said a silent thanks that he'd held his ground in the face of his contractor's city-boy scorn.

"My wife's pregnant," Gus said.

The admission explained the man's anxiety.

"First child?"

Gus nodded, looking down at the blood covering the straw on the stall floor.

"Don't get any ideas," Ryan said, shaking his head. "I'm not available for a repeat performance."

The attempt at a light moment was lost on Gus. He leaned back against the wall and raked a hand over his face. "It just made me think. You know, with birthing—there's so much that can go wrong."

"And so much that goes right," Ryan countered.

And then his words hit him.

So much that could go right.

276

He'd focused on what had gone wrong between him and Cara, and it had taken a homeless donkey to get through his skull that *he* hadn't focused on what could go right.

Worse, he hadn't even given Cara a chance to explain. Fueled by old patterns, patterns he hated, he'd launched into her without thinking, hadn't considered her pain or what she'd suffered. He hadn't trusted—hadn't trusted at all. And he'd probably scorched the path to any future he might've had with her. A future he'd dreamed about since the day he'd met her, a future he'd set to blazes in a few short, hotheaded minutes.

Ryan watched as Liza ran her tongue tirelessly over her baby, fully focused on the new life she'd brought into the world. And he knew what he had to do.

"Where you staying tonight?"

"There's a motel about an hour from here," Gus said.

"Would you consider staying here? Watching over the donkeys? Keeping an eye on these two? I've got a couple of rooms fixed up for the caretaker."

"Beats the heck out of Motel 6."

"There's a diner in town; you can run a tab on me."

The foal nuzzled along Liza's belly and started nursing.

"Now there's a mighty sweet sight," Laird said as he walked into the stall and tossed his vet bag on the straw-covered floor.

"Thank God you're here." Ryan rose and started to reach a hand out to shake Laird's, but seeing the blood still smeared up to his elbows, he drew back.

"Looks like you have it handled," Laird said as he checked out Liza and her foal. "I'll have to treat the little one's navel with iodine." He reached into his bag. "And she'll need a tetanus antitoxin shot immediately." He glanced up at Ryan. "But from the looks of how you've handled things, you probably know that."

"Nope. I got lucky. I helped my dad once, with a mare. She red-bagged, or I never would've known what to do."

"You saved both their lives, I'd say." Laird looked to Gus. "Has she been a mother before?"

"Don't know," Gus said. "She just came in two months ago. It's hard to starve a donkey, but Liza here was skin and bones. We weren't sure she'd keep the foal."

A muscle twitched in Laird's jaw. "I'll never understand the minds of some people," he said, not hiding his disgust. "Instead of connecting to the awe of life, they ignore it and harm everything in their path."

Ryan looked away. Laird couldn't know the pain those words knifed into his gut.

CHAPTER TWENTY-SEVEN

R YAN KNOCKED AT CARA'S FRONT DOOR. IN THE minute it took her to answer, he fought to counter the spikes of adrenaline surging in him.

She opened the door, and her eyes went wide.

"Are you okay?" She pointed to his head.

"That depends," Ryan answered. "Mostly on you."

She pointed again, but didn't touch him. "You have blood on your neck."

He rubbed at his skin. He'd scrubbed his arms past the elbows, changed his shirt and jeans, but evidently had missed a few spots. He'd never been one for mirrors, and he'd been in too much of a rush to talk to her to take time to shower properly.

"The donkeys arrived early. I helped one of them foal."

She took a step back, staring.

"It was an emergency, and Laird wasn't around. The foal's okay. Cute, in fact. Really cute."

She folded her arms across her chest. "Just when I'm sure that there's nothing you could say to make me ever want to speak to you again, you come up with something like this."

To his relief she stepped aside and allowed him to enter her living room. He felt like he'd passed the first gate of *Castlevania* but hadn't yet come close to facing the shadow

279

powers. Cara crossed to her desk, keeping a good distance between them.

"You were amazing at the meeting," he said. "What you did. What you said."

The words came out of his mouth, yet he heard them as if someone else were speaking, and in no way did they express the power of the feelings racing circles in him.

She picked up a pile of papers from her desk. He fought for more words, but they wouldn't come. She turned, clutching the papers to her chest like a shield.

"I thought you said you'd rather face a fast ball than go to a meeting," she said.

He couldn't read her expression, but the wavering flame of hope in his heart sprang to life.

"That part's still true."

She dropped the papers into a box beside her. The room was piled with half-packed boxes. Two suitcases stood by the door.

"You going somewhere?" He immediately kicked himself for asking such an obvious, stupid question. But his brain wasn't functioning. He thought of a dozen things to say, but none would form into words that he trusted.

She leafed through another pile of papers, then shoved them into a box that was already brimming.

"New York."

He was too late, like in one of those stupid movies where you sit through all the twists and turns and the people split up anyway.

He always hated *Casablanca*. That Ilsa would leave Rick and moviegoers thought it was a good thing never made any sense to him.

He held out the travel mug of coffee he'd brought. "This is for you. I broke down and read the directions."

She looked up, and he saw the tears brimming in her

eyes. His heart lurched and breathed flames on the flicker of hope he'd fought not to relinquish. He wanted to take her in his arms, but knew it wouldn't be the right move. He didn't know what the right move would be.

She took the mug from him.

"Thank you."

She stepped back, searching his face. He didn't know what expression would help crack her armor, would salve the wounds caused by his anger. But whatever she saw in his face sent a wavering smile across hers.

"You must've been desperate if you read the directions," she said. Her hands shook as she removed the lid and sipped. She shut her eyes and tears spilled from behind her lashes. "It's delicious."

He took the mug from her hand and set it next to the TV.

"Cara." He turned her to face him. "You can't take this all on your shoulders. My... my *projections* played a part in all this, maybe the bigger part. And my lack of trust. I wanted you to be a simple country woman—to be uncomplicated. I didn't give you a chance to be anything else. I fell into the trap of my own fantasies, and I dragged you in right along with me."

She swallowed and parted her lips. God, he wanted to just kiss her and make everything that hung between them vanish. He pulled her into his arms, and when she didn't resist, he cradled her against his chest.

"I was a Stone Age jackass," he whispered to the top of her head.

She sniffled against his chest. "Don't give the donkeys a bad name."

"You're right, the animals don't deserve such comparisons—I was a Stone Age jerk."

He stroked her hair, wishing he could stroke her heart.

"Jackie told Alex you were planning to tell me next week. You couldn't have known Henry would out you like that."

"So much for secrets," she said with a sniff.

"I should've been the kind of guy you could have trusted enough to confide in. Instead I was a bull-headed fool."

She pulled away and tipped her face to him. "I thought you were a Stone Age jerk."

Defiance flashed in her eyes. Defiance was easier to stomach than her sadness. She raised a hand and pushed her hair back from her face.

"I was a fool to think that timing mattered," she said. "The world of billionaires isn't really what anyone wants to hear about. They think they do, but when it comes down to it, the kind of money my family has doesn't build bridges. Or make friends."

"Well, *I* want to hear about it." He rubbed her shoulder. "About this one particular billionaire."

She stepped back, but he kept his hand on her. Some part of him would die if the connection between them was severed.

Her brows drew together, and she looked down at the floor. "When Jackie told me about the paternity suit, I was afraid to face you. Every time I imagined telling you, I saw the horrid similarities. Deception is the silent partner of lies—someone once told me that."

He winced at hearing her repeat the words he'd flung at her. "You'd never do a thing like she did."

"But what I did"—she looked up and held him in a firm gaze—"I know deceiving everyone was wrong, but I was dying in my life. *Dying*. And afraid." She hugged her arms around her ribs and shook her head. "I had to start over. I never imagined it'd end up like this."

He tracked his hand down her arm and squeezed. "Nothing's ended, Cara."

Spots of color burned in her cheeks. "You saw their faces. Belva... and Perk and the others. I can only imagine what Molly feels."

He cupped her jaw, gently, and kept her eyes meeting his. "You woke a lot of people up to their prejudices. And to their fantasies and shortcomings. Me included."

She bit at her lower lip.

"It was about time for me to dust off my trust engines," he added.

She nodded.

He put both hands on her shoulders. "And there are some fantasies worth testing." He released one hand and ran it down the back of her spine. "Some that stand the test of even a Stone Age jerk's follies."

She sniffed and smiled. And all the dammed-up energy he'd held in for so long rushed into the kiss he pressed to her lips.

~~✒~~

The midday sun spilled over the bed and woke Ryan. He hadn't planned on sleeping. Cara lay curled against him, still sound asleep. He leaned up on his elbow and watched her breathing. It was all he could do not to trace the relaxed smile that rested on her lips, but he didn't want to wake her. He'd seen the smudged circles under her eyes. She hadn't been sleeping any better than he had.

He inched away to slide out from under the sheet.

"No," she murmured as she reached a hand to him. "Not yet. I don't want to face the world yet."

He curled back around her. "We can face it together."

She shot up in the bed, pulling the sheet around her.

283

"You don't know what you're asking for."

"I know what I have." He kissed the worry lines at the corners of her eyes. "You're exactly the woman I was looking for."

The lines around her eyes relaxed. "Well, you aren't exactly the man I was looking for." She circled her arms around his neck and pulled him to her, pressed her lips to his. "But you'll do," she said between kisses.

"Just glad to be on the team, ma'am."

She cuffed him, and he grabbed her arm.

"One thing is true," she said. "Well, lots of things are true. But I now know this—make-up sex is even better than people say."

He tugged her against his already hard erection. "I'd prefer moving-forward sex."

"Then we should have a proper date," she said, pushing him away playfully.

The sheet slipped down, exposing her breasts, her nipples peaked with arousal. Was the woman trying to torture him?

He straddled her and lifted her to him. "How about a proper date for the rest of our lives?"

She took in a sharp breath. Maybe his timing sucked, but he was in the pond now—might as well dive.

"Marry me, Cara."

A smile crinkled the corners of her eyes. "You haven't slept and you're covered with donkey blood."

"I heard it adds to the attraction." He leaned down and nipped a kiss to her ear.

She hadn't answered him. He'd ask again. Every day if he had to. Until he got the answer he had to have.

"Well, you might feel very differently after you've had a taste of my world and my family. A taste of Caroline Barrington."

"Um, last I noticed, your parents aren't in this bed." He leaned down, caressed her lips with his. "And I like what I'm tasting right here."

She shivered as he ran kisses down her neck, to her breasts. Hooking an arm around her waist, he laid her back across the bed. The duvet puffed up around them, cocooning them in a whispering cloud of taste and touch. He needed no words now. He loved her slowly, relishing the way her body rose with her pleasure, how she met his moves with passion. And what he saw in her eyes burned away the restraints that had kept him from trusting completely.

He held her as their breathing returned to normal, as the world returned, as the need for words returned.

"I love you, Cara," he whispered against her ear. "Marry me. Marry me and we'll slay our dragons together."

"Dragons?"

"What would you call them?"

She pressed up from the pillow and turned her face to his. "I can't possibly make such a decision on an empty stomach."

The twinkle in her eyes made hope expand in his chest.

"Then let me make you breakfast and *then* you can agree to marry me."

"Cain says you don't know how to make breakfast."

"I've never been so motivated before."

She giggled. The same, sweet giggle he'd heard that day they'd struggled with Belva's squash. The day he'd probably lost his heart.

He grabbed his jeans from a chair near the fireplace and knocked the little painting off it. It tumbled toward the still-glowing embers of the fire he'd built just before they'd slept. He grabbed at it and caught it just in time.

"You just saved the three million I've earmarked for the clinic. I'm selling that painting at auction next week."

She was testing him, he knew. Testing his reaction to her world, a world where rare paintings hung in people's homes. A world of big money.

"But you love it," he said.

"I don't know how long it'll take for me to wrest funds free from the foundation, to deal with all the paperwork and red tape. That painting's a more immediate source of funds."

She wrapped the sheet around her, rose from the bed and studied him for a moment, the realization that he knew the painting's value dawning in her face. "When—when did you know?"

He hoped it was curiosity and not wariness that he saw in the tilt of her head and the furrow between her brows.

"The first morning we made love in this bed. Alex and his sister had dragged me to the impressionist exhibition at the Legion of Honor the week before."

He rested the painting carefully on the chair. "I just wouldn't let what my brain was telling me sink in. I'm letting it all sink in now. A little late, but letting it in... letting you in."

He scooped her into his arms and carried her back to the bed.

She wriggled her feet to the floor. "You'll never get my answer until I have my breakfast." She crossed her arms. "And I want to see that baby donkey with my own eyes, to make sure your alibi holds up. Women have been known to fall for stories less believable than that."

"I'll never lie to you, Cara."

"No." She took his hand in hers, closed her fingers over his. "I know you won't." She inhaled deeply. "And with the exception of the life I've lived for the past three years, I've never lied in my life. I don't plan to start now."

Ryan heard the splatter of water against the window. "It's raining," he said.

She let go of his hands and walked to the window overlooking her garden. "So it is." She opened the window and inhaled, closing her eyes. "There's nothing like the scent of the first autumn rain."

He slid his arms around her and snuggled her against his chest. "I might take issue with that." He buried his face in her hair, inhaling the intoxicating scent of her.

He eyed the bed and ran his hand along the curve of her waist. She batted his hand away.

"Breakfast," she said with a glint. "And then I'll think about whether I'm joining your team."

"Our team," he said. "But with love on the line, maybe we should call out for delivery."

"It's the country, Ryan. They don't deliver breakfast, in case you haven't noticed." The mischievous twinkle returned to her eyes. "And I'm holding out until I see that donkey."

EPILOGUE

One year later.

C ARA PUT THE FINISHING TOUCHES ON THE TRAY OF Asian spring rolls and placed it beside the others spread on the kitchen counter. Everything was ready, everything except maybe her.

She wiped her palms on the denim apron she'd worn to keep the worst of the mess off her slacks and tucked an errant strand of hair behind her ear. The chorus of voices floating in from the nearest paddock told her that the donkeys were a big hit with their families and guests.

"I thought we might find you in here." Jackie Brandon blazed into the cavernous kitchen followed by a troupe of women Cara had come to treasure as friends.

"Chained to the kitchen?" Alana Tavonesi, Alex's cousin, chided. "I've brought olives, still warm from the oven. I baked them with rosemary from our ranch. That's for remembrance, you know."

She did know. But she didn't need rosemary to remind her of the blissful happiness she'd discovered.

"Where's the guest of honor?" Chloe McNalley, Scotty's wife, bounded into the kitchen. "It's been a week since I've seen him. I'm lined up for admiration duty."

"You'll have to fight my mother for that privilege."

Cara laughed. "Or Ryan's mother. I'm not sure which of them is more formidable."

"I'm tough," Chloe said as she reached for one of the spring rolls and popped it into her mouth. "These are delicious. Don't tell me you can cook."

"Ryan made them. Hors d'oeuvres and desserts are his specialty."

Chloe laughed. "Maybe he can teach Scotty. He's still at featherweight chef level one—champagne and ramen noodles."

"Breakfast of champions," Alex Tavonesi said as he walked in and snitched one of the carefully arranged spring rolls.

"You're all ruining my artwork," Cara said, batting Alex's hand away as he reached for a second roll.

Alex glanced around the kitchen. "Where *is* the guest of honor?"

"If Ryan had had his way, *you* would've been guest of honor," Cara said.

In Ryan's mind, Alex was the one who'd suggested he look for land in Albion Bay and therefore was responsible for bringing Cara and Ryan together. Ryan had invited the entire Tavonesi clan to the party. He'd also invited every player on the Giants. She was still getting used to being surrounded by people who loved their lives, people who pursued their dreams with an energy that inspired and fascinated her and lifted her.

"Glad someone has their priorities straight." Alex grinned and devoured another spring roll before she could stop him.

Cara swallowed down the lump of emotion rising in her throat and untied her apron. "Maybe we should head down to the paddocks and find out. But I'm warning you, Alex, watch out for my dad. He's still pissed we're not having this party at the Pacific-Union Club."

Sabrina, Alex's sister, sailed into the kitchen. "Did I hear *difficult dad*? Turn him over to Alana; he'll never know what hit him."

Alana gave her cousin Sabrina a look that could be interpreted only as lovingly mock offense. Then she pulled a bottle of wine from a bag and proceeded to deftly uncork it. "Before we head out, how about a toast?" She poured a rose-colored liquid into the wine glasses that Cara had previously lined up on a tray. "My first vintage. A rose Pinot."

"And what are we toasting?" Chloe asked as she took the glass Alana handed her.

"Well, we could toast Sabrina's new film deal," Alana said with a twinkle. "Or we could toast Scotty and Chloe's upcoming anniversary—"

"Or we could toast your guest of honor," Jackie interrupted, shooting a wink at Alex. "After all, he's the cutest baby on the planet."

"To the guest of honor," Alex boomed. He turned to Jackie. "And don't get any ideas. At least not until spring."

They trooped out of the kitchen and down the path to the paddock.

Sam and Molly Rivers were feeding carrots to Liza and her foal. Both donkeys looked splendid in the garlands of roses and greens that Molly had brought as a surprise. Sam had his hands full keeping the foal from nibbling the inhaler he had strapped in a leather case on his belt and from eating the roses on Liza's garland.

Belva and Perk had Cara's dad cornered. From the look of her finger wag, Belva was giving him a full-on dose of Albion Bay common sense.

Ryan stood off to one side with his dad, Quinn, Cain, and Matt Darrington, Alana's newly wedded husband. From their gestures, Cara suspected they were planning a fishing outing. She hoped they planned to take her.

And though Ryan's dad had scoffed during his first visit at the over-the-top barn Ryan had built for the donkeys, and nearly had an apoplectic fit over the heaters, after two days on the ranch this visit he was clucking over the animals like they were his own.

Cara's mother and Ryan's stood near the tiered fountain that served as the donkey's water trough, with their backs turned, oblivious to their surroundings.

As the procession from the house reached the paddock, Ryan looked up and the smile he beamed at Cara melted her bones. She was sure no one had a better husband than she did, although several of Ryan's teammates could give a good run for a close second.

"I wondered if you'd forgotten us," he said as he reached to take her hand.

"Fat chance," Alana chimed in before Cara could respond. "We were inside rehearsing our toasts."

Ryan leaned down and brushed a kiss to Cara's cheek. "I know one toast that I'll be giving in private," he whispered against the curve of her ear. The shiver of anticipation had her wishing the party was over.

Perk clapped his hands and called the gathering to attention.

It occurred to Cara that Perk would make a great general or field marshal. Maybe he had been one. With all the hubbub of setting up her foundation office in the spacious cabin Ryan had built with the help of Alex and Matt on the east slope of the ranch, the work with Alston to do what they could to expose Dray Bender and keep him from stealing some other unsuspecting philanthropist's funds, and the effort to get the county's approval for the clinic fast-tracked, she hadn't had the time yet to find out all she wanted to know about her neighbors. But she wasn't going anywhere; she had plenty of time to discover what made her friends the wonderful people they were.

Perk spread his arms to the gathered family and friends. "I understand that there are among us some who think that the *city* would've been a more proper place to hold this ceremony." He glared at Cara's dad who, to his credit, smiled. "But if it hadn't been for the good town of Albion Bay, we wouldn't be here celebrating today." He winked at Belva. Cara was surprised to see the old lady blush. "Now, I'm no minister, but with the rights vested in me as mayor, I'd like to get this shindig started. Ladies?" He looked over to where Ryan's and Cara's mothers stood huddled together at the fountain, paying him no mind. He cleared his throat and bellowed, "Ladies, *might* we have the guest of honor, please?"

Cara's mother turned, blushing. Ryan's mother flushed too.

"I beg your pardon," Cara's mother said as she walked over to where Perk stood. "We were occupied with our grandson."

"I realize he has more charm than me," Perk said in a softer voice. "But you can't have a christening without a ceremony. And you sure can't have one without the babe."

Perk's words had to compete with the warmth flooding Cara's body as she and Ryan reached out to take Casey into their joined arms. Their son looked up at them and gave a gummy smile, his eyes wide with wonder.

As Perk concluded the ceremony, Liza escaped Sam's grasp and wandered over to lean against Ryan. Casey's curious eyes fixed on Liza's fuzzy ears, and he nearly wriggled from their grasp trying to reach for them.

They moved to the barn for the reception. The caterer they'd hired from Point Reyes served a meal made from the bounty from Cara and Ryan's garden. Bustling servers uncorked and served champagne.

Cara sat with Ryan's sister, Eve, at a table near one wall and jiggled Casey on her lap, tapping her foot to the music of the band of locals they'd hired to play. She watched, intrigued, as the new clinic doc squared off with Cain and managed to coax a dance from Molly. They'd outfitted the old dentist office and hired an around-the-clock medical staff. Until the new clinic was completed next year, at least they had a team in place for the interim.

When Alana's handsome brother Simon cut in and whisked Molly to the center of the dancers, Cara had to smile. Molly had reentered the world of romance, and it looked like she was going to have a good run at finding a man to share her life. And even though love had its shock, its bite, its ways to surprise and disrupt, she was pretty sure Molly was up to the challenge. Actually welcomed the challenge.

Molly was doing an admirable job of not being star struck over Alex's sister, Sabrina. Sabrina's second film had made her a sensational box office draw, and she'd become the new darling in Hollywood.

Cara had to admire the way Sabrina took the fame and fuss in stride. More than once they'd talked about the challenges of living in the public eye. Cara had realized that her own challenges paled when held up to the ones faced by Sabrina. The previous week she'd been grabbed by a zealous photographer and now had her arm in a sling as a result of the man's assault. Though Sabrina laughed off her brother's concern that she had only two months to recover and get in shape for an action film, Cara saw the pain and worry in her eyes. She'd joked that she could be a wounded heroine, that maybe the world was ready for reality. Alex told her not to count on it.

The musicians announced a short break, and Ryan stepped up to the stage. He clinked a knife to his glass, waving everyone quiet.

"I have a surprise." He paused and several people groaned at him milking the drama. "A surprise for the beautiful mother of our son."

He jogged to the side door of the barn, flicked a switch, and it opened on its track. There, strung with tiny white Christmas lights, was a brand new school bus with a red bow across its door.

Everyone cheered. Even Perk, who wasn't one for surprises. Cara suspected he'd been in on the planning of this one.

"But since Molly's the one who'll be driving it," Ryan said as he turned to look across the room to Cara, "with your permission, perhaps she should cut the ribbon?"

Cara laughed and nodded.

Molly had to be prodded to the front of the group by Belva. She took the scissors Ryan held out and snipped the red cord.

Over the applause of their guests, Ryan clinked a knife to the edge of his glass once again. "And now I have a confession." His tone was nearly somber.

He held out his hand for Cara.

Casey giggled as she handed him into Eve's outstretched arms.

Ryan held her in a gaze that burned with heat and passion as she walked up to the stage.

He wrapped his arm around her waist and raised his glass. "I've learned a lesson that most of you all probably already knew. I was just a bit slow to catch on." He tugged Cara closer. "When love's in the game, losing is *never* an option."

The group cheered as he met her lips with his.

Home.

Held in Ryan's arms, Cara finally recognized what it felt like to be home.

THANK YOU!

Thanks for reading *Love on the Line*. I hope you enjoyed it!

- **Would** you like to know when my next books are available? You can sign up for my new release newsletter at http://www.pamelaaares.com/newsletter-signup/
- You've just read the fourth book in the Tavonesi Series. The other books in the series are:

  Love Bats Last (Book #1, Alex and Jackie)
  Thrown By Love (Book #2, Chloe and Scotty)
  Fielder's Choice (Book #3, Alana and Matt)
  Aim for Love (Book #5, Kaz and Sabrina, available September, 2014)

- **You, the reader**, have the power to make or break a book's reputation. Reviews help other readers find books they love. I appreciate reviews from all perspectives and would love to hear your opinion. If you have the time, please leave a review and let me know what you think about *Love on the Line*.

I write so that readers may enjoy the experience of reading my books. I hope you enjoy every one!

Thank you so much for reading and for spending time with me.

In gratitude,

Pamela Aares

Another winner in Pamela Aares' Tavonesi Series. Get ready to enter the fast-paced world of alpha male, All-Star athletes and the top-of-their-game women they come to love.

Aares deftly weaves together the desires and strategies of world-class sports with the equally charged realm of the heart to create a fast-moving tale you'll wish would never end.

Mary Beath, award-winning author of
Refuge of Whirling Light

AND DON'T MISS…

Other Books by Pamela

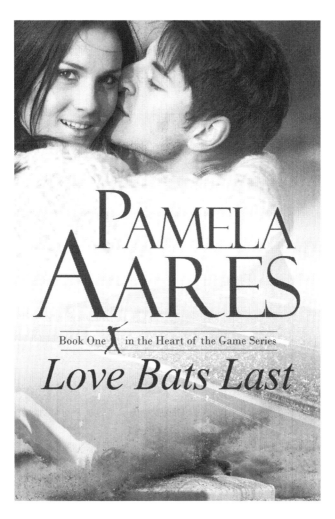

PAMELA AARES

Book One in the Heart of the Game Series

Love Bats Last

Book One in the Tavonesi Series

A stormy night changes their lives forever...

The baseball diamond isn't the only field for all-star player Alex Tavonesi; he also runs his family's prestigious vineyard. What he can't seem to run is his love life. He's closing in on the perfect vintage and the perfect game, but so far the perfect woman has eluded him.

Veterinarian Jackie Brandon is eluding her aristocratic past and memories of a soccer star who jilted her just before their wedding. She devotes herself to a marine mammal rescue center on the northern California coast, where hundreds of seals and sea lions are washing up dead.

A chance meeting in a midnight storm brings Alex and Jackie together to rescue a stranded whale. Watching her work, he realizes she's the passionate, courageous woman he thought he'd never find--he just has to overcome her deep distrust of jocks. Jackie's passion and courage lead her to discover what's killing the sea mammals. The culprits want to silence her, and Alex is the only one standing in their way. What will he sacrifice to save the woman he loves?

Love Bats Last is available online as a print or eBook at all of your favorite booksellers.

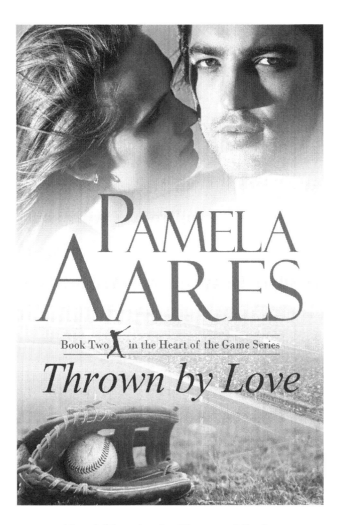

PAMELA AARES

Book Two in the Heart of the Game Series

Thrown by Love

Book Two in the Tavonesi Series

A kiss in a dark alcove triggers the greatest challenge of their lives...

Ace pitcher Scotty Donovan has been traded from his longtime team—and hates it. But to his surprise, he now finds himself in the sweetest game of his life: winning the heart of smart, sexy physics professor Chloe McNalley.

Chloe loves teaching, but she's never fit into academia. When she falls for Scotty, she discovers his arms and heart are where she belongs. They share a passion for the game, a fascination for the mysteries of the universe and an increasing love for one another.

Then Chloe inherits Scotty's new team. As player and team owner, they shouldn't be dating. They try to hide their passion, until a blackmailer threatens them personally and professionally. Exposure could be the end of everything-- Scotty's career, Chloe's team ownership, and their new love—unless they find a way to transcend the taboo standing between them.

Thrown By Love is available online as a print or eBook at all of your favorite booksellers.

PAMELA AARES

Book Three in the Heart of the Game Series

Fielder's Choice

Book Three in the Tavonesi Series

When love's the game, you can't play it safe...

All-Star shortstop Matt Darrington has more than a problem. His wife died, and now he's juggling a too-smart-for-her-britches six-year-old and the grueling pace of professional baseball. Worse, his daughter is mom shopping. When they explore a local ranch, she decides the beautiful, free-spirited tour guide is premium mom material. Matt thinks the sexy guide looks like Grade-A trouble.

Alana Tavonesi loves her cosmopolitan life in Paris. But when she inherits the renowned Tavonesi Olive Ranch, she has to return to California and face obligations she never wanted. Selling the place is her first instinct, but life at the ranch begins to crack her open, exposing the dreams hidden inside her heart.

On a lark she leads a ranch tour, where she meets Matt Darrington. His physical power and a captivating sensual appeal fire her in a way no man ever has, but he has a kid—and being a stepmom is a responsibility Alana will never be ready for. Still... she can't keep her mind or her hands off him.

When Matt's daughter goes missing from a kid's camp at the ranch, Alana organizes the search effort, knowing from experience the areas a bright child would be drawn to explore. As she and Matt work together to search for the little girl, Alana discovers that father and daughter have won her heart. Yet it may be too late for love...

Fielder's Choice is available online as a print or eBook at all of your favorite booksellers.

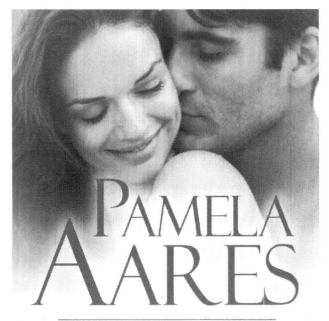

PAMELA AARES

Book Five in The Tavonesi Series

AIM FOR LOVE

Book Five in the Tavonesi Series

In AIM FOR LOVE, rising movie star Sabrina Tavonesi has only three weeks to heal her shoulder before shooting her next film. Sexy baseball pitching phenom Kaz Tokugawa has a solution—a mysterious Japanese healing method she's too desperate to turn down. Soon, they're not just working on her shoulder; they're falling in love.

But Kaz has made a promise he's not sure he can keep, and Sabrina faces inner demons that threaten to overwhelm her. When violence strikes, their secrets may destroy their dreams, their love…and their lives.

Aim for Love will be available online as a print or eBook at all of your favorite booksellers in September, 2014.

ABOUT THE AUTHOR

Pamela Aares is an award-winning author of contemporary and historical romance novels and also writes about fictional romance in sports with her new baseball romance book series titled the Tavonesi Series.

Her popularity as a romance writer continues to grow with each new book release, so much so, that the Bay area author has drawn comparisons by reviewers to Nora Roberts.

Before becoming a romance author, Aares wrote and produced award-winning films including *Your Water, Your Life*, featuring actress Susan Sarandon and NPR series *New Voices, The Powers of the Universe* and *The Earth's Imagination*. She holds a Master's degree from Harvard and currently resides in the wine country of Northern California with her husband, a former MLB All-Star and two curious cats.

If not behind her computer, you can probably find her reading a romance novel, hiking the beach or savoring life with friends. You can visit Pamela on the web at

http://www.PamelaAares.com.

Made in the USA
Lexington, KY
03 September 2014